# A Bad Place Best Forgotten

OR

EJERTINE'S TALE

## BY J. S. ALLEN

Weird Books for Weird People

# Contents

# CHAPTER 1

# The Apparition

I was alone at the bow when I saw the ghost. She was float-ing out over the slow waves, no more than a ship's breadth away, half-hidden in the morning mist. Then, all at once, the sun broke over the horizon, and the first blasting rays of dawn obliterated the vision.

But that glimpse had been enough. In that moment her eyes locked with mine; she lifted her arms toward me, the beginning of a gesture.

Leaning over the rail, I searched for any sign of her. But she was gone.

"Hava...?" I hadn't seen her in twenty years, but I would know Hava anywhere. So would you, if you'd ever met Hava.

What did it mean, this apparition? For the remainder of my watch, I turned my mind inward, remembering, worrying. As the distant coastal mountains of Lagin crept into view, I real-ized I was approaching Hava's home—or at least the place her family called home. Is that why she appeared to me? We would make port in Kortholomoth in three days.

When the mate's whistle called the end of my shift, I remained at my post gripping the rail, eyes lingering on the mountain range which now loomed purple on the horizon, its crenulations faintly visible. The way the ghost had reached out toward me, was she beckoning? Was she calling for help? Was she... dead?

"Everything all right?"

I turned to see Semetrius, head cocked. "Didn't you hear the whistle?"

I returned my eyes to the horizon, not wanting to give up my post. Probably because I was unready to return to the jostling company of my crewmates.

Seeing my mood, Semetrius came and stood next to me at the rail, saying nothing. Like most of the crew, Semetrius was a stocky Sartan with a round, pock-marked face and a beard well braided with beads, one for each voyage. I, by contrast, was a tall, wiry Soofian, with no hint of a beard to bead if I wanted to.

He studied me and said, "What is the matter, my friend? You are troubled?"

"Just thinking of someone."

A slow smile came to Semetrius. "Ah... a woman. That girl in Astina, no doubt?"

"No," I said with a frown. Semetrius was always trying to goad me into exaggerating my sexual exploits, the way he did. But I wasn't like Semetrius.

Semetrius arched an eyebrow, and his smile quickened. "But it is a woman."

"No," I snapped. Then, more gently, "I mean, yes—but not in the way you mean."

Semetrius nodded sagely and said nothing. He stroked his beard, waiting patiently for me to elaborate. But I didn't really feel like elaborating.

Several moments passed in silence. But Semetrius wasn't just going to give up. I sighed wearily and said, "Her name was Hava..."

"A Laginese woman?"

"Yes, she was Laginese. But it was not in Lagin where I met her. She came to my village."

"You have a village?"

"Of course I have a village. What did you think?"

Semetrius shrugged. "I've just never heard you talk about your home before. I've never thought of you having a home. Figured you must have been born at sea or something."

"You would hate my village, Semetrius."

"Oh? Why's that?"

"Well, for one thing, the men are made to live separately from the women."

Semetrius shook his head slowly. "I have so many questions."

"You have to understand I come from 'deepest' Soofia. As far from everything as one can possibly be. A place no one ever visited. At least not until Hava. Her visit was the biggest thing that ever happened in my village. It changed my life. In all my travels, I have never known anyone like her. There was something about her. A presence. It drew people in, rallied them to her causes. Men followed her willingly, happily. In my village, that was something new: A woman, a leader of men!"

"You loved her."

"Yes, I loved her. But not in the way a man loves a woman. I was far too young for her, hardly more than a boy. But, yes, I loved her. How could I not? Her smile was the smile of a goddess. Her laugh was like the song of kentish wind chimes. She was the kindest person I have known. Just to be around her was to be in the presence of a great person, to soak up some of her genuine goodness, to become oneself a better person."

We passed several moments with no further words, the only sound the slopping of the sea against the hull.

Or maybe there was another sound, just at the edge of hearing. I cocked my ear, listening for something far-off on the wind. A voice? Raised in song?

"Do you hear that?" I asked.

"Hear what?"

"Singing. I thought I heard..." A chill ran down by back. "She is out there somewhere, Semetrius. Something—something is not right. I must go to her."

Semetrius straightened. "What's all this?"

"Forgive me," I said, not wanting to explain myself. "I am not feeling well." I turned from my friend and stalked away, ducking belowdecks.

# CHAPTER 2

# The Cave

Ignoring the friendly salutations of my fellow crewmen, I sequestered myself in my hammock and lay restlessly swaying in the midst of a dozen boisterous Sartans sharing their supper and swapping stories of fishing, fortunes and romance. Finally someone lobbed a bread-loaf at my head and called out, "What about you, Ejertine? You always have a story for us." Another called, "What's the matter with Ejertine?" Then everyone was looking my way.

I sighed wearily. This is why I didn't want to come below-decks. With reluctance, I sat up in my hammock and stooped to pick up the fallen loaf. "It's a story you want, is it?" Breaking the bread, I said, "Well, bring me the pipe, lads, bring me the cup."

I had everyone's attention now, but I was in no hurry to tell this particular tale. So I just gnawed at my bread and made everyone wait. I could do this, because I was Ejertine. Older than most of them, I enjoyed a certain status. A pale-skinned uneducated primitive I may have been, but they all confided in me and sought my advice on matters personal and practical. Everyone liked good old Ejertine, so we all sat listening to the ship creaking and popping until I was good and ready to start.

•

I have never told anyone the things I am about to tell you. For twenty years I have sailed the South Seas trying to forget.

There were three of us: Hava, Olio, and me. I was barely a man when Hava's expedition came to my village.

To understand where I come from, you must imagine a place in remotest Soofia, far, far up the River Flegmarn, beyond Terade, at the feet of the Tharn Mountains, on the very edge of the known world. Beyond my village you will find nothing— only the impenetrable wall of the Silver Mountains, and beyond them the vast desert wastes of Central Moghia.

My village was not on the way to anywhere else and we had nothing to trade that was not readily available elsewhere. The only outsiders who came so far upriver were the king's officials who returned every year to recruit soldiers and to collect tribute.

Now imagine my father, a man with wanderlust in his heart. Long before he brought me into this world, he went to fight in one of the king's campaigns. He was one of very few veterans who returned home to our village. Most of them, having tasted the offerings of the wider world, chose to seek their fortunes in wealthier lands. But my father, he returned. And for a time he was very popular. The stories of his adventures in the outside world enthralled the men of my village.

But village life did not suit my father. Soon he became restless. Then he would take to disappearing, sometimes for months at a time. No one knew where he went or why he could not be content at home in the village. The only person he was close to was the village shaman, himself an outsider, an ascetic who lived in a sacred cave.

Well, one day the shaman was killed in a rockslide. It was a great calamity for our village because he had no successor. So it came to pass that my father was compelled to take on the shaman's role as best he could. For twenty years he was the closest thing the village had to a shaman. He knew some of the stories and rituals, but he had no powers of his own and was useless as a healer. So the men of the village had only contempt for him. He tried his best to keep the spiritual traditions of our village alive, but no one paid much attention to him. He became a solitary attendant of the sacred cave, spending more and more of his time there. Never mind that the roof of his own house was leaking, and his garden was overgrown. He preferred to spend his time alone at the cave. He came out to preside over rituals and ceremonies. And, as was his right as a tribesman, he paired with women as he chose at the Julu festival. He claimed six children as his; I was the youngest. We were raised by women, and none of us knew him.

But after my thirteenth winter I was summoned to his house for the first time. The time had come, he said, to take me to the cave for my naming ceremony and to mark my passage into manhood.

It was a cold, wet day with a stinging drizzle. I had to hurry to keep up. Even in the mire of his fallow field, the old man moved with a lively step. In such mud our sandals were useless, so we went barefoot.

To get to the cave we had to pass in front of the house of my Uncle Pto. His house was three times the size of my father's. He called out his window, "Where are you going on a day like this, old man? To the cave again? This is no day to be out on the rocks, you will fall and break your hip! Why don't you stay at home and fix your leaky roof?"

"Ignore him," growled my father and kept walking along the trail. But I could not ignore my elder, so I went to the window to pay my respects.

Pto frowned down at me and said, "Don't tell me he is taking you to play with his dolls?"

"Dolls?" I said. "What do you mean, dolls?" I didn't have any idea what he meant.

My uncle hurried out into the rain, took me by the arm and escorted me along the trail, leaning close and speaking in a hushed tone. "Of late he spends all his time up there, in that old cave. He keeps them there. His house is falling down but he is up there in that cave making dolls. Why does he do it? Is he mad? Every day he passes my house and every day I ask him, 'My brother, why do you go?' 'I'm working on my masterpiece,' he says. Masterpiece! That's what he says. He says his master-piece will bring him an ox to plow his field. An ox! Can you imagine the old fool with an ox? He can't even afford to buy a pair of sandals from the women's side of the river."

His words made little sense to me.

I found my father waiting impatiently on the rocks. When I came into sight he turned without a word and led the way, ascending stone by stone up the talus toward the cliff wall. Whenever I would pause to look up at the cliff, I found myself falling behind. The old man's feet had memorized the zig-zag way between the piled-up boulders and he moved quickly, ap-parently without effort. I felt ashamed to be so young and yet out of breath.

The way to the cave was treacherous: a tortured route through the maze of boulders piled high at the cliff's base; to a crumbling trail that hugged the sheer cliff wall; and over slippery-wet rocks which had a way of shifting underfoot, threatening at every moment to send me tumbling down onto the jagged fingers of rock waiting to impale me some thirty or forty feet below. But the old man did not slow down. I think it was partly his intention that a sensation of mortal danger permeate my journey to the cave.

When finally the old man stopped to take a break, I collapsed on the ground next to him. After I caught my breath, I asked him about the dolls. He gave me a sharp look and said, "Don't listen to Pto. He knows nothing."

The rain had slackened off by then and from up there on the cliff I could see the great River Flegmarn zagging like a serpent across the land. I could see the women's houses where my childhood was spent. Looking down on those houses, it came to me suddenly that I was no longer a boy and would no longer be allowed on the women's side of the river. My life would be different from now on. This was the way of things in our village, the way it had always been.

From his bag my father produced a few beads, a citrus, and some bauble or another—I don't recall. He laid these on a flat stone before a menhir. "What's that for?" I asked.

"For the dwerrig," he said with a frown. Seeing my blank expression, he became enraged. "What, have the fools taught you nothing? When I am gone, who will be left to make offerings? Pay attention, boy. You must always leave something for the dwerrig when you pass this place. He is the keeper of these lands, and it will not do to displease him. Understand?"

I nodded, eager to please. He looked at me hard. I do not think he was impressed.

"Come," he said. "The cave is not far." Coming round the bend, my first sight of its wide-open maw caught me off guard. It was not what I'd expected. Through the gaping hole sunlight fell onto the floor of a great chamber below. We had to climb down a ladder to descend into the chamber which was shaped like a great egg.

Inside there was an airy openness and an eerie silence and a distinctive smell of must. I was duly impressed that this was indeed a sacred space. A great stone idol was enthroned in the wall, and I felt its old eyes upon me, judging me. Scattered around the cave floor were perhaps a hundred smaller figures made of wood and adorned with feathers and painted with ochre. When I saw them up close I was amazed by their lifelike detail. The largest of the wood figures stood as high as my belly and his features were so lifelike that I reached out to touch him to make sure he wasn't alive. His eyes gleamed, black and intelligent. His hands seemed as though they might open and reach out to me at any moment. My father came to stand behind me and said, "My masterpiece."

# CHAPTER 3

# All Eyes

That night before the witness of the idol my father conducted my rite of passage, calling upon the spirits to recognize the start of my second life as a man. On this night he gave me my name, and ever since I have been called Ejertine, which in my village's dialect means something like All Eyes. I did not like the name at first because it made me think of the non-men who sat in their tree houses overlooking the river, sentries against men who attempted the crossing over to the women's side. I did not wish to be associated with such an unenviable and unpopular authority. But my father made me feel better when he explained the name called back to an ancient demon with eyes pointing in all directions, preventing his enemies from sneaking up on him.

Afterward we spent the night in the cave. We sat close to the fire pit and the old man was feeling unusually talkative. My interest in his wooden figures had tickled his pride and he was eager to tell me about them. In a candid moment he told me where the inspiration for his work came from. When he was a young man, before he went to fight in the king's army, he climbed up through the high pass over the Tharn Mountains and descended all the way into the Deep Valley Durez. No one lived there, he said, except for some monsters. So he was very surprised when he came upon a lone house in the jungle. He took shelter there during the rainy season and was a guest of a man named Korieski. Korieski was a kind but reserved host who spent all his time in his workshop making tiny wooden dolls. My father found that Korieski would tolerate his presence in the workshop if he was very quiet and didn't get in the way or block the light. So he spent a few rainy weeks watching a master craftsman at work. He watched Korieski as he transformed a floor-to-ceiling pile of Yeber wood into dozens of little dolls, each one a detailed little naked person, just a few inches tall. He would string tiny splinters together to make little fingers and toes. Their teeth were individually carved. The dolls seemed very much alive.

But the strange thing was that Korieski used to go out in the middle of the night, when he thought my father was asleep. The next day my father would notice that one of the dolls was missing. Whenever Korieski would complete a doll, it would disappear during the night. My father wondered where Korieski went at night, in the rain, with nothing but jungled mountains all around? But when my father put this question to him, Korieski was evasive. Finally one night when Korieski sneaked out, my father got out of bed and went into Korieski's workshop to look around. He didn't touch anything, he just looked around to see which doll was missing this time. It was a little man with a bow which Korieski had completed the night before. Like the others, gone. My father went back to bed bemused.

The next morning Korieski burst into my father's room and pulled him out of bed, demanding to know whether he had been snooping around the workshop? My father denied it at first. But Korieski was beside himself and insisted that my father leave at once. My father apologized and pleaded to stay just another few days until the rain passed. He promised not to go into the workshop again.

Reluctantly, the old man agreed to let him stay a few days more. He went back into his workshop and closed the door.

Then my father heard the strangest sounds coming from the workshop. He heard things that didn't sound right—some hideous breathing, something rasping for breath.

He shuddered at the memory, and this seemed to jolt him out of his story. He looked over at me and remembered his audience. I could tell he regretted saying too much, and he quickly changed the topic. I was disappointed at such an abrupt and unsatisfying conclusion to the story but could get him to say no more. But he had said enough. If not for that little story of his—if my father's tongue had not been so loose that night—then my own story would have turned out very differently.

# CHAPTER 4

# Payment as Agreed

That night would prove to be my father's last visit to the cave. On the return trip he fell on the wet rocks and broke his hip.

So it was that I became his caretaker. I moved into his disintegrating home, swept it out and patched the leaking roof. Uncle Pto came from time to time to look at our one-room house and to gloat. He told us all about his plans to build a second house for his servant. Even with my father bed-ridden, Pto took every opportunity to mock him. He was always asking when he could expect to see the new ox. The truth is we did not have even a chicken and had to live on fish and whatever I could gather from the forest.

During this time my father was a changed man. He tolerated Pto's visits because he had nothing else to look forward to. He no longer talked about his masterpiece. He had no interest in rituals or in reciting the village history or telling the stories of our forefathers. Sometimes he would stare blankly at me, as if he had forgotten who I was.

It was many months before my father was ready to be on his feet again. One day I helped him out to the river. I thought it would do him good, and indeed he seemed to respond well to the sunlight and the wind and the closeness of the slow-moving river. He was pointing out the birds to me and telling me their lore when suddenly he stopped what he was saying. A light came into his eyes.

"Do you hear that?" he said, grabbing hold of my shoulders and staring into my eyes with an intensity that took me by surprise. "Do you hear it?" he demanded again and gave me a little shake.

I heard nothing out of the ordinary; I thought he was still talking about birds. But then I heard it, too: Singing! A group of people singing, their voices carrying over the smooth surface of the water. Someone was coming up the river.

When he saw that I had heard it too, my father's face became the visage of joy. He spoke quickly: "Listen to me, boy, this is the day I have waited for. Go to the cave—run!—and bring my masterpiece down to the landing."

I could make no sense of any of this. All I knew was that my father was happier than I had ever seen him. But despite his command I did not want to leave him there, barely able to stand on his own—that is, until he gave me a vigorous push and cried, "Go, fool! I will meet you at the landing." So I went.

Now, remember, the way to the cave was not easy. I had to double back several times to find my way through the maze of rocks. When I finally made it to the cliff-top I paused to look out over the river and caught my first sight of the expedition paddling up-river. A string of longboats was rounding the bend, carrying goods and livestock and dozens of men and women, a mix of foreigners and natives. Every voice was lifted in song. This was my first time to hear an Alyonic chant and I was struck dumb by the beauty of it. At the fore of the lead boat stood a tall foreign woman, her voice rising above all the others. This was my first time to see a Laginese woman with her skin golden-brown, her long black hair flowing freely, her uninhibited smile. As I stood staring dumbly down at her, she caught sight of me on the cliff: Our eyes met. She kept singing and opened her arms in greeting, and it seemed then that she was singing to me directly. This was too much for me and I quickly hid myself among the rocks. I did not know what to think.

Soon the women on the far bank caught sight of her, too, and they did not much like the look of this free foreign woman; first one or two of them started ululating, and in no time the foreigners' song was drowned out by two dozen women expressing their loud disapproval of the visitors.

I hurried on to the cave. I did not want to disappoint my father. The trail was overgrown now that no one came here anymore. I discovered the cave by very nearly tumbling into it. I steadied myself on the ladder and hurried down into the great open chamber. My father's masterpiece stood waiting just where it was before. I tested its weight and found it lighter than expected. Among my father's abandoned tools I found a piece of rope and used it to tie the figure onto my back. Then I climbed up the ladder and hurried back down toward the village.

But I did not make it far before I was stopped in my tracks by a fearsome stench. Oh, what a foul stench! It crawled up into my nostrils and, I swear, still to this day it festers there, coming out now and again to haunt me.

The source of the stench was a twisted stump of a creature, one eye larger than the other, with wiry hairs bristling here and there at random. He was blocking my way, fixing me with a gaze most malevolent. Until that moment I thought the dwerrig was merely one of my father's stories.

When he glimpsed my father's masterpiece on my back, the dwerrig's expression softened. "What's that you've got there?" he purred, his speech gravelly but fluent.

I opened my mouth but could not speak for my shock.

"Is that for me?" said the dwerrig. "And here I thought you had forgotten me. Show me see what it is you've brought me."

I took a step back. "I'm sorry," I managed. I was not about to give the statue over to him. The thought of my father's disappointment was too much for me to bear.

"What do you mean, 'sorry'? Have you an offering or not?"

"Of course I brought you something," I said, thinking quickly. "I'm only sorry my people have forgotten the old ways."

"Well then, give it over. It looks like a fine offering, the finest I've seen."

"This?" I said, swallowing. "No, you don't want this. I have something better for you."

"Oh?"

"My first born son," I said. It seemed a clever idea at the time, since I never planned to have children of my own.

The dwerrig considered my offer. "Hmmm. One boy is not enough. My offense is not so cheaply healed. No fewer than three children shall I require before I am satisfied."

"Then I shall give you my grandchildren," I said.

"All of them?"

"Certainly. In fact, why settle for grandchildren? I will give you my great grandchildren instead. Think of how many that will be."

"Very well," said the dwerrig, stepping aside for me to pass, and I went on my way, feeling very satisfied with myself and glad to escape his stench. That was the last I would see of him, I was sure. I planned to leave my village behind and travel the world, like my father.

But at the moment I was in a hurry to get back down to the village, eager to see the visitors. The statue's weight, though, threw me off balance and I had to tread with painstaking care to avoid sliding down the crumbling cliff-side.

When finally I made it down to the landing I saw the men of the village standing around grinning dumbly, charmed by the tall foreign woman. She was passing out flowers and gifts and spoke in respectable Soofian with a voice that was like honey in the men's ears. Meanwhile her followers, Soofian and Laginese alike, busied themselves unloading the longboats, smiling and joking amongst themselves, clearly glad to have arrived at last.

None of the villagers knew why the strangers had come, but they were welcomed as honored guests. None of the men even bothered to bring their weapons because they had heard the singing and knew these strangers could not be dangerous. It was impossible to hear such song and be afraid. Even the women had ceased their lamentations after one boat went across the river laden with gifts of Laginese spices and tobacco.

My father was waiting for me impatiently, just out of sight of the main group. When I arrived he unfastened the wood statue from my back and looked it over appraisingly, smoothing out the feathers and polishing the stone eyes. Still breathing heavily from my trip to the cave, I watched him as he worked, glad to see his hands busy, his mind engaged. "It'll have to do," he said, pretending at dissatisfaction, but I could tell he was proud as ever of his masterpiece. "Come," he said, and I followed after him, carrying the statue.

When the foreign woman saw my father, she called him by his name and embraced him warmly, much to my surprise and to the surprise of the village men. My father introduced me as his son and her eyes touched mine a second time. "I believe we have met already," she said with a smile. But as soon as she spoke her eyes moved on to my father's masterpiece. Then she seemed to forget all else. Her face went slack and it was her turn to be dumbstruck. I put the statue on the ground for her, and she knelt to inspect it up close. "It's perfect," she said. The men of the village gathered round and added their praise, applauding my father as the local genius, forgetting for the moment his status as an outcast. My father stood up straight and smiled grimly, absorbing this long-awaited moment. "It is all you promised," said the foreign woman. "And more. Now here is your payment as we agreed." She motioned over a foreign man with an ox; he passed the reins to my father.

# CHAPTER 5

# A Bad Place, Best Forgotten

Head held high, my father led his ox away while the foreigners set up camp. This morning he could barely stand on his own; now his limp was barely noticeable.

I walked alongside, full of questions. Who was that woman? Where does she come from? How do you know each other? How did she know to bring you an ox? He said nothing but was obviously enjoying himself.

Coming the other way along the trail we encountered my Uncle Pto. "What's going on?" he wanted to know. "I thought I heard singing..." Then his eyes fell on the ox and he stopped in place. "What is *that*? Where did *that* come from?"

My father did not slow his pace, forcing Pto to hop aside to make room on the trail for the ox. Pto stared agog at the animal as it passed. I emulated my father and simply walked on in a dignified manner, saying nothing. And the ox for his part stepped lively, glad to be off the boat at last.

•

Finally when we were home and my father in his bed, he took mercy on me and told me about the woman.

Her name was Hava, he said, and she came from the far side of the known world, from the land of Lagin. He told me the story of how he met her years ago in the sea-port of Harta. They made fast friends, recognizing in one another a kindred spirit and a shared love of wandering. She was on a voyage around the world collecting dolls for her father, a famous doll-maker in the land of Lagin.

In her father's ship Hava had amassed an astounding array of dolls collected from the shores of the Carolyn Sea. All of these dolls were very fine, to be sure, but to my father's eyes none compared to the ones he saw during that rainy season of his youth when he was a guest in the house of Korieski.

My father thought to himself, "I saw how Korieski made those dolls. I am clever with my hands; I could do that myself." And aloud he promised Hava a doll far superior to any she had in her collection if only she would come to his home in the remotest corner of Soofia to collect it. Intrigued—and not one to pass up a challenge—Hava promised to some day make the journey inland up the River Flegmarn. And if the doll was everything he said it was, she would happily pay him the price he requested: an ox to plow his field.

•

That night my father smiled in his sleep. The morning found him weak from the exertions of the previous day—but still smiling.

He needed my help getting out of bed. I walked him to the doorway so he could lean against the doorframe and gaze out at his ox in the field.

That day Hava came to visit bearing gifts of tobacco and dried cactus. She sat at my father's bedside and told him the story of her journey upriver. They laughed together like old friends.

I brought food and water, then faded into the corner. I found myself watching our guest in amazement. Her very presence seemed to fill our home with light and air. To me she was some exotic creature from another world.

Hava asked about the foods offered to her, wanting to know what each was called and where it grew. She asked about the lay of the land to the north, east, south, and west. Smoking the tobacco she gave him, my father spoke at length with great authority on these matters. And though she didn't ask, he also told her all about the lore and traditions of our village.

Finally Hava came round to asking what was foremost in her mind. In Lagin scattered rumors had come to her family, telling of an old madman who lived alone in the deepest wilds of Soofia, making dolls of an extraordinary nature. It was said these dolls mimicked life in such exquisite veracity that they were in fact alive, possessed of a true living spirit.

To search out the truth of these rumors, Hava's father financed her expedition to Deepest Soofia. Her purpose was to find the master doll-maker if he was real and, if possible, acquire some of his work to bring back for her father's collection.

Hava came to our village seeking my father, to honor the agreement they made years ago in Harta, but also to find out what he knew of the rumored doll-maker.

But for once my father was quiet. He shook his head slowly and said, "No, I have never heard of such a thing before. Perhaps it was only me they spoke of." I was about to open my mouth when he silenced me with a sharp glance.

•

After Hava left for the night, I confronted my father. "Why didn't you tell her about the doll-maker, that Korieski?"

In his eyes I could see my question made him very tired. "I should never have told you about that," he said. "It is a bad place, best forgotten."

# The Wrong Idea

"A bad place, best forgotten," I repeated grimly, pausing in my story and surveying my crew-mates, meeting their expectant gazes.

I took a long draw from my water skin and wiped my mouth with the back of my hand. "I have said enough about my father. He died soon after. His part of the story is at an end and my story begins."

•

Hava's expedition returned to my village some weeks later, after a long but fruitless exploration of the surrounding hill country. The expedition was greeted with much joy in the village, particularly by me.

Since my father's death, I had gone every day to check on the boats and supplies that the expedition had left neatly stowed in a lean-to near the village center. I would sit there, a self-appointed guardian, and dream of their return. There was no doubt in my mind what I wanted: to join the expedition, to become an explorer like my father.

Already I had given away my father's ox to his brother Pto. Now I was merely waiting. In my mind I was already gone.

When word came that Hava's expedition had returned, I dropped what I was doing and ran to meet them.

I found Hava cheerful from her journeys but no closer to finding what she sought. She was sorry but not surprised to hear of my father's death.

Her expedition was breaking up, she said. Their supplies were running thin. Half her people were to return downriver to Qarat. The other half would take the remaining supplies and press on for one final drive, deep south into the Ucheti. She thanked me for my offer, but said there was no space for me in the smaller, leaner group.

But I was not so easily deterred. "I will hunt for you," I said. "I don't need supplies. I am used to living off the land. I will show *you* how to live off the land."

In the end she had little choice but to take me on. "You are your father's son," she told me.

•

A week later I was living my dream, on the trail with Hava, passing into territory beyond the farthest wanderings of my childhood, seeing the places I knew only from my father's tales. These days were a joy to me, my first taste of the wanderer's life. I loved it, and loved Hava best of all.

Not that I spent much time with Hava on the trail. Her man-at-arms, a surly mustachioed Laginese by the name of Olio, kept himself perpetually between us. The more excuses I found to linger in Hava's presence, the more I found Olio's stout body between us, his eyes glowering at me from beneath great bushy eyebrows. "Why don't you make yourself useful, lad," he would say in broken Soofian, thrusting a bucket into my hands to fetch water. Or, "Don't you have roots to gather or some such?"

One night without warning Olio seized hold of my arm with a terrible grip, his ogre of a thumb digging unnecessarily into my armpit, and he dragged me away from camp. Once we were out of sight, he put me up against a tree, crumpling my vest in his grip. "I think it's time you and me had a private talk," he said. "You think I'm blind? I see the way you look at her. You need to understand one thing: You will never. Ever. Lay a hand on her."

I could see that he was serious. "All right," I said, trying to get my arms up in a defensive posture. "You've got the wrong idea. It's not like that at all."

His eyes drilled into mine until he was sure my intentions were harmless. Only then did he loosen his grip a little. His eyes softened. "Okay then. So long as we're clear." He unrumpled my vest and tried his best to straighten it. "Sorry. You have to understand, I work for her father. And her husband. Just doing my job."

After that, Olio and I were the best of friends. I think that what Olio realized in that moment was that the love I had for Hava was not so different from his own feelings toward her.

●

One night at the fire I overheard the two of them arguing. I was starting to pick up some of their Laginese and could make out the gist of their words. There was a disagreement about our course. Hava had been leading us west, ridge by ridge, over the shoulder of the mountain range. Olio felt that we should veer south-west and begin our descent toward the confluence of the Durez with the Flegmarn. But Hava wanted to press on and higher along the successive ridges to reach the remote jungle valleys beyond.

"There's nothing there!" decried Olio.

"Exactly," said Hava. "That's why we should go there."

There followed a murmured back-and-forth, hunched over a sketchy map whose accuracy had already been called into question. They debated my father's words about the contours of the mountains. Hava's eyes fell on me. "Let the boy settle the matter," she said.

A lazy eavesdropper, I was alarmed to find myself thrust suddenly into the center of attention. Olio glowered at me.

"Ejertine," said Hava, "you must have heard your father's travel tales a hundred times. And did you not overhear when he told me of this route? I have counted seven ridgelines since leaving your village. Four lie ahead. What's in store for us is an easy climb followed by a steep descent into the jungle. There are no tribes anywhere along the route, at least not when your father passed this way. Would you say that is correct?"

I nodded, a little flushed. This was the first time Hava had consulted me on anything. I felt like I was being treated as a man—although she'd just referred to me as the "the boy."

"Now Olio would have us head downhill tomorrow and be out in the open plains the following day."

"We would make faster time," said Olio. "We can still reach the Ucheti by going around the mountains. And there'll be game and roots to be had along the way." This last point resonated with me. Up here on the slopes, I was going hungry.

"But that whole region is full of tribes," countered Hava. "That way might be faster, but it is the more dangerous route. We do not want to get caught up in some local war. The place we are seeking is a remote one, a place without tribes."

"I'd be more worried about grithies or renegades up in the mountains," said Olio, his voice rising. Now they were staring each other down. I tried to melt into the background while the other members of the camp pretended not to notice.

"Admit it, Olio, you just hate mountains."

"The only thing worse is the jungle—and now you mean to drag us into a place that is both mountains and jungle! What kind of man-eating monstrosities do you suppose lurk in a place like that? Will I hear you speak of safety then?"

"Why, Olio... can it be that you are afraid? And I thought I had hired a hardened adventurer as my man-at-arms!"

"With respect, my lady, you did not hire me. Your father hired me to protect you. That's what I'm trying to do. Here is the question I must ask myself: Is this a hazard really worth undertaking? Do you have any reason to believe that this mythic doll-maker of yours even exists?"

Then it happened. My mouth opened, words spilled out. I don't know why I said it exactly. Maybe it's because I missed my opportunity earlier to say something clever and impress Hava when she turned to me for advice. Whatever the reason, I said it; I told them, "The doll-maker's real."

Now both of them were looking at me. I remembered my father's words: a bad place, best forgotten. But there was no going back now.

"My father did not tell you everything." I talked fast and told them everything I knew: how my father went over the high pass and descended into the Deep Valley Durez, how he found the house of Korieski, how Korieski made tiny dolls that seemed so real as to be alive. "This is where my father's inspiration came from for his own work."

Hava's reaction to my words gratified me. Her smile outshined the campfire. "I knew that man was holding something back," she exclaimed, leaping to her feet. "In the morning we turn south and begin the climb to the pass. Sleep well!"

And so it was settled. I did not care that I would be hungry in the days to come. Hava's approval was nourishment enough for me, and I lay down to sleep with a great smile. What a fool I was.

# CHAPTER 7

# Not in My Village Anymore

I will spare you an accounting of the hardships that followed. It is enough to say our new route took us over disagreeable terrain. Instead of following along the ridgelines as my father advised, we now confronted the slopes head-on. Over each ridge lay a higher ridge beyond it. At each ridge top we were rewarded with a view of our destination high above, taunting us.

During this time I stayed true to my pledge to live off the land. I refused food even when it was offered. I lived off scorpions mostly. On a good day I would find a rabbit or a bird and kill it with a well-aimed stone. I always shared what I killed, even though there was never enough. By necessity my hunting skills did at least improve.

Worse than the hunger was Olio's grumbling. Hava was right about him and mountains: They just didn't get along.

But Olio was right to fear the mountains. This became abundantly clear to all of us when, picking our way along the top of a ridgeline, a silent shadow flashed over; and just like that, we lost one of our pack mules, picked off by the great roc that inhabited those mountains.

After that incident, we had to think twice before exposing ourselves on the ridges that way. We moved cautiously and kept our eyes on the sky. Losing the supplies with the mule was bad enough, but worse still was the skittishness of the two remaining mules. As the way became steeper, their restiveness made the going all the more difficult and treacherous.

The pass was tantalizingly close now. Hava called a halt from a vantage where I swear I could have thrown a stone and had it land in the pass, but a dizzying abyss yawned between us and our destination. There was no way for the mules to get across unless we lowered them with ropes, and the prospects of their getting up the far wall seemed improbable.

I watched Hava and Olio exchanging measured words as they looked down upon their weary crew, most of whom seized upon this respite from climbing in welcome collapse, unused as most of them were to the high mountain air. I, too, was tired to the bone and ragged with hunger, but I was not about to show as much with Hava looking on.

Hava came among the members of her expedition, the wind whipping at her hair, and called out, "Listen up. You have got me this far, to the very edge of the known world. You have done more than enough. I go the rest of the way alone, with Olio as my guard. There's not enough supplies to feed us all. The rest of you will return the way we came and bring word to those who wait in Qarat. Tell them I am close to finding what I came for. He is no fable: His name is Korieski, he lives in the jungles beyond this pass. I will find him. I am not about to return to my father in Lagin with empty hands, to tell him I came this far only to turn back again."

And so it was decided. Hava kept the climbing gear but sent the remaining supplies with her crew. They wept, they embraced Hava, but no one argued. I stood silently by as the expedition set off back down the way they had come. "I'm staying with you," I said matter-of-factly.

Hava looked at me sidelong with a smile. "I was hoping you would," she said, giving my shoulder a squeeze. It was enough to make my young little heart burst.

Olio laid his heavy hand upon my other shoulder. "We're going to need you, lad."

We moved quickly without the mules and extra bodies. In a few hours we attained the pass, lightly dusted with snow—the first snow I'd ever touched. Two mighty peaks towered on either side, covered in the stuff. Between these two walls of snow and stone we had an easy trudge and soon enough we were through to the far side.

What greeted us there was a view more spectacular than I can begin to say. There were no ridge-lines beyond this one, just a great, single slope plummeting downwards into a vast cavity: The Deep Valley Durez stretched before us, vivid green, choked with life piled atop of life. Even at this height we could hear the calls of bird and beast rising from the jungle.

Ringed by mountains, the valley was no less than a hundred miles long and nearly as wide, emptying into the greater Ucheti far to the southwest. Few men can claim to have seen the Valley, much less from such a height.

We stood for perhaps half an hour, just taking it in with our eyes. I remember Olio muttering, "How do you expect to find one man, if he even exists, in that great mess?" Hava just smiled that radiant smile she had and started down the slope.

Two days we spent on the slope and had a relatively easy time of it. A great many birds made their nests on the cliffs, and there were eggs to be had. For the first time in more than a week, our bellies were satisfied. We were merry, we swapped stories. Hava sang softly for us while the moon rose. This was, I think, my happiest time. I felt for the first time part of a family.

At the edge of the jungle, we made a spear for each of us. When the foliage closed around us, we found it surprisingly dark even at noon, but we did not lack for game: monkeys and boars and spangas. We made fires and feasted on meat. When it rained we sheltered under broad-leaved trees that funneled every drop of rain into repositories in their trunks, leaving us utterly dry beneath.

It was the insects that were the bane of us, with their thousand varieties of bites and stings. Once I saw a mantis tall as my waist; we kept it at bay with our spears and marveled at it while it watched us with equal interest, its alien eyes measuring us. Olio joked it was sizing us up and would return later with its mother to nip off our heads.

The jokes ended when we became the intended prey for real. We were crossing a mucky channel, ankle-deep in mire, when what I thought was a log lurched forward across my way, making a lunge for Olio. I gave a shout of warning and Olio leapt up onto a rock just in time as mandibles the size of my arms slid out of the sides of the monstrosity's head, snapping closed in the place Olio had been standing. It was a good twelve feet long, this beast, with six scaly legs. I broke my spear on the armor of its back, and its tail came whipping around, knocking me off my feet.

Olio pulled me up to safety. The beast slithered or crawled straight ahead twenty feet or so before turning itself slowly back to face us. "Come on," called Hava, urging us back up the embankment where we could get some height over the monster.

"What the hell is that thing?" growled Olio, gripping his spear.

"A barrakapa," I told him. My father had told me about them: creepers of the jungle, ambush hunters.

The thing was returning our stares. It took a step forward.

"Come on," I said. "Let's outdistance it." We moved quickly, leaving the beast behind. I looked back over my shoulder, saw no sign of pursuit.

That night we made a fire. Olio was in a foul mood, crankier than usual. I think the barrakapa had shaken him up. "With things like that lurking in the weeds, how am I supposed to protect you?" he demanded of Hava. "One snap and you're bit in two. What will I tell your father then?"

"We shall have to be careful," was her reply.

Then, all at once, the thing erupted from the dark. It had followed us. Straight into the fire it dived, snapping and thrashing, knocking us aside. I think the fire must have blinded or confused it; lucky for us. I don't need to tell you the terror it gave us. Olio and Hava scrambled up into the trees. I was already holding my knife, and without really thinking I reacted, sticking the blade into the barrakapa's eye. It didn't much like that, or the fire either, and in its thrashing I was thrown well clear. My thigh was bloodied from the rough horns it had along its neck. I still have those scars as a reminder.

The fire had been scattered and was more or less out as the barrakapa found me with its one good eye, my knife still protruding from its other socket. I decided this was a good time to join Olio and Hava in the trees, and I scampered up out of the creature's reach, heedless of my injury.

"Are you all right, lad?" called Olio from his tree.

"Splendid," I said.

Then the barrakapa charged my tree. The impact nearly shook me loose. I was sorry I hadn't chosen a more established tree.

"Look out," warned Hava. "He means to fell you."

The monster was backing up for another charge. I could see where his mandibles had closed on the trunk, splitting it to its core.

I climbed as high as I could; the tree bent under my weight. As the barrakapa charged a second time, I closed my hands on a neighboring vine hanging down from the high reaches of the canopy. The tree shuddered and snapped, flinging me even as I tightened my hold on the vine. My back slammed into another tree, I spun around. The vine did not hold me; my weight pulled it down and I landed roughly in a spiny fern. I heard the monster coming for me. I was too stunned to find my feet.

Then there was Olio with his spear, sparring with the beast.

My head spinning, I pulled myself up. Olio was stabbing at the barrakapa, targeting its good eye. It charged, he stepped to the side and came at it again from the side. The beast was slow to turn, and Olio used this to his advantage. It tried pivoting the other way and struck with its tail, but Olio was ready for that. He jumped over its body and struck on its blind side, jamming his spear between its scales. It had had enough then and rushed off into the dark, taking Olio's spear with it.

"Come on," said Olio, pulling me along. "Let's get out of here before it changes its mind." Hava shimmied down from her tree and together we made speed through the jungle.

"It followed us," I said, incredulous.

"Are those things territorial?"

"I—think so," I said without much conviction. My father told me they liked to lie about in riverbeds. But we were nowhere close to a river or even a stream.

Olio kept us moving, though the nighttime jungle was darker than pitch. We walked into an army of biting ants that got into our clothes. I kept running my face into webs, and who knows what kind of poisonous spiders lurked in those webs? But Olio kept pressing us on.

"What if we run into another of those barrakapa?" I wanted to know.

"It won't be as mad as that one," he answered. "I'm beginning to think it's got something personal against us."

"That's preposterous," said Hava. "It's only looking for its supper."

But I was starting to believe Olio was right. There were no people in this jungle so far as I could tell, so where would this beast have developed a taste for human flesh? We were not its natural prey. This was some other type of aggression.

When dawn came, Olio finally called a stop. "You two get some sleep," he said. "I'll keep watch."

When I woke, I saw Olio had made four or five more spears from bamboo. Hava was still asleep. "This is madness," he said quietly. "No doll is worth this. If I ever make it back to Lagin, I will find someone else to work for. The whole Nipalto family is crazy."

But when Hava woke, Olio was full of sweetness. He found some fruit and told her about a nearby waterfall and pool where she could bathe. "That was quite some excitement we had last night," said Hava. "You all right, Ejertine?"

I was pretty stiff and sore, truth be told. My breeches were torn and bloodied, and my gouged thigh was muddy. She took me down to the waterfall and cleaned me up while Olio stood guard. Embarrassed though I was to take down my pants with Hava looking on, there was no question my wound needed tending. In my village, a woman was never allowed to look on a naked man, except during the appointed times. But then we weren't in my village anymore.

"I'm sorry I got you into this," said Hava gently.

"Are you kidding?" I replied. "I'm having the time of my life." Which was true.

We pressed on, deeper into the valley, coming finally to the River Durez, full of snakes big enough to swallow a man. There were crocodiles, too, and elephants who regarded us warily from across the river, flapping their ears with trepidation.

"There's no crossing this," announced Olio. "Not without making a raft."

Hava shrugged. "I'm not sure we need to cross. For all we know, our Korieski lives on this side of the river. But a raft is an excellent notion, the better to conduct our search. We can cover a lot more area by raft."

So Olio cleared the snakes out from a patch of bamboo and I went about selecting mature canes for a raft. Here's where I came in useful again, having manufactured more than a few rafts in my day. Olio and I chopped down the canes and laid them out on the bank while Hava kept watch for crocodiles and other perils. We put our rope to good use as lashing and finished the raft in a few hours.

"We'll test it in the morning," said Olio.

"No, we launch it now," said Hava as she approached, her face pale.

"What is it?"

"I saw tracks." She pointed back the direction she had come. "It followed us, I think."

"What!" Olio made her show him the tracks.

"See here? That's no crocodile, I think. It came, looked at us, then slunk into the undergrowth there."

"Ye gods, she's right," declared Olio. "Let's get that raft in the water."

"No way," I said. "We haven't a chance against that thing in the water."

Olio and Hava exchanged glances. "Then we end this here," said Olio. "We stand our ground and we kill it."

We used our remaining daylight to prepare our defenses. We picked our spot on the bank near our raft and dug a shallow, circular trench about twelve feet in diameter. We emplaced sharpened bamboo spikes at an angle around the perimeter of the trench. "Let's build a nice heaping fire in the middle," said Olio. "That seemed to confound it last time. It'll probably wait for nightfall, but watch yourselves, now, don't let it sneak up on you."

As darkness fell, we waited next to the fire. "Let's lay down, pretend to sleep," suggested Olio. "Keep your spear in hand, though, he'll come at us quick, maybe from the water below, maybe from the jungle above. Keep your wits about you now. If things go bad, find a nice big tree and climb it."

We waited.

An hour passed. Then another.

The rain took us by surprise. One or two drops, and then it was pouring. "Keep the fire going," urged Olio.

Our fire was big enough to survive the rain, but before we knew it, the river was lapping at our trench. "This is no good," I said. "We've got to make for the trees."

"The raft!" called Hava, pointing. The raft was sliding into the rising river.

I leapt up to save the raft. "Leave it!" shouted Olio, his voice drowned out by a sudden clap of thunder from a nearby lightning strike, which cast a blinding light over the scene.

And there, on the other side of the raft I saw the barrakapa lying in wait for me. I lost my footing in my panic. The monster scrambled over the top of the raft at me, but the motion of the raft saved me. I rolled backward. Olio was there, saving me once more. He pulled me back behind our defenses.

A surge in the river swept over our feet, washing away our trench. Our sharpened bamboo spikes did little to slow the giant barrakapa; it swept them aside like toys.

"Run for it!" screamed Olio to another clap of thunder. He reached into the fire with his bare hands and threw the burning mass of wood atop the monster while Hava and I ran for the trees. I glanced back and saw Olio circling around the beast with his spear even as it threw off the burning logs.

"Olio!" I shouted. "Forget it! Come on!" I saw one of the burning logs roll into the rushing river and there I spied three or four crocodiles closing in on the turmoil. "Behind you, Olio! Look out!"

Olio couldn't spare a look behind him. He drove his spear point home into the barrakapa's flank, putting all his weight into it. The monster threw him off, then caught Olio with its tail, knocking him into the river.

I was sure that was the end of Olio. I couldn't see him for the dark and the rain, but in a mad rage I charged the barrakapa where it lay among a scatter of still-burning logs. I heard Hava scream at me from behind but I did not care. I did not even have my spear. The monster saw me coming and it charged to meet me, head to head. I realized then my tactic was perhaps not the most prudent. At the last possible moment I leapt as high as I could, just clearing its snapping mandibles, and I landed on its back and fell sideways, cutting my head on one of the bamboo points.

As I righted myself, the beast slithered forward where I now saw Hava, spear in hand. She stood her ground and let the monster charge her. I was horrified. The expression on her face... she didn't even look frightened... just determined. She stabbed the thing right in its open maw. Her spear broke, she fell, the beast was upon her. I found my spear where I dropped it by the fire and went as fast as I could.

Hava was lying on the ground. The beast was disappearing up the embankment. I rushed to her, fearing the worst.

"I'm all right," she said, though she was bleeding from a deep gash in her arm and I could see a massive footprint on her bosom where the monster had stepped on her. "I think I got it good."

"Come on," I said, lifting her onto my shoulders.

Then, to my amazement, Olio was at my side. "I thought I told you to climb a tree."

"I thought you were dead!"

"I don't die so easy. Give me your spear, I'm going after that thing."

"Are you crazy?"

He took my spear. "Look after her," he said and scrambled up the embankment after the barrakapa.

●

At dawn, the three of us—Hava, Olio, and me—huddled together in the hollow of a giant tree, where we had some shelter from the pouring rain.

"It's still out there somewhere," said Olio grimly.

"It was mortally wounded," answered Hava. "I got it right in the mouth."

Olio shook his head. "That probably just made it madder."

"Suppose it *is* still out there," said Hava. "Do you think it will be coming after us now? After all the hurt we've heaped upon it?"

"That thing, it's no ordinary animal. It's got the heart of a demon in it, I'm sure of it. It intends to end us. It hates us now more than ever."

"Where does all that hate come from?" I asked.

Olio shrugged. "Don't try to understand evil, lad. It's got no reason to it."

"I can't believe that," said Hava.

"Believe it. Hava, listen: This doll-maker you want to find for your father so badly... You've got to see that a doll, even a living doll, is not worth dying for. Your father would much rather have you alive."

Hava smiled weakly. "At least now you admit the doll-maker exists."

"Fine. He exists. Look, I'm not saying we give up. I know that's not in your nature. What I'm saying is, with that monster out there, hell-bent on killing us, and us in the shape we're in... I'm just saying we need to retreat. Stay ahead of it, get out of the jungle before it can catch up to us again. Regroup."

"Regroup," repeated Hava hollowly.

"Olio's right," I put in. "The rainy season's started in, anyhow. The smart thing to do is get out of the jungle, wait out the rain, resupply. Korieski will still be there after the rainy season."

Hava looked from one of us to the other. "It seems I have no choice. But where to go? We're closed in by mountains."

"We make southwest for Aymad," said Olio firmly.

"Aymad! That must be three hundred miles from here."

"We can pick up proper supplies. Rations, weapons, traps, a mule."

"But Aymad..."

"It's a place you've never been. The city of a thousand tribes. Think of the romance of it. When will you ever be in this far corner of the world again to see it?"

Hava shook her head slowly. Olio smiled; it was not often he won an argument with Hava.

# CHAPTER 8

# Aymad

So we marched day and night through the mud, keeping Olio's brutal pace. It may have saved our lives. Maybe the beast was after us the whole way. Or maybe it was dead. We never knew for sure.

When we emerged from the jungle, Olio continued our death march until we were well clear of the foliage and had nothing but open plains all around. Only then did he let us rest.

The next day we made for Aymad. The rain fell on us every day.

The sodden plains were rich with nomadic tribes, and among these we found our share of friends as well as enemies, including the Trngste who laughed at our story of the demon-beast in the jungle, taking us for fools; and the Musaab who coexist with elephants as full members of their tribe; the Dzrnyelki whose chief wanted Hava for his bride after hearing her sing; the Chernobvabve who made Olio fight to prove his worth; and the Chakls, famous for their rock-stacking skills, who gave us shelter, food, and good company.

But it is in Aymad where my story gets interesting. Aymad, the one great city in the wildlands of the Ucheti. Trade capital of a thousand tribes. Here the King's power was second to tribal power. I was excited as Hava to see the place. I knew it only from my father's descriptions: a sprawling conglomeration of huts and hovels and tents with no discernible beginning or end, like a thousand villages thrown into a hopper and scattered haphazardly, all jumbled up, people and livestock and all. You'd see people walking in twos or threes with matching tribal markers—piercings, tattoos, feathers, axes, helmets—but no one set the same as another, it seemed, and each group conversing in their own weird dialect of Soofian. They came from all over Bvosoly to barter in the vast chaos of Aymad.

We were not long in Aymad before we found our niche. Every night Hava's singing summoned massive audiences of men, none who could understand her Laginese but who were nonetheless entranced (as I was) with her voice. They showered her with gifts and more than a few marriage proposals.

By day Hava would send me out with a handful of the gifts she'd received the night before, and I would see what I could find in trade. In a few days we had machetes, a fine bow, new boots for Olio, and whole bagfuls of salted meats. Within a week I'd even found us a pack mule. Aymad: that's where I learned my knack for commerce.

Well, one day in Aymad I was coming out from a trade tent, my arms laden with eggs, when a passing young man jostled me roughly. "Out of my way, cretin," he snarled, and I lost my eggs, every one.

"Hey, watch where you're going!" I shouted at his back, but he didn't even deign to glance back.

A slave girl from the sex market stopped to help me brush the broken eggs from my breeches. "Call me a cretin, will he? He's the cretin."

"Don't mind him," said the girl. "That's just Korieski."

It was like she'd thrown cold water on me. "What name did you name him?"

"Korieski," she repeated. "He's no good, that one, believe me."

"Thanks," I said, pressing a bronze ring into her palm by way of appreciation. I hurried after the man before he was lost to my sight. My mind raced. Korieski? Here? A heavy bag tossed over his shoulder, he charged through the maze of trade tents pitched in the grassy commons. He was tall and young... too young to be our Korieski. But still I followed at a distance, trailing him out of the tent city and down into a rocky ravine. There an ancient ruin lay collapsed; some of its tumbled stones had been repurposed to build a wall of a crude, half-subterranean dwelling. A malicious-looking dog chained outside the door lifted its head as the young Korieski approached. He kicked a loose stone at the dog, rousing it to its feet with an angry snarl. He shouted something at it before passing through the arched doorway and into the ominous-looking dwelling. I noted several chimneys snaking up from the place along the wall of the ravine, issuing smoke of several different colors.

The dog turned a suspicious eye toward me, and I moved on. I hurried back to our camp to find Hava deeply engrossed in negotiations with three old women. I caught Olio's eye and motioned him over.

"What, no eggs?" he said, disappointed.

"I found us something better than eggs. I found us a Korieski."

"What?" Glancing over his shoulder at Hava, he took me aside. "What's that now?"

I told him about my encounter with the surly young Korieski and how I trailed him to his lair.

"Hmmm," said Olio. He grabbed his sword and fastened his sheath to his belt. "Let's go have a look."

"What about Hava?" I asked.

"Awww, she's happy as can be with these makers of porcelain dolls. She's arranging for a whole passel to be shipped off to her father in Kortholomoth. I say let's leave her out of it for now, until we've scouted out the situation. Could be dangerous."

So the two of us sneaked off. I showed Olio to the ravine. "There, you see? Where the smoke is coming from." We crouched at the top of the ravine, scoping out the ruins and Korieski's subterranean lair.

"Only the one door in and out?"

"As far as I know." The dog still sat on his haunches outside the door, biting his fleas.

We watched for a while, to see if anyone would come or go. We did not expect someone to come from behind.... A shadow fell over us, we turned... and there was a figure, arms raised, a black cloak, a staff topped with twin serpent heads. Before my eyes, I swear to you, these carved serpent heads came to life and turned their horrible gaze upon us.

Those eyes… those eyes got hold of us and wouldn't let us go. Olio and I both fell under their power, frozen in place. We were helpless, unable even to lift our arms to defend ourselves when the man with the staff came to cudgel us over the heads. He had to club Olio twice before he went down.

I don't even remember getting hit. But I do remember the headache that greeted me upon waking. I was tied to a rough bench, my bonds cruelly tight. The room was spinning as I tried to focus. I remember the smell of fumes, the sound of something sizzling. Low voices saying something about us. Olio was beside me, half awake.

A bucket of tepid water in our faces roused us to full consciousness. "Who are you? Who sent you?" demanded a mad face, his eyes wild and round, a gray-black shock of hair ringing his face like a mane. It was the man with the serpent-headed staff.

"No one," I stammered. "No one sent us."

We were inside the lair. I glimpsed the young man named Korieski standing across the way before a great iron oven, wearing giant insulated mittens, attending to his work but watching us curiously.

Our interrogator held Olio's sword, fingering its point. "I have no patience for games. Talk quick now, or die."

"The boy speaks the truth," said Olio. "We represent no enemy of yours. We simply heard the name 'Korieski' and came to find the man. Are you he?"

The man looked sharply at his assistant across the room, then back to Olio. "Korieski?" He lowered Olio's sword, disappointed. "Of what interest could you possibly have in that one?"

Korieski took off his oven mitts and approached, bemused.

"We are looking for a Korieski," I said, "but maybe not you."

"I have no time for such nonsense," declared the older man, dropping Olio's sword and pulling up his hood of black. "Korieski, they are yours to dispense with as you please. I expect the rest of the mandrake processed by nightfall." And he took his staff and went out the door. I heard the dog growl as he passed.

We were left with young Korieski, who eyed us shrewdly. He was a pallid boy, lanky in body, with cold eyes.

"Well," he said, "what do you mean you were looking for a Korieski, but maybe not me? There are no other Korieskis about, I assure you. And if you've asked around about me, then you know I'm not one you'd want to seek out. Explain yourselves, or I'll drag you outside and let the dog have at you. We keep him hungry and angry just for such situations."

"Take it easy, lad," said Olio. "It's like this: We're looking for a doll-maker, that's all. A Korieski who makes dolls."

"A Korieski who..." The boy burst into laughter. "What, you mean my father? You seek that old fool?" He laughed at some length, stopping only to choke for breath. Olio and I exchanged glances.

"That is rich," said Korieski. "My father, the maker of dolls. I'm not so sure you would like them so well as you think."

"I'm sorry for the mix-up," I said. "We didn't mean any harm."

"How about untying us," suggested Olio.

Korieski ran a hand through his hair, still chuckling a little. "Why not?" He came around behind and worked on loosening my knots. "Because you amuse me, I shall let you live. Hemech is not so gracious as I."

"Hemech, that's the other fellow?" asked Olio.

"He is the master, I am the pupil. Cruel though he be, Hemech is ten times the man my father ever was."

I got my hands loose and set to untying Olio. Korieski took up his mittens again and went back to the great oven that dominated the laboratory. "All those years out in the jungle in that little house of his... I couldn't take it anymore. Always with the dolls. He expected me to stay and carry on the legacy. Pshaw! This Korieski was made for better things." He took up tongs and opened up the oven, reaching within and flipping something over. I could hear it sizzling.

When Olio was loose, he rubbed his wrists where the rope had cut into them. He opened and closed his hands, getting the blood flowing as he eyed Korieski. He picked up his sword.

"Come on," I said, tugging Olio's sleeve.

"Wait a minute," said Olio. "Tell me, Korieski. Where can we find your father's house?"

Korieski started to say something, but he broke into laughter before he could get the words out. He waved us away.

We heard his guffaws even over the raging of the dog against its chain as we edged by just out of his reach.

# CHAPTER 9

# Don't Thank the Gods

The mate's whistle interrupted my tale.

A general groan of dismay rippled through the Sartans as they gathered themselves up to go back on deck. "Well, what about the rest of the story?" whined one.

"Don't worry, mates," I called. "I'll finish the tale tomorrow."

As the men climbed up onto deck, I saw Semetrius standing in back.

"You got off early," I observed.

"Wanted to check on you. Sounds quite the tale."

I sighed. "I'm sorry about before, Semetrius."

He raised a hand to forestall my concern. "She must have been some woman."

"Yes, she was. Or is. I don't even know if she's still alive."

The men of the third shift were coming belowdecks. I pulled Semetrius aside and whispered, "Listen, my friend. Back there, when I was on watch, I saw something."

Semetrius raised an eyebrow.

"Just for a moment. I saw her."

"Saw who?"

"Her. Hava."

"What, you mean...?"

"I don't know. Maybe it was her spirit. Or maybe she was projecting herself. It was like she was calling for help. Like I was being summoned."

Semetrius searched my eyes. "You believe in such things?"

"When I knew her, Hava was studying to be a Mystan. She is capable of magic. Anything is possible. All I know is… I must go."

"Go? What do you mean, go?"

"Day after tomorrow, we'll be in Kortholomoth. My two-year contract is elapsed."

"What kind of talk is this?"

"She needs me. I can't explain it, Semetrius, but I know it's true. I must go to her."

"Let's not be rash," whispered Semetrius, tugging on my sleeve and pulling me back out into the sun, away from the ears of the crew. "You can't *leave* us. You'll miss Logoss. I can't go to Logoss without you."

The first mate, seeing us conversing in confidence, narrowed his eyes and approached. "What are you men doing on deck? Neither of you is on shift."

"Sir," I said, "I'd like to volunteer to help out this shift. Whatever needs doing."

"Shouldn't you be sleeping?" muttered Semetrius.

The mate considered my request. "Captain doesn't approve his men missing their sleep."

"I won't be sleeping either way, sir. Might as well be useful."

"Very well. You can assist young master Ferrio changing the topsails. What about you, Semetrius?"

"I'll be belowdecks on my rest," said Semetrius with a frown. He shot me a wounded look before turning to go.

"Be sure Ferrio inspects the sails for damage before stowing them," said the mate.

And so I kept myself busy, trying not to think about Hava.

It was well after dark before the mate's whistle blew again. Bleary-eyed, I went to my post at the bow. This was now the beginning of my watch. I served as primary watch on most boats, because my senses were keener than anyone else's. I was almost always the first to detect land, bad weather, another craft, or any of the great variety of trouble that present themselves on the south seas. Most days this work suited me. All Eyes indeed.

But on this night the solitude of the watch was an unwelcome invitation to self reflection, forcing me to face up to what I'd been avoiding. In a few hours I would have to tell the second half of my story. I was going to have to talk about the horror of what happened when we returned to the Deep Valley Durez. About what happened to Hava. Because of me.

There was a reason I'd never spoken of these events before then. My shame was too deep to bear, certainly, but more than that, the sheer terror of the things I experienced was more than I could manage. I was surprised at how much I'd already said, telling the crew even about the dwerrig. These were matters I had not yet reconciled within my own rational mind. It was easier to put them aside and pretend they weren't part of me, though of course they were. I never married, never had children—that was because of the dwerrig. But that's not what I told myself. I never really fell in love—that was because of Hava, but I had never admitted that to myself, either. I had simply taken up the sailor's life, kept moving, and never looked back. Until now.

It was too dark to see land, but I could smell the land and the forest pollens as we sailed north along the coast. The miles couldn't pass quickly enough for me. A dread sense of urgency gnawed at my gut.

Only a few minutes had passed since the start of my watch, and already I was in trouble. Despair was coming for me and I had nowhere to hide.

It was then I became aware of Semetrius, silent at my side. "Oh! I didn't see you there." All Eyes, indeed. I sniffed and blinked back the tears that had started to well up in my eyes.

"It's all right, my friend. I got special permission to join you on watch."

"Thank the gods," I said with a nervous laugh.

"Don't thank them," said Semetrius. "You know I don't believe in gods."

"Neither do I, but thanks to them nonetheless. I didn't want to be alone just now."

"So thank me then."

"Very well. Thank you, Semetrius. You're a true friend."

"I haven't told anyone what you said."

"About the apparition?"

"No, fool. About your leaving the crew. I have a plan to talk you out of it."

"Ah, Semetrius. It's been a good run. I will miss you most of all."

"So," said Semetrius, "since we have this time together and suddenly you're talking about your past, I have some questions about your upbringing."

I groaned. "This is why I don't talk about my past."

# CHAPTER 10

# The Lantern

Semetrius got me through the end of my shift, bless him, and followed me belowdecks. "Don't you have to work *your* shift?" I asked him.

"Are you kidding? I traded again. I'm not about to miss the end of your story." Semetrius settled into the hammock beside mine, normally occupied by Regge, and cheerfully set to rolling himself a cigar.

All the men were quick to grab their soup and stale bread and find their places.

"I suppose you lot will be wanting the rest of the story," I said.

"Don't leave out the sex parts," urged Meyer.

"Quiet, you," bellowed Ugly Tom. "Let him tell it. We want to hear."

"Thank you, Tom." I looked at the cauldron but felt no desire to eat. "I will cut right to it," I said, swallowing.

•

It was in Aymad I left us, where by some odd luck we'd found Korieski's son. When Hava learned of our encounter with Korieski the Younger, there was no stopping her. She knew for certain now that we were on the right trail.

We returned to the Deep Valley Durez well rested, resupplied, and with renewed determination. A guide and three porters joined the expedition. Back across the plains and into the jungle, one adventure followed on the heels of the other. In those days and weeks we must have run up on a dozen barrakapas, but none came hunting after us like the other. Our porters laughed at us and dismissed our recollections as the exaggerations of hysterical foreigners.

Greater perils than barrakapas lurked in that Deep Valley: great bears and blood-vines and pond-things; and a thousand predators of the sky, from the great roc to the swarming striges and harpies; and worst of all, the insects. One by one, men died or left us, until finally our fellowship winnowed again to three: Hava, Olio, and me. By then we knew our way around the valley and had learned our survival strategies well.

We'd spend a week or two at a campsite, sallying out by day to map the features of the region. Then we'd move on to the next region and start over again.

One day, to gain a high vantage, we climbed a peak jutting out like a promontory, forming part of the valley's southern wall. From a cliffside we sighted it a last: Two, perhaps three, miles below us sprouted the roof of a structure, pressing up through the trees like some giant mushroom. The house of Korieski, it had to be!

The rest of the day we spent picking our way down the cliff and then slogging through the jungle, trying to rediscover the house we'd sighted from above. Here in the southern wall of the valley, the jungle was a jagged maze of vine-choked gulches, and the house that had stood out so plainly when viewed from the cliff now defied finding.

Dusk caught up to us and we decided to make camp and resume the search at dawn. Hava was calm and focused, her goal within reach. It was Olio and me who were beside ourselves with anticipation. "This had better be worth it," grumbled Olio, but I could tell he was just as excited as I was. Hava went to sleep while the two of us stayed up with our nervous energy.

Then I saw it. Or maybe it was Olio who saw it first. A light in the jungle, winking between the trees in the gully below us, perhaps five hundred yards distant. We soon lost direct sight but could still see a faint glow reflected in the canopy. It seemed to be moving away from us.

"Faeries?" whispered Olio with dread. We'd seen those before and wanted nothing more to do with them.

But this light was no faerie-glow. It was a lantern.

We woke Hava and told her about the light. Rubbing the sleep from her eyes, she said, "Well, come on, quick!" And we abandoned our camp to go chasing after the light, taking only our weapons with us.

The meager glimmer of a slivered moon did little to illuminate our way, but we soon discovered a well-trod path. "This way," I whispered, leading them along the path in the direction I'd seen the light moving. The path climbed up out of the gully but soon turned sharply to follow along the top of a much deeper ravine. We heard water rushing below, and ahead in the faint moonlight we made out a fantastic land bridge spanning the ravine; and on the trail ahead, the figure of a man with a lantern, treading unhurriedly along the trail, following it out over the natural bridge.

We had a clear view of him silhouetted against the starry sky as he traversed the bridge. His gait and posture made him an old man, and a large, wispy beard glowed yellow and white in the lamplight.

"Korieski," breathed Hava. We hurried after him, easily catching up on the far side of the bridge, but we hung back so as not to startle him. We followed at a distance, as the trail wended slowly uphill. Finally the old man came to his house, jutting from the side of the hill. It was a fine if austere house, taller than it was wide. When the old man went inside, his light made the front windows glow, like two eyes that seemed to glower out at us in judgment, skulking as we were like some robbers in the dark.

"We've found him," declared Hava. "Come on!" And we went up to the front door.

Through the window, I saw the old man struggling out of his cloak and draping it over a chair.

Hava put her hand on the front door, tracing a symbol inlaid in metal. She glanced back at Olio with her eyebrows raised. It was the sigil of Morphid upon the door, though I was ignorant of such things then.

Hava grinned back at us, then she rapped three times upon the door.

# CHAPTER 11

# Korieski's Workshop

The old man stood in the open doorway, blinking at us.

"Hello there," said Hava cheerfully. "Please forgive the intrusion, master. I know the hour is late."

He opened and closed his toothless mouth in consternation, looking at each of us in turn.

"My name is Hava. I've come all the way from Lagin to find you. And these are my stalwart companions, Olio and Ejertine. You are Korieski, I presume?"

"How did you...?" His voice trailed off and he just stood looking at us, trying to comprehend.

"Again, I'm very sorry to surprise you like this. You are a hard man to find. Will you let us in?"

"What?" He shook his head, trying to clear it. "Yes. Yes, of course," he stammered, shuffling aside to let us pass.

We entered into a close den with scarcely enough space for the four of us. Olio jostled the chair with the old man's cloak. A small table held the lantern. "Forgive me," said the man. "I've had no visitors in some years." He moved to close a heavy, arch-shaped door at the end of the room. It made a great thunk when it latched shut. A narrow stairway climbed the opposite wall to a loft above.

"Please, make yourselves comfortable." Our host gestured to a padded bench covered with threadbare cloth.

"Thank you," said Hava, closing the front door behind her. She sat, taking in the unadorned room.

The old man stood next to the heavy door, wringing his hands and looking at us.

"You all right?" asked Olio.

"What?"

"You seem nervous."

"No. Yes. No, it's just I'm unaccustomed. To people. I've been alone such a long time."

"Poor dear," said Hava. "You must be ever so bewildered. Let me explain. We're here about the dolls. My father sent me from Lagin to seek out the best work of Soofian doll-makers. I was hoping I might see some of your work."

"Oh," he said, with some hesitation. His eyes darted to the arched doorway. "No... I'm afraid I don't really.... What I mean to say is, my workshop is private. I'm not able to... I can't share... The dolls I make, they are not for sale."

"What are they for, then?" I interjected.

"What?"

"Why do you make dolls? What is their purpose?" I was thinking of my fool father and his obsession.

The old man looked back to Hava. "Then this is the only reason you've come? To see... dolls?"

She smiled radiantly. "My father is quite the collector."

"And she likes a good quest," groused Olio.

Korieski closed his mouth into a tight line, and I saw some complex emotion I did not understand pulse like a wave over his features.

"I understand you are a private man," said Hava. "I'm sure you have your reasons for living here in isolation. You remind me of my husband; I'm quite sure he'd prefer this arrangement himself. I say, are you part of an Order? I noted the sigil upon your door."

"Something like that..." said Korieski, stroking his beard nervously.

"We'll leave you, master, if our presence offends. All I ask is this: Before we go, give us a little peek at your work." She rose and sidled up to him. "Just the smallest of peeks. We have come so far." She took hold of his hand as she said this last.

"Oh, very well," he said, reclaiming his hand. "A little peek. But you must touch nothing. And keep your voices down."

He turned back to the heavy door, unlatched it, and pulled it open with a groan. "Come and have a look, if you must. Bring the light."

Hava snatched the lantern and followed with all eagerness through the door. Olio came close behind, hand resting on his sword hilt. "Keep your eyes open," he whispered as he jostled past me, glancing up at the stairs.

I nodded and kept an eye on the stairs, in case there were anyone else hiding up there. Olio always was the suspicious type.

Through the arched doorway, over Olio's shoulders I could see the lantern's rays falling across neat bundles of sticks lined up on shelves stacked to the ceiling. Inside the workshop, I heard Hava take in a sharp breath. "This is amazing," she exclaimed.

"Please," hissed Korieski. "You must keep your voice down."

"Of course," whispered Hava. "Olio, have a look at this. They are utterly lifelike! And so small. I see no joints in the wood! Sir, how have you achieved this? I've never seen their equal."

"The technique was passed down from one Korieski to the next," answered the old man in a hushed voice.

"Is it all wood? Look at the hair! What is it made from?"

"All materials gathered from the forest," he said impatiently. "Careful," he chastised Olio whose elbow came too close to something.

I could contain my curiosity no longer. I went in to have a look for myself. The workshop was deeper than I expected, full of work spaces. It smelled of wood and oil.

I stood on tiptoe to try and have a look over Olio's shoulder. My first glimpse of the dolls disoriented me. The scale was all wrong; I felt I was looking down from some height upon a field of people—casualties after a battle, bodies all lined up in neat rows, arms and legs scattered about.

These were no crude, colorful dolls like my father made. They were the color of living flesh, naked, each one's skin tone a little different from the others. Each one was a person, unique. Several dozen of them, in various states of completion.

"This is the greatest work I've ever seen," said Hava, stunned. "My family, the Nipalto family... We have prided ourselves for generations on our craftsmanship. But our best work does not rival these. They are magnificent, sir, simply magnificent."

Korieski wrung his hands together, seemingly indifferent to her praise. He kept glancing over to his left at the wall of his workshop.

Olio noticed it, too. He borrowed the lantern from Hava and turned it to the wall in question. "What's over here then?"

"Nothing," said Korieski hastily.

"What's that, a closet?" The light fell across an ornate door-frame engraved with symbols that were strange to my eye. If it was a door, it was not a door that anyone had used in many years. It was painted over, and a workbench was parked in front of it, bolted to the wall.

"Oh, you mustn't do that," said Korieski, a palsied hand reaching for the lantern.

"Oh, and why not?" said Olio, holding the lamp up out of Korieski's reach.

"Olio," scolded Hava. "Behave yourself."

"Quiet!" hissed Korieski. "Please. This is sacred ground. Sacred ground! I'm going to have to ask you to leave now."

Olio turned the lantern back on Korieski. "You're going to have to ask me to leave? Is that so?"

The old man's jaw quivered.

"Olio," said Hava sharply, grabbing back the lantern. "Out, now. You, too," she said to me. When she used that tone, we knew we'd better obey. "Master Korieski, please forgive our intrusion. Thank you for allowing us this glimpse."

"Out please," he said, glancing again at the old sealed-up door. He took the lantern from Hava and motioned her out of the workshop, and then he closed himself back inside, pulling the big arched door closed with a thud.

That left the three of us in utter darkness in Korieski's den.

"What just happened?" asked Hava.

"I don't like this guy," said Olio. "What's he hiding in there?"

"Quiet," I said, putting my ear to the door. I could hear something on the other side. A little musical sound, and the old man's voice, hushed and sing-songy, like you might use to soothe a crying baby. And that strange little music, I'll never forget. Like one of the dolls was playing a tiny piano.

"I think he's singing to them," I said.

"Singing?" said Olio. "He's singing to the dolls? He's been out here a little too long on his own, I say."

"I'm going to sit down," said Hava, feeling her way in the dark to the bench.

"What do we do now?" I asked.

"Let me do the talking," said Hava.

We waited in the dark, but Korieski did not emerge from his workshop until it was nearly morning. He bore a candle that showed the deep lines in his face. His hair was disheveled, his shoulders drooped. He seemed surprised to see us. I truly think he had forgotten about us.

"Master Korieski..." started Hava.

"It is best you leave," said the old man with as much conviction as he could muster.

"Of course. Before we go...."

"Just go," he said. "I am old and I need my sleep."

He went to open the front door.

"I can't go without a doll," said Hava flatly.

"That is absolutely out of the question." He flung the door wide. The sounds of the jungle spilled in with the night air. "Out with you! Begone from this place."

What could we do? We went. But just before Korieski closed the door behind us, I opened my mouth and out came these words: "We spoke to your son in Aymad."

With that, the old man's demeanor shifted completely. He stood up straight and looked at us, truly looked at us, for the first time. "My son?" He ran a hand through his hair. "Please. Come in. Come back, sit down. I will make a fire. My son, you say...."

# CHAPTER 12

# A Mysterious Errand

The old man drank up what little we could offer him concerning the younger Korieski. Yes, he looked well, we told him. Employed, yes, very focused on his work. We left out the bits about the unpleasant company he was keeping in Aymad. And when pressed about whether he said anything about returning home to the valley, we only said, no, he didn't say.

"He'll be back," said the old man, half to himself. "I know he'll be back."

By then the morning light had begun to show through the window, and we heard monkeys heralding the morning.

Korieski allowed us to stay as guests in his home—so long as we promised to stay out of his workshop. His little house was crowded with all of us there, but we were glad for the shelter. Our first respite in some weeks from the biting flies of the Ucheti. Our sleep was long and glorious. We woke at midday, and Korieski opened a trapdoor under the stairs and showed us the kitchen under his house, open to the jungle in back. He hastily removed a few snakes before inviting us down. He made us a breakfast of honey yams. He was a kind enough host.

Hava sent Olio and me back into the jungle to gather up our gear. She wanted some time alone with the old man. Olio didn't love the idea, but in the end Hava got her way.

By the time we returned it was nearly evening. We found Hava and Korieski sitting in the den laughing at some joke. Two or three dolls were sprawled on the table in front of them. Sure enough, she had worked her charms on him, same as the rest of us.

That night I lay sleepless on the padded bench in the den. My mind kept returning to my father. A bad place, best forgotten, he'd said. What was the old man hiding in his workshop?

I sat up. In the dark I could just make out the shape of the arched doorway that led into the workshop.

The others were asleep in the loft. I would hear if anyone started down the stairs. So I got up and slinked over to the door. I listened. All was quiet. I hesitated with my hand on the handle. Could I open it without waking anyone?

I heard a footfall overhead. Someone was coming down-stairs! I rushed back to the bench and lay down.

It was the old man, trying to move quietly on the stairs. I pretended at sleep as he tiptoed past where I lay. He went over to his workshop door and pulled it open.

I'm not sure how long he was in there. I might have drifted off. But I woke again when I heard the front door close. Some-one had just gone out. I went to the window, saw Korieski in his cloak skulking away into the night with an unlit lantern.

What the hell...

I waited until he was away. Then I went after him.

Once out of sight of the house, he stopped to light his lantern. He was easy enough to follow after that.

I followed him a long way into unfamiliar territory, a treacherous landscape full of sudden plunges in the dark. I risked getting a little closer, just on the edge of his light, so I could see where I was putting my feet. He never once turned around to look behind him.

Finally, he stopped and put his lantern on the ground next to a tree. I hid myself and watched from a distance as he knelt and put something into a hollow in the tree. Then he struggled back up to his feet, rested a moment, and picked up the lantern and started back toward me.

I crouched out of sight and waited for him to pass. When he was gone, I went over to the tree. It seemed no different from a thousand others we'd passed. Why this tree?

It was too dark to see into the hollow within the tree. So I had to reach in blind, not without some trepidation.

My fingers found the form of a little doll nestled in the hollow. I could feel its little hairs against my fingertip. I jerked my hand back, a little spooked.

I stood up and watched Korieski's light winking between the trees. What in the world was going on here?

# CHAPTER 13

# No Monkey

I managed to circle ahead of the old man and slip back into the house just ahead of him. I lay down on the bench and tried to catch my breath.

Korieski came in quietly and draped his cloak over the chair. By then it was nearly dawn. "Good morning," he whispered. "I did not mean to wake you. I'm an early riser."

"Good morning," I said, trying to sound drowsy, hoping he would not light the lantern and see how filthy I was from scrabbling in the jungle all night.

But I needn't have worried. Straightaway he opened the trap door and started down into the kitchen. "I gathered some mushrooms," he said hastily. "You have to get up early to find these ones, or the boars will get them first. I'll make us an omelet."

Upstairs, I heard heavy footsteps. That would be Olio. "I heard voices," he grumbled, coming down. "It's still dark outside. Where's your decency?"

"Olio," I hissed. "Come here."

"What?" groused Olio.

Korieski had the fire going down in the kitchen, and a little of its light spilled up through the trap door, showing the contours of the room.

I took Olio by the arm and pulled him toward the front door. "Come on, I need to show you something."

"Ejertine... I'm not even awake yet."

"Shhh. Come on, put your boots on."

I dragged Olio complaining through the jungle. I had some trouble finding the tree again; everything looked different in the morning light. And when I did find it, I reached my hand into the hollow—but the doll was gone.

"It was here," I said.

"What was?"

"A doll. One of Korieski's little dolls."

"Why would he spend all that time making a doll just to dump it out here?"

"Exactly!" I said.

Olio threw up his hands. "This is what you dragged me out here for?"

"Well, what's it about? The doll, it was here just a few hours ago.... Someone's come and taken it. Why would they do that?"

At that moment we heard a rustling up in the tree. "What was that?" We both looked up.

"There!" We glimpsed something skittering along the bough above us. "Did you see that?"

"Probably a monkey," said Olio unconvincingly.

"That's no monkey—look!" We spotted it leaping the gap between two trees. There it was: the tiny doll, giggling as it scurried up a branch.

Olio's jaw dropped. "You're right—that's no monkey!" He hurried after it as it leapt down from the tree and sped across open ground.

The thing led us on a manic chase, disappearing periodically into cover only to come bursting out a moment later. I had the feeling it was toying with us, leading us along.

Olio drew closer and closer, close enough almost to grab it before it darted sideways and disappeared into the foliage. Finally, when the doll showed itself again Olio lunged for it, crying, "I've got you now," but his confidence turned quickly to horror as he found himself tumbling over a hidden precipice. The doll leapt aside at the last second, giggling maniacally as Olio tumbled forward into a chasm.

"Olio!" I called and went after him, stopping short at the edge. It was a long way down. I saw only treetops below, and no sign of Olio. "Olio!" I called again, but no answer came.

I saw the doll running away along the edge of the cliff. "What have you done?" I shouted after it.

I called again for Olio, but it was no good. He was somewhere down there, hidden in the foliage. I would have to find another way down.

I don't know how long I searched. It seemed like hours. When I finally found him, he was in bad shape—broken bones and barely breathing.

Somehow, I don't know how, I lifted him up and over my shoulders. Olio was no small man. I guess I was more determined than I was strong, but that was enough. Once I had him up, I moved quickly, knowing if I faltered I probably would not be able to lift him again.

I made it perhaps half way back to Korieski's house when I heard the pitter-patter of tiny feet overhead and saw the branches move. A chill ran down my spine. I hurried on, stumbling a little in my haste.

Then—pow!—something struck me in back of my head. I don't what it was, a pebble maybe, but thrown with such velocity that it impacted like a sling stone.

I don't remember falling. I just remember blackness. And then the black gave way, slowly, to leaves. An inchworm. An ant. I became dully aware of a tremendous pressure on my head, pinning me down: Olio had fallen on top of me. He was awake now, screaming from the sudden pain.

I tried to get out from under him, to little effect beyond causing Olio even more pain. My head and arms were pinned firmly to the ground with Olio lying sideways on top.

Then suddenly the doll was standing right before my face, almost touching me. Only it was no doll anymore, clearly; it was a real person, a tiny little girl with a wicked smile. Very much alive she was, her chest heaving with exertion and exhilaration. She had a tunic and little boots that Korieski had fashioned for her. All this I took in during that instant when she scurried up to my face. And then she seized hold of a handful of my eyelid and yanked with such viciousness that I screamed in horror.

I think my scream must have snapped Olio into sudden clarity, because his hand darted out like lightning and grabbed hold of the little doll. He rolled off me, and I was greeted with a new wave of surprising pain, blinding me as the blood rushed back into my head.

When I could see again, Olio came into focus, struggling to keep hold of the squirming doll. "Oh, no you don't," he said, and pulled it in close to his body, firming up his grip. He had only one good arm, but he wasn't about to let it go.

The doll with its one free arm scratched at Olio's hand and made him bleed, but he only smiled at it wickedly; then the doll had just the briefest instant to squeal in mortal terror as Olio thrust it into his mouth and bit off its head. And he just kept chewing. He ground that doll up between his teeth until there was nothing left of it but sawdust and splinters in his mouth.

I sat up, holding my eye. Olio was breathing hard, still gnashing his teeth like some animal, his mouth covered in the remains of the doll.

We made eye contact briefly, then he passed out.

# CHAPTER 14

# The Music Box

How could something so small cause so much harm?

I tried moving Olio but no longer had the strength. I don't think I had the strength to begin with. But I couldn't just leave him there, not with all the opportunistic scavengers about.

So I set to manufacturing a primitive sled from young trees, lashing them together with lengths of vine. It took longer than I wanted, but the make-shift sled allowed me to drag Olio's weight without having to fully lift him.

We'd already lost half a day in the jungle. Hava would be worried. But more than that, I was concerned about her alone with Korieski. What kind of monster purposely created such malevolent beings and released them into the world?

The closer I drew to Korieski's house, the angrier I became with Korieski. Olio was in a bad way because of the old man. Maybe I desperately wanted to blame him so I wouldn't have to blame myself. I don't know. I wasn't thinking very clearly. By the time I reached the house, with sweat and blood burning my eyes and blurring my vision, I kicked open the door and dropped Olio's sled on the floor, crying "Korieski!" from the back of my throat.

Inside, I saw that the door to the workshop was open, and Hava and Korieski came rushing out to see what was the matter. She had evidently sweet-talked her way back into the workshop.

"What happened?" cried Hava upon seeing Olio. She untied him from the sled, which was already falling apart.

I turned my rage on the old man. "You did this! Tell us what is going on here, right now!"

Hava got between us, protecting Korieski. "Ejertine, what happened?"

"Tell us! Why do you make these dolls? Why do you hide them in the jungle?"

"Please," begged Korieski. "Lower your voice."

"What do you keep in your closet?" I shouted. "Tell me, now!"

There came a thumping from the workshop.

"Oh, no," moaned Korieski. He turned and rushed through the workshop door, and tried to pull it closed behind him, but I stopped the door with my foot and went after him.

Another thump. Paint chips fell from the edging around the closet. The old man's tools rattled on his workbench.

"Oh, no," repeated Korieski, arms flapping, as he scurried to the far end of the workshop and pulled down a little carved box from the shelf.

Thump. The whole wall shook, pieces of half-finished dolls fell from the shelves. The workbench bolted in front of the door—I saw it flex and creak under some tremendous pressure pushing from behind. I stood there stupidly, just watching. I didn't know what else to do.

With trembling hands Korieski opened the lid to his little carved box. It was a music box, and out came a tinny little repeating melody, that same song I'd heard through the door the night before.

Korieski tried to hum sweetly along with the melody. A bead of sweat broke on his forehead. He looked at me, his eyes desperate, and he motioned for me to hum along.

I couldn't do it. I just didn't have it in me to hum at that particular moment. But Hava was there behind me, and she picked up the tune.

Together, Hava and Korieski calmed the thing in the closet. I could hear it breathing in there, a monstrous rasping breath. Its breathing slowed, and then finally it was quiet.

Korieski closed the music box and slumped against the shelf in exhaustion. Hava helped him into the den and sat him down at the table. She exchanged glances with me, put her hand on my shoulder. "Go, stir the fire. Brew some fresh coffee."

# CHAPTER 15

# Last of the Morosovan

When I returned, Hava had the front door open and was making a splint for Olio. Korieski was still slumped over the table.

I poured the coffee and sat next to him. He cupped his hands around his mug and stared dismally into his drink.

"What is that thing?" I asked, my voice quiet and calm this time.

He shook his head. "He is not a thing. He is called Enyin. A great demon once, a Duke of Kaphador."

Hava drew nearer to listen.

Korieski looked up at her, his eyes glistening. "When first I saw you at my door, I thought... What a fool I was! Every morning I prayed to Morphid to send someone. I thought He had sent you. I thought someone had come at last." He looked back down into his coffee and wept quietly. "I thought...."

"You poor dear," said Hava, putting her hands on his shoulders. "You have been alone here with that thing for such a long time."

He shook his head. "I am not equal to the task. Maybe once, but not any more. I am not my father."

He looked up at me, wiping his tears on his sleeve. "But my son.... My son has much of his grandfather in him."

He brought his cup up to his lips and took a tentative sip. "He has the strength to contain the beast. I need him. I cannot do it alone, not anymore. Of late, the beast, he has grown stronger. I feel him waking. I think he senses my weakness; I think he knows his time is drawing near."

"What happens if he gets out?" I asked.

He slammed down his cup, slopping hot coffee over his hand. "We cannot allow that to happen." His eyes seized mine, apparently heedless of the scalding coffee on his hand. "It would be the beginning of the end."

"I don't understand," said Hava. "How did it get here to begin with?"

Korieski shook his head helplessly. "It matters not."

"It matters," I growled, trying to imitate Olio. "You'd best tell it all."

"Maybe there's something we can do to help," suggested Hava. She brought a rag and mopped up the spilled coffee.

He sank back into his chair, defeated, and let Hava dab at his hand. He had dark, sunken bags under his eyes. "Let an old man sleep. I will tell you all when I wake."

But I said, "No." I was not about to let this moment pass. "Tell us now. Make it quick, then you may sleep."

He smiled a little at that. "Make it quick? A thousand years of history is locked in that cell." Korieski ran a trembling hand through his hair. "A thousand years ago. That was when En-yin was banished from Hell and first came crawling up into our world. He started off small enough, but still large enough to slaughter and consume a man, and with each man he ate he grew larger. And he took the heads of his victims and melded them onto his body. Soon he had dozens of heads sprouting from different parts of his body, with eyes that could see in all directions. And with each head he grew smarter. In the middle of his body was one great maw, his original mouth, grown large enough to swallow a man whole. This terror ran free in Lagin, and none could destroy him, though many tried. He gathered about him the forces of darkness and made war on the world of men. This was after the fall of the Ancients, and in this day Lagin was in great decay and could not stand before Enyin. He enslaved the people and made Thansby his seat of power."

"That's what you've got in your closet?" I said, incredulous.

"...Thansby?" said Hava. "You mean Dhalmadhi?"

Korieski waved his hand dismissively. "Whatever they are calling it these days."

"But how can it be I've never heard this before?"

He shook his head sadly. "Humans forget so quickly. Enyin's rise was quick. His purpose was to make our world ready for his allies in Hell; for he had friends among the other demon lords who defied Kaphador, and together they plotted to flee Hell and come to the surface world to join Enyin and rule over the children of Morphid. No doubt they would still rule today had not Morphid intervened. True, mankind had fallen from favor with its Creator, but when He looked down from Alyon and saw what had become of the holy land of Lagin, His wrath was stirred anew. And though the sacred order of the Morosovan, His earthly instruments of justice, had long since passed from the earth and now served as His Palatine Guard in Alyon, still there was one mortal man—my great grandfather—who acted as the last of the Morosovan. He was not himself knighted, but Morphid had chosen him as steward of the Order, and he alone among men possessed the power to wield the holy brands of the Morosovan. Morphid called upon him, a humble builder of temples in foreign lands, and He commanded him to take up the holy brand and raise an army against Enyin."

"Now, hold on," I said. "Just wait. Your grandfather... was alive a thousand years ago?"

"My great grandfather. We are a long-lived family. The world may have forgotten him, but a thousand years ago my ancestor earned the name Korieski the Great. Against Enyin's dragons and warlocks, Korieski brought strange allies from overseas... In the end, the armies of Enyin were defeated or scattered, but Enyin himself could not be destroyed. Instead my great grand-father imprisoned him."

"...And brought him here, to the edge of the world?" said Hava.

"And here he has remained through the centuries. Each gen-eration of Korieskis must learn anew how to keep him con-tained. He is no easy prisoner. He boils with rage. He dreams of our destruction. But we keep him sleeping, we keep him con-fused, we keep him weak."

"Weak?" I said. "I thought your workbench would snap in half!"

"Shh... I told you, he is growing stronger, even as I weaken. I cannot keep up with him anymore."

"You mean you can't make dolls fast enough?" guessed Hava.

He nodded.

"I don't understand," I said. "Why do you make the dolls?"

He sighed and rested his chin against his chest. "They are not dolls."

"Well, what are they then?"

He looked like he was about to slump forward. "Hey," I said. "No sleeping yet. First tell me, what are they if they are not dolls? Then you can sleep."

He lifted a feeble hand. "They are homunculi. My family… we learned to siphon the energy from the demon lord. But this demonic energy, it does not simply dissipate into the air. It must be contained, or it will be drawn back into its source."

"Demonic energy," I said, nodding my head. That's what the little thing had in it. It was starting to make sense.

"I take the evil of the demon lord and diffuse it into many small packages and release them into the wild. The unspeakable evil of the demon I trade for the smaller mischief of the homunculi."

"Small mischief! That thing nearly killed us both!"

"Shh! Please lower your voice. If it should wake again, I do not think I could put it back to sleep."

"Hava," I said, "we have got to get away from this place."

"You're in no shape to go anywhere," she declared. "Let me see that head. And take a look at Olio. He is not going anywhere for a long time."

"You want to stay here with that thing?"

"Until Olio is fit to travel." Hava blinked a few times. I could see her mind turning. "We will all need our strength," she said, "if we are to return to Aymad."

"Aymad? We're going to Aymad?"

Hava touched Korieski on the shoulder. "Come, dear man. Let me help you to your bed. We'll stay as your guests if you'll have us. Let us ease your burden. I will help you as best I can in the workshop. And when Olio is mended, we shall return to Aymad and find your son."

# CHAPTER 16

# The Thump

So it was we stayed in the house of Korieski. We put Olio upstairs to lie in Korieski's bed. Hava and I took turns looking after him.

Otherwise I saw little of Hava. She and Korieski worked furiously in the workshop together. I came and went from the house, doing the hunting, gathering, and cooking. I kept a wary eye out for any more of Korieski's demon dolls, though he assured me his little homunculi were predisposed to scatter themselves far and wide. They repelled one another, he said, and most of all they were repelled by the place of their origin. Each one was a little demon in its own right, imbued with an instinct to distance itself from Enyin lest it be reabsorbed. I found myself wondering just how many of these little monsters Korieski had put out into the world and what had become of them all.

For some weeks we stayed with Korieski, as Olio gradually recovered. He slept mostly, but when we was awake he made for a very grumpy patient.

We settled into a routine, and things seemed better for a while. With Hava's help, Korieski was producing twice as many dolls, and his spirits ran high. For the first time in years he felt he was getting the better of the demon in the closet. And with Hava's promise to find his son, he clung to hope for the future.

But then things went horribly wrong. To this day I don't know what it was that woke the demon. I was under the house in the kitchen slicing tubers for a stew when I heard a terrible wrenching sound overhead.

I rushed up through the trap door and was greeted by an unnatural howling. The whole house convulsed with a great rending of wood and metal. I rushed to the open door of the workshop to see Korieski's shelves and workbenches tumbling over—and there was the beast tearing its way out of the wall. The door to its prison hung badly askew, still fixed to the broken workbench. Hava was backing away through the door just as I arrived. I got in front of her, trying to protect her. Inside, Korieski was on the floor, clutching desperately at his music box that now lay in pieces.

As I looked upon the beast emerging from the wall, I could not comprehend what I was seeing. He was big—taller than the biggest man and twice as wide. His hands were huge, his arms had too many joints. He didn't seem to have a head, just one great mouth in the middle of his torso, and from this giant, fetid hole came a second shriek, a rage-howl that shook my bones.

I was transfixed. Hava was tugging on me, urging me out of the workshop, but I couldn't move. What I was seeing was so beyond the context of my world, I suppose my mind must have just shut itself off. I had faced the barrakapa, but that at least had made sense to me—an animal, a predator. But Enyin was something else entirely, something that was not part of nature. Something that did not belong in our world.

The demon picked up the old man by an ankle and slung him across the room, still clinging to his broken music box. That was enough to snap me out of my shock. I crouched down and picked up a heavy tool, one of Korieski's vises.

"Get out of here," I said to Hava. "Run!"

I couldn't tell if the demon was looking at me or not; I didn't see that he had any eyes. He screamed again, showing me a ring of sword-like fangs. Then he turned to go for Korieski, who lay crumpled in the corner.

"Hey," I called and hurled the heavy vise, two-handed, and smack! I hit him square. It didn't seem to hurt him much, but it did get his attention and made him even madder.

I noticed then Hava was still standing behind me. "What are you doing? Run!"

Next I knew, a workbench was hurtling at me. My reality slowed down. I remember the pattern of the woodgrain on the countertop as it loomed toward me. I saw Hava diving to the side, but I could not get out of the way. It was just too big, and I had nowhere to go. The best I could do was throw myself under it and avoid being crushed between it and the wall.

I don't know what happened next. I'm not sure how long I was out. Only a few seconds, I think. I found myself pinned under the workbench. Hava had managed to dodge, but now she was alone in the workshop with the beast. I couldn't see from where I lay, but I could hear...

"Shhh," Hava was saying. "It's all right now." Her voice was cracking, but she had managed to calm the demon. I could hear him breathing. She began to hum the melody from the music box.

In the far corner I saw Korieski begin to stir. I was glad to see he was alive. But for my part, I lay still and played dead. I don't think I could have got the workbench off myself if I tried.

But from upstairs there came a thump. It was Olio. He had managed to roll himself out of bed, and was coming down to see what was the matter.

That one thump was enough to startle the demon out of its dreamy state. With a snarl he fell viciously upon Hava.

I couldn't see... but the sounds... It sounded like he was killing her. It went on and on. It was the worst, longest moment of my life. I closed my eyes. I wanted to die. I wanted it to be over. But I could hear him breathing and grunting, I heard Hava's clothes tearing, I heard her cries, her sounds that were not quite speech. And it did not stop.

I saw Korieski in the corner, bleeding from his head, sitting up now and still fumbling with his damned music box.

I heard Olio on the stairs.

Hava fell silent, but Enyin still grunted and growled and thrashed, until finally he howled or screamed and was still at last, breathing rapidly.

Korieski held his music box in one hand and turned a screwdriver inside it, making it play a distorted version of its original melody. The beast, spent, slowed his breathing.

"That's right," said Korieski, his voice quavering. "Sleep now." He hummed along with the distorted tune.

CHAPTER 17.

# A Prayer

I think I must have passed out. I don't remember the next several minutes.

The next thing I do remember clearly was Olio's face, reddened, his eyes swollen like he'd been crying.

"Hold on, lad," he said, lying alongside me. He braced his one good knee under the workbench and lifted it a little, and he pulled me out with his good arm.

The two of us lay there in a heap, breathing. Dolls and bits of dolls were strewn everywhere. I could not bear to look in the direction of Hava.

Olio seized my head in his two hands and looked me in the eyes. "I need you to carry her out of here. Can you do that?"

"Is she…?"

"I need you to carry her."

I took a deep breath. I checked myself over. I couldn't feel anything. But my bones seemed unbroken.

I rose unsteadily to my feet. The room spun around me. It didn't even look like the same room anymore. I saw Korieski tucking the beast into what remained of the closet. I saw it curled up in there, sleeping. It seemed so much smaller now.

A blanket, blood-soaked, covered Hava. She was lying so still. I went to her, picking my way through the ruins of Korieski's workshop, stumbling a little. My body didn't seem to work quite right.

I reached out my hand to pull back the blanket. But I couldn't bring myself to lift it.

"Never mind," said Olio gently, trying to pull himself upright. "Just get her out of here." He looked like he was about to pass out.

I did as I was told. I took her in my arms and lifted.

Korieski was looking at his mangled closet door, shaking his head in dismay. A steady stream of blood flowed from a gaping hole in his scalp, matting down his hair and dying his beard with streaks of red.

"You, too," said Olio, looking at the old man. "Let's go."

"I think I'd better stay," whispered Korieski, rubbing his hands together.

"I'm in charge now," said Olio through clenched teeth. "You'd better come with me."

"Oh, dear..." Korieski looked back and forth between Olio and the sleeping demon. "Oh, no," he said, kneading his hands. "Oh, no." Meekly, he limped toward Olio.

We followed Olio into the den, where he held himself upright at the table. "Give me your stick," commanded Olio, and Korieski hastened to comply. "Outside." He pointed at the door, breathing heavily as he leaned on the stick.

Olio was the last out the door. "Down there," he said, pointing down the slope into the jungle. Then he turned back to hop into the house.

"Where are you going?" gasped Korieski, blinking in the sun.

"Never you mind."

"Come on," I said, holding Hava, struggling to stand on wobbly legs.

But instead of following me, Korieski dawdled at the door, then went in after Olio.

I carried Hava away from the house and laid her down. I crawled a few feet and retched up what little I had in my stomach. The sensation of pain was returning to me, and every part of me hurt.

From the house came raised voices, then the sound of something breaking. I rose unsteadily to my feet and stumbled toward the house.

Smoke came pouring out the open door. I ran to the door, heard something else breaking inside. I heard Korieski's voice: "Stop! Listen to me, this will do no good!"

I rushed into the smoke-filled den. The workshop was on fire; I saw flames crawling up the door. From within the workshop I heard Olio cry out and fall.

The smoke drove me to the floor. I crawled across the den and peered into the chaos of the flaming workshop. Olio was passed out on the floor, dolls shriveling up and catching fire around him. Korieski was on his knees in front of the beast's closet, praying to his god.

The room was going up quickly. All the wood pieces made for kindling, and Olio had spilled lantern fuel over the workbenches and shelves.

I had only seconds to drag Olio out. I took one last look behind me and saw Korieski still bent in prayer, heedless of the fire that was even now engulfing his cloak.

Olio came to as I was dragging him across the den. The fire was spreading rapidly along the ceiling. The two of us crawled out the front door, coughing and blinded from the smoke.

We got ourselves a safe distance from the house, then sat and watched it burn. Soon, it was entirely engulfed, a raging furnace. Part of the roof fell in upon itself and flames shot over the tree-tops into the sky.

I helped Olio up and took him to Hava. New blood showed on her blanket. Kneeling beside her, I saw her face wet and bloody. Gently, I turned her head toward the light, and my hand came away bloody; her ear was missing, blood pulsing from the exposed wound. Her heart, at least, was pumping.

Olio pulled me away. "Not now. Not here." He glanced back at the inferno. "We need to get away from this place."

# CHAPTER 18

# My Accomplishment

We were in no condition to go far. But by then I had the lay of the land, and knew just where to go. I fashioned a sled for Hava, Olio found himself a good stick, and we dragged ourselves through the jungle.

I brought us to a small cave, on the side of a slope behind a great boulder. It was a defensible spot, with a good view of the surrounding land. It was in fact the same hillside where we first spotted Korieski's roof. Now a line of smoke snaked into the sky from the site of the house.

I lay Hava down in the cave. But once again Olio pushed me away. "I need you to stand watch." He put himself between us, the same way he did when I first joined the expedition. Only this time he wasn't protecting Hava. He was protecting me. He didn't want me to see.

But I did not want to stand guard. I did not want to turn away and go sit by the boulder and keep a look out. I did not want to be left alone with my thoughts.

*It was my fault. I did this to her.*

I knew this. There was no denying it.

If I had listened to my father, this would never have happened to Hava. *A bad place, best forgotten.* He foresaw this, I believe that. He did not want Hava touched by the evil of that place. But, because I wanted to impress her, I told her my father's secret and where to seek for Korieski. I led her to this place. I woke the beast. And when he woke the second time, I provoked him, and then lay under a bench playing dead while he savaged her.

I did this to her. This was the culmination of my short life's work. I left the village to follow Hava, and this is what I had accomplished. I destroyed her. I destroyed the most wonderful, lovely, courageous person I had ever known.

Hava possessed the spirit of twenty ordinary people. She was a goddess so far as I was concerned. All I wanted was to follow her, to be around her, to bask in her light. But all that was gone now. Hava would never be the same.

I did this to her. I couldn't stop saying it to myself. Because it was true. It's a truth I've had to carry ever since.

These were my thoughts as I sat motionless watching the sun sink below the horizon. Finally Olio came out and leaned on the boulder. He had dirt caked on his face, with deep streaks where he'd been weeping. "It's not good, lad."

"Is she... going to die?"

"I don't know. Maybe."

We stood in silence looking out over the jungle. The gloom of night fell quickly over the landscape. A sliver moon peered through clouds that rushed silently overhead. The forest was still. No monkeys called. The birds and frogs were quiet.

"It's too quiet," observed Olio.

"Shh." I thought I heard something. Then we both heard it, more clearly this time: Some kind of... wail. Some kind of sound I could not understand.

# CHAPTER 19

# Blood and Water

I spent a sleepless night listening to the jungle. Sometimes I could hear something out there, moving. Or the sounds of wildlife snorting, crying, or fleeing.

In the morning, Olio rose up and declared he was going back down to the site of the house, to try and recover his sword from the ruin.

"I'm not sure that's a good idea," I said. "That thing might still be down there."

"I don't think so. It burned up in the fire."

"But we heard it."

"That could've been anything. You know as well as I this valley is full of strange monsters. All the more reason I need my sword."

There was no dissuading him. "Let me go," I offered.

"No, I need you to stay and look after Hava."

So Olio went down into the jungle and I stayed with Hava. The morning's light fell into the cave, and for the first time since the attack, I got a clear look at my friend. She was hardly recognizable. Both eyes swollen shut, her mouth and nose broken and torn, one of her ears missing. Olio had done what he could to staunch the bleeding and clean her up. The still pool in back of the cave was more blood than water.

I did not cry. Instead I felt a grim determination to see her through this. I was responsible, I knew, and the only scrap of honor I could salvage was to see that she made it out alive. I set myself to collecting stones which I planned to use to defend the cave if necessary from any predators who might show themselves.

Then, from the direction of the ruined house, I heard a shout. Voices raised in anger! The sounds of fighting.

I stood, strained my eyes, trying to see. I heard a cry—Olio? The jungle fell silent once more.

What in the world was happening down there?

Then, from behind me, I heard Hava stirring. I rushed to her side. Her mouth was moving.

I gave her water. She took a little, then tried to speak again.

I put my ear close to her broken mouth. What was she trying to say?

"Encho," is what she said. The name of her husband in Lagin.

# CHAPTER 20

# Two Well-Balanced Stones

When Olio failed to return I knew he was in trouble.

Much as I hated to leave Hava alone, I had to find out what was happening down there. So I crept through the jungle, keeping under cover and moving quietly.

I went to the smoldering remains of the house but saw no one. All that was left of the old house was the chimney and a heap of ashes and debris caved into the trench that was the old kitchen. Then, from very nearby, I heard a sharp cry—Olio!

I followed the sound, keeping low to the ground. There, in a clearing, I saw Olio tied to a tree with two men standing over him. I recognized them: Korieski the Younger and his dark master Hemech.

Korieski was holding Olio's walking stick, and he used it to jab Olio's bad leg, eliciting another scream.

"Careful, or he'll pass out again," counseled Hemech.

"I don't care. I'll have the truth. Why were you seeking my father? Why did you burn the house? What did you do with the old man? Where is the demon? Speak, damn you!" And he jabbed him with the stick again.

I found two good, balanced stones and crept in as close as I dared. My plan was to throw both rocks in rapid succession and try to take out both men.

My first shot knocked Hemech out cold, but Korieski swiveled just in time to deflect the second stone with Olio's stick.

"You!" cried Korieski. "I remember you as well. I should have killed you when I had the chance." He came after me with the stick, but Olio thrust up his good leg and tripped him up, just enough to give me the advantage. I got round behind him, slipped his own knife out of its sheath and pressed it against his neck. And a nasty, double-edged knife it was, all curved and jagged.

"All right," conceded Korieski. "You've got me."

I kicked the staff away and made him untie Olio, keeping the knife pressed against him the whole time. Olio collapsed to the ground but presently struggled his way upright. "Now it's your turn to sing, little parakeet. What in Nevik is going on here?"

"We have come for the demon," said Hemech, awake now and on his feet. I spun round with the knife, startled. How did he get up so fast? He was half demon himself, if you ask me.

"Well, you're too late," growled Olio. "We killed it already."

Korieski the Younger laughed. "You mean with the fire? That one comes from a place of fire. Fire cannot harm him."

"Fools," said Hemech. "You have unleashed him."

Nobody made a move. I held the knife at Korieski's throat, all too aware that Hemech could strike us down with his magic.

"What now?" I asked.

"Now," said Hemech, "we find the demon. Before it is too late."

# CHAPTER 21

# A Bad Idea

As bad an idea as it seemed, I joined with Korieski and Hemech to try and track Enyin. I suppose I was the closest thing we had to a tracker.

We started by sifting through the remains of the house. I found the melted hinges of the closet door from the workshop, but there was no sign of the demon. I did find the bones of Korieski the Elder where he died in prayer. The younger Korieski came and stared down at his father's bones, saying nothing.

"He died trying to protect us, I think."

Korieski the Younger seemed unmoved.

Olio gave a little cry of happiness when he found his sword, damaged but salvageable. He used the sword to poke around the ashes, but came up only with the sigil of Morphid that had hung on the front door.

I circled the rubble, searching for any sign of the demon's passage. I did find some bent stalks, but any one of us could have left those traces.

I thought back to the sounds I'd heard in the night from the jungle and made a guess as to the direction the demon might have gone. "This way, I think."

Korieski and Hemech followed me. Olio, with his bad leg, stayed behind. We exchanged glances as we went our separate ways. I knew he would return to Hava's cave. Korieski and

Hemech knew nothing of Hava, and we planned to keep it that way.

"What will we do exactly when we find the demon?" I wanted to know.

"Leave that to us," said Korieski.

I tried to put myself in Enyin's frame of mind; which direction would I go? But the truth was Enyin's mind was entirely alien to me. All I had to go on were the sounds I'd heard in the night, but with all the ravines and hills, sounds had a way of playing tricks. I kept looking for signs of destruction, or some kind of strange footprints. But I couldn't even say what Enyin's feet looked like exactly. Did he have hooves? I was too busy staring into his gaping maw to notice much else.

"He could be anywhere," I had to admit finally. "Our best bet is to climb to higher ground and see if we might see or hear him."

"You're not much good, are you?" said Korieski.

I threw up my hands. "You guys are supposed to be the demon experts."

We stopped finally on a hilltop with a view in all directions. We waited, silent, watching. At dusk Hemech left us, making no explanation for himself. Korieski and I sat on the hilltop. Trauma and lack of sleep caught up to me, and my eyes grew bleary. A sudden rain pelted us, and I sat motionless and miserable in the downpour.

"I should have come sooner," said Korieski suddenly.

"What?"

"The doddering old fool. He must have known he was fighting a losing battle."

"He did. He was just trying to hold out until you returned."

"He told you that?"

"He told me you had the strength to contain the demon. He said you were like your grandfather."

"I am nothing like the Korieskis before me. They were part of the old world. Morphid's world. That world is gone. Morphid may be king but his power is in decline. The days of the Morosovan are done. Today the only things His priests are good for is healing and blessing babies. Mastering a greater demon, that is hardly within a Morphidian's capability. No, the true power today lies with Kaphador, the son and heir to Morphid. My father, or his father before him, could never understand that."

"What about your mother? What became of her, if you don't mind my asking?" A sinking feeling came over me then, as I realized that may have been the wrong question to ask.

But Korieski snorted and shook his head. "You wouldn't understand."

I let the matter drop.

"This way," said Hemech, startling both of us with his sudden presence.

We got to our feet and followed Hemech down the hill. The way was dark and treacherous. Though the rain slackened, heavy clouds obscured the moon and stars. More than once we lost sight of Hemech in his dark cloak, until distant sheet lightning would reveal him to us again. Once I saw him reaching up to the sky, and I thought I glimpsed a small bird or a bat alighting on his glove.

"What was that?" I asked Korieski.

"That would be Tobias, his familiar."

"I will have silence," said Hemech, suddenly in our midst again, glowering with disapproval at Korieski.

# CHAPTER 22

# Lullaby

Hemech and his bat led us in a wide half-circle. I became aware of a sinking sensation in my heart as I recognized that we were headed back in the direction of Hava's cave.

I found myself asking again what exactly I was doing with these unsavory characters. If I was no longer their guide or tracker, then what was I to them? My answer came soon enough, even as I contemplated how best to extricate myself.

Hemech sent Korieski and me ahead into a ravine, and as I was picking my way down the slope, Korieski close behind, I felt a sudden searing blast of heat on my hindquarters, propelling me forward with a yelp. A rapid series of crackling bursts of energy followed the first, flicked from the fingers of Korieski, aimed at my legs and feet. Singed and indignant, I fled into the ravine as he continued the assault from behind. I quickly found myself alone, heart pounding, my buttocks burning. What the hell? I kept moving, trying to stay ahead of them. The walls of the ravine closed in on either side. I was all too aware that I was trapped and was no doubt being sent ahead as... bait.

I was also keenly aware of an unusual silence in the jungle. Even the neeker-beekers lay quiet.

In fact, as I stopped in my tracks, I heard no sounds of pursuit. I seemed to be alone in the ravine.

I decided to climb a tree. Dark as the night was, I might be able to see something, and at least the tree might afford me some measure of safety.

Once in the treetop, a flicker of distant lightning showed me two figures running along the top of the ravine: Hemech with his staff and his disciple laden with big sacks. He didn't have those before; where did they come from?

The next flash revealed movement in the ravine ahead of me—foliage bending, something large moving in my direction.

I was frozen in a moment of indecision. Did I have time to climb down and make a break for it? Or should I stay still in the tree and hope to stay hidden in the dark?

My hesitation decided it for me: I stayed in the tree. Unfortunately, the demon came right to me. I was horrified to see how big he had grown; he must have been *twice* the size he'd been in the workshop. He stopped right under my tree and looked up at me. He had new heads—the heads of beasts he'd consumed in the jungle, and his big mouth was capacious enough to swallow a cow whole. He roared up at me, and the fumes of his breath made me dizzy. I clung desperately to the trunk as he shook the tree, holding his mouth open expectantly.

I closed my eyes, I held my breath, I thought of Hava. Enraged, the demon set to destroying the tree. Each swipe of its claws shook me violently. I remembered the barrakapa, when it had me treed. I readied myself for the tree to come down.

When it fell, I used my forward momentum to roll and land running. The demon was at my back, shrieking unnaturally. I ran deeper into the ravine, leading the demon toward where I had spotted Hemech and Korieski running.

At first it was easy to stay ahead of the beast. But as it came to speed, its progress was terrifying. It was breathing down my neck by the time I leapt over a brook.

From above, Hemech and Korieski threw down burning baskets of incense. The demon stopped at the brook, surprised by the smoke. Hemech stood on a rock above, lifting his staff and addressing the demon in what language I could not say. Korieski continued to throw down more and more burning baskets of incense.

I just kept running. I could hear the rising, insistent voice of Hemech commanding the demon. I climbed up out of the ravine and kept running and running. I headed up the slope toward Hava's cave, astounded to be alive.

It was almost dawn by then, and the clouds were clearing from the sky. Midway up the slope, I turned back to look. I heard the demon roar. From my vantage, I could see the tiny figures of Hemech and Korieski moving around the demon in the predawn light. They had ropes around its arms and they were pulling on the ropes while standing on opposite sides of the demon, keeping his arms taut. As I watched, Enyin roared again and threw them off. Korieski was flung some twenty yards or more and lay motionless. Hemech kept the demon at bay with his staff. He struck at it twice, and I could hear a zapping sound as some great energy was discharged. The demon roared in pain and rage and rushed at Hemech, throwing him back into a tree. Hemech crumpled, and the demon roared once more in triumph, then he took Hemech and tore his arms and legs off and devoured them in greedy gulps, leaving the torso behind.

Then he looked up, all his beast-heads fixed directly on me! And he made straight for me.

I ran.

I headed for the cave. I found Olio next to the boulder, wide-eyed, leaning on his stick. "What'd you bring it here for?" he said. It was a fair question. I was panicked, I wasn't thinking clearly. But some part of me told me that the demon was seeking for Hava, that he was going to find her regardless.

"Come on," I said, out of breath. "We've got to go." I went to get Hava from the cave.

"It's no use," said Olio. "It's nearly upon us! Time to fight."

"We can't fight that thing!"

Olio backed into the cave and drew his sword, for what it was worth. I stood in front of Hava with my knife, protecting her where she lay next to the pool of water mixed with her blood.

We saw the long shadow of the demon in the morning light as he came to a stop beyond the boulder. But he came no farther. Instead, he stood just out of sight, breathing. We saw the dust stirring from his breath, but he did not come around the boulder.

I heard Hava stirring. She was conscious, aware of the proximity of her tormenter. I saw her shaking, whether in rage or pain or fear.

His breathing slowed. He seemed to be calming down. Olio and I exchanged glances, standing ready.

Hava managed to sit up, propping herself against the cave wall, frowning bitterly. She began to hum under her breath. At first, the sound caught in her throat. But then she was humming the melody from Korieski's music box, her voice sweet as ever.

Olio and I stood gripping our weapons, but the demon was breathing calmly now, in and out. Hava's voice faltered, and I found myself picking up where she left off. I looked to Olio and motioned for him to hum along. Soon we were all humming the tune.

We heard the beast lay down. He was soon asleep.

Olio and I went out to look at the demon. "How do we kill it?" asked Olio quietly.

Korieski the Younger came puffing up the hillside, his head swollen and bleeding. "Get out of the way," he commanded. He drew a circle in the soil around the demon, chanting under his breath. He circumambulated the demon time and time again, scattering a yellow powder. We watched gravely.

"Come on," said Olio. "Let's get out of here." I went in to lift Hava, but she waved me away. She wanted to rise on her own. She started to stumble and I reached out to catch her, but she aggressively waved me away. She wanted to walk out under her own power.

She went out and looked down at the demon. Korieski was still walking in rhythmic circles around the demon, ignoring us.

Hava's whole body shook as she looked down at the demon. He lay sleeping peacefully, innocent as a baby.

# CHAPTER 23

# Companionship's End

We left the demon to Korieski.

The three of us departed the Deep Valley Durez and did not look back. All the joy was gone from our companionship. My sole remaining purpose was to see Hava safely home.

We travelled by raft, following the Durez to its juncture with the Flegmarn, and rejoined the remainder of Hava's party in Reiz Nohl; and from there by boat to Kharoth and Gwalnn. There were no more songs on the river, and I was shunned by the rest of Hava's crew, no doubt blamed for what had befallen their beloved leader. I deserved no less and spoke little to anyone, not even Olio who spent his time beside Hava in the boat, grim and silent.

It was said we might find a Morphidian in Harta who could heal Hava, but he was absent from the city when we came there. Hava's crew booked passage across the strait to Tross where her brother Belchamp resided. But in the morning when I went to board the ship, Olio put up his hand and stopped me. "This is as far as you go," he told me. My passage had not been paid, it seemed. He put his hand on my shoulder and told me, "Have a great life, lad."

I did not even get to say good-bye to Hava. I stood stupidly there on the dock watching their ship depart.

I am not ashamed to say I wept. My heart was broken. I had no more purpose and no idea what to do next. Returning home was out of the question. I spent some aimless weeks in Harta before joining an Astinian crew as an oarsman, and so began my life at sea.

And thus ends my sad tale. Now you know how a landlocked tribesman from deepest Soofia came to be a seaman. Now you know what I have spent these last twenty years trying my best to forget.

•

"That's it?" said Meyer. "Well, what happened then?"

"That's it," I said. "I never saw them again."

"Well, that can't be the end. That's a terrible ending."

"What do you want him to say," said Ugly Tom. "He's just telling it like it happened."

Semetrius shook his head sadly. "This Hava. No wonder you've never fallen for any of the girls in port. I understand you so much better now. But let me ask you this, my friend. Why have you never looked for her before? This is not your first time in Kortholomoth."

I had asked myself this same question. "I don't know," I said. "I never spent more than a day or two in Kortholomoth. I suppose it didn't really occur to me that she would want to see me."

Semetrius shook his head even more sadly, closing his eyes. "You were afraid."

I looked at my friend. He wasn't wrong. "Afraid of finding out. I guess I still am. Maybe it was better to hold out the possibility that she bounced back and went on with her extraordinary life, than to find out the truth. She might well have died all those years ago."

Except for one thing: The apparition that appeared to me did not look like Hava as I remembered her. No, the contours of her face had matured, the corners of her eyes marked by crow's feet.

# CHAPTER 24

# The City of Crossing Paths

I was the first to spot the lights of Kortholomoth. Presently the bay opened before us, thick with vessels from many lands. Prowbeam Rock loomed invisibly in the dark, blotting out the stars and dividing the South Port from the North. We made for the South, the larger and primary of the two ports.

My mates were jolly in anticipation of going ashore. Kortholomoth was a sailor's city, where a crew of Sartans could expect to be made welcome. I, on the other hand, was no Sartan; I was a foreigner among foreigners here in the homeland of Hava. The memory of the Great War was somehow still fresh here, although a generation had passed, and I had learned to watch my step in such places.

In an hour's time the ship was made fast in its berth. The mate erected his table on the dock, and the eager crewmen lined up for their pay.

Word had gotten round it was my last stint with this boat, and the crew were all determined to give me a proper send-off, with Semetrius as their ring leader. But I was in no mood for a night on the town. "I have my own business tonight, my mates," I said, putting my arm around Semetrius, who immediately began to weep. "A finer crew I've not known, nor a sounder ship. You took me into your family and treated me like a brother. It's been a lovely two years. Raise your cups to me tonight, my mates, and remember me well." And I walked away, an unencumbered man, carrying only a bag of personal items and a purse of silver on my belt.

I did not look back at my mates. I was eager to leave behind the sailor's quarter and find some place where the locals gathered. *Maybe I can find someone who knows Hava's family.* That was the extent of my plan.

I walked for half an hour, in no particular direction. The streets were dark and mostly empty, punctuated by lit plazas full of people and the sound of music and laughter. *In Lagin it is a party every night.* I smiled; I'd always liked the Laginese. *Not that they always like me back.* Two men stared hard as I crossed over to the other side of the street to avoid them.

I followed my stomach into a kitchen where an old woman was baking meat pies. A pair of bar wenches shooed me out of the kitchen and into a humid tavern hall full of murmuring Laginese. A long bar ran the length of the hall. I wasn't the only foreigner in the room; I spotted a lone Ckorrmanian at the end of the bar, gnawing earnestly on a drumstick.

I edged along the bar, looking for a spot. Keeping a tight hold on my purse and counting the knives and swords as I went. I swear one man *growled* as I slid behind him; his broad shoulders and general bearing reminded me of Olio. I made for the Ckorrmanian at the end of the bar, who slid over a little to make room. We foreigners had to look out for one another.

But just as I was about to settle in, the growling man demand another drink. I knew that voice!

"Olio? Is that you?"

"Eh?" Olio turned and looked at me without really seeing me. "Who wants to know?"

"It's me, Ejertine!"

"Ejertine?" A blank look. Slowly he stood up straight and faced me. "Ejertine from *Soofia*?" He pulled me in and grabbed me by the shoulders and gave me a shake. "Ha! Look at you. What ever are you doing here?"

"I'm a sailor man," I said with a grin.

"A traveler. You would be, wouldn't you? Well, come on, nestle in. Make room, make room," he grumbled at the man next to him at the bar. "Well, they call Kortholomoth the City of Crossing Paths. If you wait around long enough, you will cross paths with everyone, sooner or later. That's what they say. And here's the proof: Little Ejertine, all grown up!"

"I never thought of myself as 'little,'" I said with a frown. With an apology to my neighbor, I crowded in at the bar next to Olio. "It's the strangest thing, seeing you here... I was just talking about you to my mates."

"What's it been? Twenty years?"

"So it has."

We stood silent for a moment, leaning on the bar. Olio broke the silence with a call to the bartender. "A drink for my friend! What does it take to get a drink around here?"

I shook my head. "No thanks. It's a meal I'm wanting. I'm starved."

"Pshaw! Ale's a meal, is it not? Trust me, you don't want the food here. My friend will have an ale," said Olio to the bartender.

"And another for me as well, if you please." Olio drained what was left in his leather cup.

"You are drunk," I observed.

"Not yet I'm not."

# CHAPTER 25

# Olio's Bottom

"I can't believe it," said Olio. "Look at you, all grown up!"

"And you, looking fit as ever, I see. A little more gray in the mustache perhaps. What are you doing here, drinking by yourself?"

Olio frowned deeply. "I don't want to talk about it." He downed the rest of his ale and called for more.

Something bad had happened. I felt my heart sink. "Olio, it's no accident, the two of us meeting like this."

"No?"

"No. Some fate, or some force, has brought us together. I saw something out at sea, a spirit..."

"You're right, lad. It's destiny sent you to me so I wouldn't have to drink alone. For that I am thankful. By the gods, it's good to see you again, you old rascal. A sailor! I should have known. Another ale for my friend!"

I smiled weakly as the bartender refilled my blackjack. "Olio, please tell me, has something happened?"

Olio groaned and put his head down on the bar. "I'm ruined. He'll crush me. There's no rock I can hide under where he won't find me. He'll quarter me, he'll gouge out my eyeballs with his thumbs and make me eat 'em."

"Who will? What are you talking about?"

Olio pulled his head up again and looked dismally into his cup. "It doesn't matter. I deserve whatever he dishes out. I failed in my duty."

"What *happened?*"

Sudden tears burst forth. "She was just a little girl," he bawled. He grabbed hold of me and squeezed, forcing the air out of my lungs.

"Oof! Easy there, big fellow. Just slow down and start from the beginning."

Olio shook his head sadly and let me go. "It's a bad business, I'm afraid. I was supposed to protect her."

I swallowed. Was he talking about Hava? "Who?" I ventured.

He picked up his blackjack and drew deeply, peering at me with one eye over the rim of the cup. "Layona Tower. As in the daughter of Mizen Tower."

I stared blankly; Olio planted his cup on the bar, disappointed with me. "You have no idea who I'm talking about. Never mind. You're not from Lagin." Olio rubbed his eyes a moment. "Forget it. It doesn't matter. The short version of the story is the girl is gone, I am doomed."

"...I wish I knew what to say. What happened to her?"

"Swoosh!" He gestured violently, jostling the man next to him. "She was gone, just like that!" Indignant, his neighbor took one look at Olio, then closed his mouth. By way of apology, Olio took the man's shoulder and shook it, saying, "It was a desert twister! Did you see it? What a devil it was! Came down right on top of us. There was no time. I tried to get everyone away, but the horses... everything went to Hell. The wheel came off, girls were spilling out everywhere, and the horses, they just kept running. By the time I got them reined in, I had a trail of bumped and bruised girls stretching half a mile. When we got everyone gathered back up together again and Etebe counted heads, we were missing one girl. And who do you suppose it was? One girl missing, and it had to be the Tower girl."

"That's terrible—I'm sorry."

"Not as sorry as I'm going to be." He motioned for the bartender. I looked on dubiously as the bartender refilled Olio's blackjack from the tap. "But enough about my woes. We should be celebrating, you and I. Ejertine! Right here before my eyes. What were you saying, something about a spirit, you said?"

I said nothing for a moment, pursing my lips. "Olio—what happened? To her?"

"Oh," said Olio slowly, standing up straight. He considered me anew. "Of course. You don't know."

"The last I saw the two of you, I was standing on a dock in Harta."

"Yes, of course. I'm sorry. Let's…" Olio looked around. "Let's get out of here." He gulped down his drink and dropped a few coins on the bar. The bartender looked at him askance, and Olio added a few more coins with a frown. "I know a classier place, not far from here."

# CHAPTER 26

# A Classier Place

Already regretting the cheap Laginese ales on my empty stomach, I followed Olio into an unpromising-looking alleyway and through an archway of stone. Crumbling stairs led down into the bowels of some ancient warehouse. We followed a long, subterranean corridor smelling of must. "Where exactly are you taking me?"

"Trust me," promised Olio. Soon enough he showed me through a finely painted door which opened into a warmly lit great hall, full of well-dressed gentlemen who sat in earnest clusters in overstuffed chairs, smoking pipes and playing Gritz.

"Oh," I said, impressed.

"What'd I tell you? Come on." He led me to an engraved cabinet with brass handles and opened it to reveal tiered shelves of liquors and wines. He started rifling through the bottles, scrutinizing the labels.

I looked nervously at the other patrons but no one seemed to pay us any heed. "Are you sure we're supposed to be here?"

"You mean do they allow the likes of us in a place like this? Normally, no. But don't worry. I work for Mizen Tower. He's a dues-paying member here. The way I see it, that entitles us to all the booze we want. I better enjoy this while I can. Here we go," he said triumphantly, having found the bottle he'd sought.

"Come on, this will knock your sailor-boy socks off. Grab a couple of those glasses."

"I thought you said they had food here?" I said doubtfully, following Olio to a remote table.

"Don't worry. They have the best food here! Someone will be by."

I sank back into the embrace of an armchair while Olio poured the drinks. "Not so bad, eh?"

Across the way I saw a striking man with long, white hair and a tall hat laughing amiably with two elderly gentlemen sucking on kanis-cigars. I noted an ornate smoking box on the table in front of him. "I didn't know places like this even existed!"

"Drink up, little man," said Olio gravely. "The story I've got to tell you is not an easy one, but one you deserve to know."

I winced a little but reached for the glass. "Just tell me this, Olio. Did she make it? Did she live?"

Olio blinked a few times, then said simply, "Drink."

I drank.

"You mean, did she live—after what happened? Yes, she lived. She lived a long time."

I nodded slowly. "But now she's dead."

"I'm afraid so. Not so long ago now." He refilled my glass.

"Tell me what happened," I said, sitting up in my chair. "I want to know."

"Well, she fell ill. Coming back from one of her fool journeys. She died in the forest, just a few days from home."

"I saw her."

"Eh?"

"Her spirit came to me, two days hence. She was beckoning… summoning me here to Kortholomoth. It's like she was asking for my help."

Olio stared steadily at me for a moment. "What are you talking about, her 'spirit?' Like she's some tortured soul trapped in this plane? No. Trust me: She's gone from this world. A spirit like Hava's belongs in Alyon with the gods and goddesses." He tossed back his drink.

"That may be; but nonetheless I know what I saw."

"I reject that," shouted Olio, slamming his glass down. "You don't know what you saw."

Lowering his voice, he added, "Besides, don't you think, supposing Hava's spirit were wandering this plane, don't you think she would come to *me* before you? I mean, she barely knew you."

I pursed my lips and looked coolly at Olio. "What, now you're jealous?"

"Don't be ridiculous." Olio rubbed his eyes. "Just let me talk, will you? There's things you need to know…"

●

That day we left you back in Harta, Hava had taken a turn for the worse. She lay still and unconscious, cold to the touch. That's why we were in such a hurry to go. I wanted to get her across the strait to Tross, the land of healers. Straightaway after landing in Wahl Dahldin I took her to the temple of Morphid.

Well, turns out the Morphidians weren't so helpful after all. They wouldn't even let us in the gate. I had her in my arms, but I could not lift my foot to step through the gate. Some unseen force stopped me. The hand of Morphid, I suppose. The priests came out and clucked over us, but in the end it amounted to this: The taint of the demon-thing was upon her, and the protective spells of the priests barred her from entering sanctified grounds.

When I raised a ruckus, the High Morphidian came out to see what was the matter. He was a peace-loving man, and he spoke softly so I had to lower my voice and listen to what he said. By the by, he had me calmed down. No, he couldn't let Hava into the temple, but he agreed to come with us to our lodging. Hava's crew had already made the arrangements.

Well, we laid Hava out in the biggest room in the lodge. The High Morphidian looked over her injuries and listened calmly to my tale. I left out the particulars, didn't even tell him our names for some reason. He seemed like a good man, but something told me not to trust him.

He sent me out onto the balcony while he prayed over Hava. I stood out in the wind with the seagulls for an hour or more, contemplating the canal—a clean and tidy canal such as only can be found in Tross. Beyond the canal the city marched up the hillside, all the way up to the great crack in the mountain you see on all the coins.

Well at long last, the High Morphidian joined me on the balcony, and here is what told me: Hava was pregnant, he said. The demon had planted his seed within her.

I could not even understand what I was hearing. "Well, can you heal her?" is what I wanted to know.

"You don't understand," he said. "There is no healing. She shares blood with a demon, of Nominian ilk, festering within her. We must do what must be done."

I did not like the sound of that one bit, and I told him so.

"I am sorry, but in this matter there is no luxury of choice," he said. "We cannot permit a demon birth into this world. And as for the woman, the woman you knew is gone; you must accept this. This one may look like the one you knew, but she has been changed." That's what he said. "If we do nothing and allow this unnatural process to unfold, then we will have unleashed not one but two demons into our world. You must understand: We must do what must be done. It will be a mercy upon her. My acolytes will perform the purging this same day before the sun is gone."

Well, that cinched it, I'm afraid. I bopped the High Morphidian on the head, I'm ashamed to say, and I dragged him into the room and tied him up and locked him in the wardrobe.

I was not about to just stand by and let harm come to Hava, demon-tainted or otherwise.

I gathered up Hava's crew and put them to work. Two went to the stable and readied a couple of mules; I dispatched another to the temple to make excuses for the High Morphidian; and the rest schemed to smuggle Hava and me out of the lodge without being seen. I told them to scatter from Wahl Dahldin, to take separate ships and meet up in Kortholomoth. Should the Morphidians come looking for us, I hoped that would throw them off the trail. My real plan was for me and Hava to travel overland to Shamp where Hava's older brother Belchamp lived.

I put Hava on a mule and we fled into the green hills beyond Wahl Dahldin. Once I had turned my back on the city of men, I went looking for kents of the wood. If the Morphidians wouldn't heal her, perhaps I could find a healer among the kent-kind. That's how my thinking went.

Well. It's not a hard thing to find kents in the woods of Tross. But finding decent, trustworthy ones is another matter altogether. These ones I found were a bunch of scoundrels. They gave me some sweet wine that knocked me out. I woke up, who knows how many days later, stripped of all my clothes and belongings, half-submerged in a stream, surrounded by crawfish who had taken up residence under my naked body. I was parched and starving and all my joints were stiff. Those dirty kents had had their fun with me, and they had taken Hava away.

The next several days I lived like an animal, eating whatever I could catch with my hands and cursing the kentkind. I could hear them sometimes, somewhere out of sight, laughing at me. Sometimes they would leave me little offerings tied up in leaf-packages. But I was no fool. I wasn't going to eat any more kentish offerings.

Finally, they sent a kent child to gather me. She led me to a hut where I found Hava sitting up and laughing with some old kent. "Olio!" she said. "Where are your clothes?"

I didn't even care that I stood naked before her. I was so happy to see her well again. Her mouth, her face, her ear were all healed, and she had something of her old glow returned to her.

I'll say this for the kentkind: They took good care of Hava. They also gave me my sword back and some balm for my bad leg that took away my pain for weeks. Come to think of it, I wish I could find those kents again—that leg still bothers me.

When she was well enough to travel, Hava and I left the hill country and headed out into the vast stretches of Yahr toward Shamp. The weather turned dismal and the mud was too much for our mules. Our way was slow and the horsemen of Yahr proved of little help. The ill weather disagreed with Hava, and she fell into fever again. We stopped and rested, days at a time, until she was well enough to travel a little more. All the while that demon child was growing inside her, poisoning her. By the time we arrived at the house of Belchamp, even I could see she was pregnant. I had to carry her up to the gate and bang with my scabbard until someone finally came to let us in.

"Don't tell my brother what happened," she whispered before the servants came and took her away.

I wandered the house of Belchamp, wringing my hands. The house was a sprawling affair. Belchamp was forever adding new wings. One room spilled into another as if it all were some terrific accident. He drew his money from the old Nipalto well, coupled with the new commercial wealth of his Tross-wife.

I found a quiet sitting room away from the bustle of the servants. On the walls hung portraits, paintings of Hava and Belchamp together—on a ship, at the peak of some mountain, standing before the Ankbar Palace.

"Our trip to Anbactica," said Belchamp from behind me. "Hava was just a girl."

Belchamp looked older than the last time I'd seen him. He still filled the room with his personality, though, and it was impossible not to be swept away by his presence. "See here," he said, showing me a display case with shelves of clay dolls they'd gathered on that excursion to the far north. "Father financed the trip, of course. As always, we promised to bring him dolls from the places we went."

Belchamp had long since settled down, but the love of travel and adventure never left his little sister. The elder Nipalto was disappointed, of course, that neither of his children stayed in Lagin. Belchamp loved his father well, but he loved his wife Meida more, and his life in Tross most of all.

"Are you the father?" Belchamp asked me, just like that. I could feel his eyes burrowing into me.

"What? No," I blurted. "Of course not."

"Tell me what happened." I could see him sizing me up, searching for any weakness. "If ever you were a friend to this family, tell me what happened."

But I could tell him nothing. He pressed me well, but I could not betray Hava's trust; she had sworn me to silence.

After that, things were a little tense between Belchamp and me. I tried to make myself scarce. I stayed out of Shamp, too, in case the Morphidians might be on the look-out. Mostly I hunkered down on Belchamp's grounds in the empty kennels and kept to myself. I earned my keep by walking the grounds at night to discourage trespassers and groundlings.

I did not see much of Hava during these months. She was pretty sick for the rest of her pregnancy and not much interested in conversation with anyone.

The birth was difficult. She almost didn't make it through. But the baby was... beautiful. I must admit, the words of the High Morphidian had been haunting me, and I half expected something all claws and fangs to tear its way out of her womb. But instead we got a perfect baby girl who would fall asleep in the nook of my arm, just so. The servants used to give her to me to hold when they couldn't get her to stop crying. She just took to me somehow. Our connection did not escape Belchamp's notice and only fanned the fires of his suspicions.

Hava was in no hurry to recover. She shunned the baby. She would not even look at the beautiful child she'd created, much less hold her or feed her.

So Belchamp hired this Soofian nursemaid to care for the girl. It was the nursemaid who came up with the name Elevaer. A very pretty name, I thought.

It was clear enough Belchamp didn't want me about the house, so I kept to the abandoned kennels. But from time to time I'd find an excuse to check in on Elevaer. The nursemaid—well, she thought I was coming round on *her* account. When she knew I was coming, she used to put on this little… heh. Never mind about that. Suffice it to say, the Soofian nursemaid and me came to be on intimate terms. I loved her, or thought I did; now I can't even remember her name. One time I embarrassed myself by earnestly suggesting we could be a family, the three of us—her, me, and the baby. Hava clearly did not want the baby. It just made sense to me, but the nursemaid, she looked at me like I was crazy. "This is my job," she told me. "I don't *keep* the babies."

But she did worry herself over Elevaer's future well-being. She didn't think Hava would ever grow to love the child.

"She'll warm up, you'll see," I told her. "She just needs time."

"I don't think so. She thinks Elevaer is *evil*; she told me so." She was afraid Hava would try and do harm to the child. I took offense to that notion and stormed off. Maybe I was also a little mad about her rejection of my proposal. But later when I was alone with my barrel-fire beside the kennel, the nursemaid's words about Hava returned to bother me, and I found myself beginning to have doubts of my own.

A few days later, Belchamp came to see me in the night. "I've had a letter from my wife. She's returning with the dogs any day now. Would you mind helping the lads in the morning to make the kennels ready?"

I wasn't sure if he was offering me a job or just trying to get me to clear out. But I kept my mouth closed, on account he was still standing there clutching some letters, like he had something else he wanted to say.

"It's time, don't you think, for Hava to return home? Look," he said, handing me the letters. I looked, to be polite, noting the Nipalto family seal—but of course I don't know the first thing about reading. "From her husband," he said. "And this one from her father. But she makes no answer to them. What am I to do?"

Not that he was asking my advice. "There is nothing wrong with Hava, physically," he said. "She is well enough to travel. Hiding here longer will not serve her interests." He had already sent a letter ahead, promising to book Hava's passage with a trusted captain who would deliver her all the way to Kortholomoth. "The open sea will do her good," he said.

I didn't disagree.

"Olio," he said. "Here's how it is: We shall say the child is the bastard of my daughter Yerve. We shall say I've asked Hava to foster the child in Lagin to avoid scandal here in Shamp."

So that was the story. He was insistent that we get ourselves straight on all the particulars. Yerve was a wayward child and no one in Lagin would question the tale. He had even browbeat poor Yerve to go along with the story.

"So," I said. "Does this mean I'm to be trusted after all?"

Belchamp nodded without hesitation. "I know about the trouble with the Morphidians in Wahl Dahldin. If it weren't for you, Olio, we would have lost Hava altogether. It's true she may not be her old self, but I know my sister. She is in there. She just needs time. I also understand your silence. And I commend your loyalty to my sister. She needs one such as you at her side." I admit it felt good to hear that from him. I didn't realize how much I craved his approval.

We boarded the ship within a few days. Dockside, I watched as the nursemaid passed the baby to Hava. Grim but resolved, Hava accepted the child, holding Elevaer away from her body like she was some adder. The nursemaid caught my eye. I kissed her goodbye and didn't care who saw. "Watch out for the child," was the last thing she said to me.

And so I did. I kept close to Hava and Elevaer. When the baby cried, I was on hand to take her. Hava was moody and depressed but had resigned herself at least to taking basic care of Elevaer.

We sailed south through the Strait of Harta without stopping. We resupplied in Hajan and then made the long, lonely voyage among the Nohads to Astina. The final leg took us west across the Green Sea, back home to Kortholomoth.

A few days shy of Kortholomoth, I started to relax. I didn't realize how much I had missed home. It had been nearly three years. Nearly three years since Hava had last seen her husband. That's a long time for a husband to wait. Would he even recognize her, I wondered? But Hava was still Hava, and the closer we came to Kortholomoth, the more her old self began to show. When we spoke of her husband, her mood improved. And she spoke of her second cousin Elevaer as if she herself believed the myth Belchamp had concocted.

So I relaxed a little. I let my guard drop. I fell asleep, dreaming of home. Well, when I woke up, they were gone from the cabin. No Hava, no Elevaer. I had this sinking feeling. It was not like Hava to leave the cabin and take the child with her. In a panic, I searched the ship and finally found Hava at the stern, standing at the rail... She was holding Elevaer at arm's length over the rail, as if to drop her into the tossing sea. She had this crazy, far-away look in her eyes, like she was in a dream.

"Hava! What the hell are you doing?" is what I said, or something close to that. She turned her head a little toward the sound but otherwise didn't react, just stood there holding the baby over the rail.

"Hava, this is not you," I said. "Give me the baby."

But she did not give me the baby. "You don't understand," she said. "Don't you know what she is? What she will become?"

"What are you talking about, she is a beautiful little girl."

Hava's eyes hardened. "Olio. This is no harmless child. You saw what her father was. Her blood is demon's blood. No good can come from this life. That is certain, Olio. What must be done, must be done."

Well, I'd heard that line before. I wasn't going to stand by and let Hava drop her own baby into the Green Sea. I'm a man of action; I gave up on words and just grabbed the baby from her. She did not resist. She could have dropped her if she wanted. For that matter she could have easily tossed her in the sea while I was still asleep in the cabin. But she didn't. She knew it wasn't right and couldn't bring herself to do it.

I kept a close watch on mother and child for the remainder of the voyage, but the danger was passed.

# CHAPTER 27

# A Look Over the Edge

Hava's husband Encho met us at the docks. Who knows how long he'd been waiting there? He was a scrawny little specimen, his eyes all twinkling with joy at the sight of Hava. Even before the ship was tied he leapt aboard and seized hold of her. They both wept, and I admit I cried a bit myself. It was a sweet reunion, and good old Encho lavished the baby with kisses, accepting her into the family at once. "Has she already been blessed? If not, we'll get her to the temple tomorrow..."

"No need for that," said Hava, laughing. "She's already had ample blessings in Shamp. Tross is nothing if not rich in Morphidians." I have to say, I was a little surprised how smoothly Hava lied.

Encho suspected nothing. Here was a man with not a drop of guile in his blood. He was ever the simple apprentice, utterly unchanged by the wealth he married into.

See, before he was Hava's husband, Encho was her father's apprentice. He was the son Nipalto never had. An urchin, actually, who first started coming round the shop years before. Nipalto used to put him to work when he came around, and he proved clever with his hands. Years later, when it was clear that neither Belchamp nor Hava were going to settle down long enough to carry on the family legacy of doll-making, Old Nipalto decided to take on an apprentice, and there was Encho wearing an apron now, learning the craft in earnest. This was the Encho who finally caught Hava's eye. Seeing him together with her father in the workshop, month after month, she began to take a shining to him. This unassuming little man, the only man who ever captured Hava's heart. He was everything she wasn't: patient, focused, there for her father. Old Nipalto gladly blessed the marriage and granted Encho the family name and named him heir as well, no small detail when you are talking about one of Kortholomoth's founding families; the Nipaltos owned most of the South Port and still do to this day. But none of that mattered to Encho. He was not interested in business or society; he was interested only in his craft.

Old Nipalto still ran the family's business—or he had, last I heard. He was my employer, the one who charged me with seeing Hava safely to Soofia and back. But apparently a lot had changed while we were gone. Old Nipalto was old indeed, having outlived his sisters and wives, and his age was finally catching up to him. "He is so frail now," Encho told us, wringing his hands. "He doesn't leave the House anymore."

The "House" is the Nipalto mansion, a century-old castle hidden in the heart of the city. That's where I was man-at-arms before I was assigned to protect Hava. Apparently in my absence, I had been replaced by some fancy gentleman swashbuckler by the name of Alakhar, whom I disliked immediately. I was eager to go to Old Nipalto and set matters right, get my old job back, you know? But when I finally came into the presence of Nipalto, such petty thoughts evaporated at once. He was just this frail little thing, bonier than before; and he exuded this infectious calm. He had with him that big doll your father created, you remember? And he was full of questions about it. Hava came in and they talked at length. But there was no talk of living dolls or demons.

At a lapse in the conversation, I put in, "I expect you'll be needing me back at my old job straightaway."

"Certainly, just report to Alakhar," he said. *Report to Alakhar.* That did not sound much like getting my old job back. Turns out, Alakhar was being groomed not just to be in charge of security but to take over all management of the family holdings. "Steward" they called him. That is to say, Encho would be the head of the House, but Alakhar would actually run the show. I am not sure where they dug up this Alakhar guy… I'm sure he was somebody's uncle. I guess he had the right breeding and all, but to lay eyes on him, he wasn't much to speak of. All that fancy fencing school doesn't substitute for real combat experience, but he liked to pretend he was some kind of master swordsman. Funny, though, how he never seemed to have time to spar with me and my simple broadsword, though I invited him many a time. He tried to keep me out of the way, putting me to work at remote properties, rousting squatters, collecting rent, doing odd jobs, anything to avoid squaring off with me.

But I always found an excuse to come by the House, to check on Hava and Elevaer. I used to bring sweet mash for the baby. Well, maybe the third time Alakhar started to give me the stink eye. "Since when does a henchman care for the welfare of babies?" A henchman! That's what he called me.

He must have said something to the Nipaltos, pouring his vile slander in their ears, because they started looking at me askance too. Who knew it was a crime to bring sweet mash to a baby? Then one time Encho saw me with Hava, we were sitting together just talking, quiet like. I think we were talking about Soofia; I don't remember exactly. Well, he didn't say anything, just smiled in that way you do when you're being polite, and went about his way, leaving us to talk. But I could tell it bothered Encho, how close I was to Hava. All those experiences we shared that he wasn't part of and could never understand.

It wasn't long after that Alakhar found some excuse to discharge me from service, and Encho did nothing to try and keep me. By then, Old Nipalto was dying and everyone was much distracted.

But good old Hava came through for me. She got me work with the Mystans. Soon after Old Nipalto died, Hava herself was finally initiated as a Mystan, so I got to see her from time to time. I would always ask about Elevaer.

But the truth was Hava did not see much of Elevaer. She spent most of her time away from home, delving into the Mystan arts, doing whatever Mystans do (I still don't know after all these years); and when she did go home she mostly avoided Elevaer. It fell upon Encho to love and nourish the child. After Old Nipalto's death, Encho had taken to sleeping in the back room of the doll shop, on his old apprentice's cot, and he kept Elevaer full time with him, only going back to the House when Hava came around. He refused servants, insisting they were in the way. All by himself, he made his dolls and ran the shop and cared for the little one. She took her first steps in that workshop. I saw her soon after that, toddling about the shop, making trouble. It was madness, with all those priceless dolls lying about, but Encho was full of patience and forgiveness. I couldn't help but notice that the presence of the adorable toddler in the shop turned out the wealthy lady customers who would come specially to dote on her and, while they were there, buy a unique item as a gift for some foreign dignitary they needed to impress. When I visited the shop, Encho was always kind to me and let me bounce Elevaer on my knee. He asked how the Mystans were treating me, I said everything's great, and we left it at that.

Hava and Encho may not have seen much of each other, but they were as much in love as ever they had been. Those two were just fools for each other. And a few years later, they had a child together. Another beautiful little baby. They named her Ichito. And how Hava loved her Ichito! She would hold her in her arms and coo, give her milk from her breast, sing to her.

Well, little Elevaer saw all this. She saw the love lavished upon Ichito where there had been none for her. I believe this is when something shifted inside her. I think this is when Elevaer started to go bad.

Now I wasn't there, mind you. I can't claim to say what did or didn't happen. I know only what Hava told me. She was convinced that Elevaer had become obsessed with harming Ichito. It started off like this: with Elevaer picking up a pair of shears from the shop and looming over the baby. Hava saw what was happening and quickly intervened. "I just wanted to give her a pretty haircut," is what Elevaer had to say for herself. She must have been five or six at the time.

After the incident with the shears, Hava insisted Elevaer be kept separately from the baby. Encho thought this was an overreaction. "She'll grow out of it," he said. "It's natural she should be envious of Ichito."

But there was nothing natural about Elevaer, not in Hava's mind. When she looked at the child, all she could see was the memory of where she had come from.

There was some tension between Hava and Encho on this matter, but in the end they agreed that Elevaer would stay full time at the workshop in Central Market as Encho's apprentice, while Ichito was kept at the House proper. Hava ceased her travels and her politicking with the Mystans to care for her baby. She kept the windows bolted and a guard on duty. Encho didn't think these precautions necessary; he thought—we all thought—Hava had lost her ability to think rationally when it came to Elevaer. The notion that a six-year-old girl would find her way across town, slip into the House unnoticed, to act on a grudge against a baby... it did not seem reasonable or plausible.

Well, time rolled on. The months passed. Elevaer for her part was all smiles and sweetness, and popular as ever with the customers. An intense child, to be sure. But she gave no indication she even remembered her cousin Ichito or the incident with the shears. Still Hava sensed a darkness within the child. When she looked into Elevaer's eyes, she felt an adversary returning her gaze—a calculating intelligence, sizing her up. "She is biding her time," Hava told me. I admit, I had my doubts about Hava's state of mind; my memory always returned to that moment on the ship when Hava was ready to drop baby Elevaer into the sea.

But here's the truth of it: Hava was right. Elevaer *had* been biding her time, waiting for her opportunity; and that opportunity came on the occasion of Ichito's first birthday, when she saw Encho about the workshop making a special doll. Elevaer caught wind that this special doll was to be a gift for Ichito. Well, Elevaer managed to slip something extra into the hollow head of the doll. I don't know where or how she came up with the scorpion. She must have captured it. It was one of those little red kind, you know the ones I mean? Yeah, you don't want to mess with those. Well, this particular scorpion, as it turned out, was pregnant. And while little Ichito played with her beloved new doll, locked inside the head of this doll was an angry, pregnant scorpion. And in the night, when the doll finally lay still against Ichito's little body, then the scorpion gave birth, and a dozen or so tiny babies found their way out of that doll's head.

It was Alakhar who noticed something was wrong. Hava still insisted on a nightly guard, and Alakhar himself was on duty that night. And when he went to check on Ichito, he noticed something tiny and red moving on her cheek. He did the right thing, he got the scorpion off her but got stung himself in the process. If little Ichito had been stung like that, on the face as it were, it would have likely killed her. Old Alakhar got himself stung, not by the scorpion he saw on Ichito's cheek, but by the one he didn't see when he plucked her out of her infested crib.

Hava immediately suspected Elevaer, of course. And when Encho opened the doll's head and found the mother scorpion inside, it was hard to deny that it had been put there deliberately. But when he confronted Elevaer, her denials were so convincing that he was persuaded of her innocence. Encho and

Hava argued fiercely over Elevaer and what, if anything, was to be done about her.

Hava wanted to take Ichito to Ragne to live with the Mystans, but she could not do that to Encho. He loved both his girls and didn't want to lose either of them. So things stayed more or less as they were, with Ichito living at the House and Elevaer banished to the doll shop.

These were hard years for Hava. She was afraid to travel, afraid of what would happen if she left Ichito. She had a wanderer's heart, like your father, and it did harm to her soul to be bound down in one place for so long.

Encho, on the other hand, flourished. He was at the peak of his powers as a master craftsman, his reputation had swelled beyond even that of Hava's father. By day he worked in his shop with Elevaer at his side, and at night he returned to Hava and Ichito. He had everything he wanted, and he was surrounded by those he loved.

Elevaer stayed in the workshop, with a guardian to watch over her—someone whose job it was to look after the girl, make sure she was safe through the night and that she stayed out of trouble. Sweet as she was to Encho, Elevaer was hard on these guardians. One after the other, she used to drive them away, until finally she got one she liked. Someone she could work with.

Mistress Kella was her name. She was a smart one—smart enough to know how to say the right things to Encho and Hava. They resorted to her only after rotating through every reputed caretaker in Kortholomoth. Mistress Kella was a middle-aged widow of a disgraced tobacconist who killed himself some years prior. She had raised seven of her own children, and for whatever reason Elevaer behaved for her, and for this Encho and Hava were grateful. How could they know Mistress Kella and Elevaer would form an unholy alliance against them? For what Elevaer saw in Mistress Kella was darkness, a willingness to look evil in the face and ask, unflinchingly, what could they do to help each other out? Mistress Kella was a woman turned wicked, and further encouraged into wickedness by Elevaer.

For several years Kella served the Nipalto family as Elevaer's guardian. In Hava's absence, it was Kella taught Elevaer how to be a young woman. And at night, after Encho left the workshop, then would begin Elevaer's second, secret life. We don't know at what age she started going out into the city. Evidently Central Market's night watch was not so watchful after all if they allowed a little girl to come and go freely from the doll shop in the dead of night. Kella protected her secrets in exchange for money that Elevaer skimmed from the sales. (Encho was a dreadful accountant and never noticed the missing money.) We don't know exactly what Elevaer did on the streets of Kortholomoth. We know only what Kella told us later under Hava's interrogation.

It seems Elevaer had been surveying the House Nipalto for some time. And not only that, she'd made contact with Ichito. They had a secret correspondence, and Elevaer got Ichito to agree to sneak out of the House and meet her. Elevaer was perhaps thirteen winters old; Ichito must have been maybe eight or nine.

The sun was not yet risen before it was noticed Ichito was missing from her bed. Then began a frantic search of the House, but of course Ichito was not to be found. Encho dispatched a servant to the shop and soon found out Elevaer was also missing. That's when they knew: Elevaer had taken Ichito.

Hava and Alakhar took charge of rapidly mobilizing a search team, while Encho departed the House, headed (he thought) toward his shop. The sun had not yet broken over the horizon but its first rays were already grazing the top of Prowbeam Rock, that giant rock that overlooks the city and separates the South Port from the North. Acting on a hunch, Encho made for the Rock. *That's where she'd go*, he thought to himself. There was no more denying it. Hava had been right about Elevaer. He made speed for the Rock. If Elevaer meant to harm Ichito, he would have to catch up to them before they reached the top.

Why Prowbeam Rock? I don't know. It's the obvious place a child would think of, I suppose, looming over the ports as it does. Captures the imagination, right? Or maybe it's because Encho spent so much time with Elevaer, he knew the way her mind worked. One reason or the other, Encho's hunch was right. Elevaer had in fact taken Ichito up to Prowbeam Rock. At first, Ichito had come willingly, but when they started climbing, she cried and wanted to turn back. Elevaer had to more or less drag her up to the top. Once she was up top, Ichito was dazzled by the sunrise over the Green Sea and the view of Kortholomoth emerging from the last shadows of night.

"You can look straight down and see the beach," said Elevaer. "Take a step closer and have a look over the edge…"

That's when Encho arrived, all out of the breath from the climb. As he came upon them, Elevaer had her hands out to push Ichito over the edge. Encho came up from behind and took hold of Elevaer's upper arm, even as Ichito was leaning forward to peer over the precipice.

"Get back from there," said Encho sternly.

Ichito turned and ran to him. "Papa! Papa! Look at all the boats."

And that was that. Encho gathered Ichito in his arms and glowered down at Elevaer. Elevaer, for once, was out of lies and just stared back at him, aghast.

On the way down, before they reached the base of Prow-beam Rock, Elevaer turned down a different path, separating herself from Encho and Ichito. He made no attempt to go after her. They took one last look at one another and went their separate ways. And that was the last anyone saw of Cousin Elevaer. At least that's how Encho told it.

Elevaer skipped town, we think. Hava worried, of course, that sooner or later she would show up again, jump out of the shadows to snatch up Ichito. But at least Encho and Alakhar now knew the truth and would take Ichito's safety more seriously.

Months and years passed with no sign of Elevaer. Hava resumed her travels. She was a proper Mystan now and had responsibilities in the world. Though, as I've said, I still have no idea what Mystans actually do. Go to a lot of conventions and talk a lot about "balance," as far as I can tell.

I saw less and less of Hava, toward the end. Last I saw her, she looked something of her old self, but more... tired. Still that same determined look in her eye. I'm not sure what exactly she was up to, but something important, I'd say. Something more important than collecting exotic dolls, anyway. She didn't want to talk about it, whatever it was. She was headed north to the Isthmus, she told me that, but nothing more.

I was working in Ragne when I got word a few months later. Hava was dead. I didn't believe it at first. I came back here to

Kortholomoth. I was here in this club and I saw Encho across the room, there where those gentlemen are now; he was meeting with Alakhar and a couple of other high-and-mighties. When I saw the look on Encho's face, that's when I knew it was really true.

# CHAPTER 28

# Fleggar

"Thank you," I said to Olio. "Thank you for telling me."

Olio nodded slowly. "Well, I think we've finished the bottle," he said sadly.

I looked around. The last of the other patrons had left a few minutes earlier. "I never got any food."

"What are you going on about?" Olio found his feet but lost them again just as quickly, falling back into his armchair. "Look out, I think the floor is a tad unsteady in this place."

I rolled my eyes. "I'm half your weight, but I hold my liquor better."

"What!" bellowed Olio and leapt to his feet, trying but failing to draw his sword.

"Come on," I said, laughing. "Let's get out of here."

"Holds his alcohol better than I do… ha! I'll have you know," said Olio, leaning on me as I tried to steer him toward the exit. "I'll have you know… Wow! Walking is hard."

"I've carried you before."

"Pshaw! A scrawny thing like you? I think I would remember that."

"Well, you were pretty unconscious at the time. One of Korieski's little demon-dolls had done a number on you."

Olio frowned, trying to remember, as I negotiated him through the doorway and into the long, ancient stone corridor.

"Where are we going, anyway?"

"This is the way we came in."

"Yes, I know *that*. I mean, where are we going next?"

"To find a bed, I should think. Where do you live?"

Olio laughed. "You don't get it. What I do for a living now… the pinnacle of my career… I travel about with a bunch of little girls! We go from town to town, singing. So you see, Ejertine, I don't have a home. I don't have a bed. The ground is my bed." As he said this last, he sagged away from me, reaching for the ground. "The ground is my friend."

"No, no—keep going," I said, straining to keep the big man on his feet. "Just up these stairs here. I don't think this would be a good place to sleep."

"Who said anything about sleeping?"

"You did. You just—never mind. So you travel about with a bunch of singing girls, do you?"

"I do."

"And I take it they hired you on, not so much for your singing voice as for your sword hand? So you go along with the girls to keep them safe."

"That's the theory."

"First of all, that's honorable work. Nothing to be ashamed of, my friend. Second of all, it's not your fault a freak twister storm snatched up one of your girls. Your sword hand is not much good against an act of the gods. If it had been robbers or rapists, I would be the first to condemn you."

"And well you should."

"But a twister? No. That's no reflection on you."

"Let's hope the girl's father sees it the same way."

"Third of all," I continued as we emerged into the cool night air, "if you're here with me, then who, pray tell, is watching the girls?"

"I took the night off," grumbled Olio. "Don't worry, I left them in good hands. Hey, you know what? Let's go see old Encho. I haven't talked to him. Not since."

"It's the middle of the night."

"Pshaw! This is Lagin. Encho Nipalto is like family. All this talk about him reminds me what a decent man he is. I should very much like to shake his hand and throw back a drink in his honor. What do you say, lad? Are you with me? Good old Encho Nipalto! I'd like to introduce you. He'll want to meet you, too, you know. Your father was a great doll-maker. He'll want to talk shop, I'm sure."

"…You can't call me 'lad' any more, you know…"

With renewed purpose, Olio's stupor disappeared, replaced with a lively gait. He locked arms with me and more or less dragged me along through the dark, empty streets. "Encho spends all his time in his shop these days, I hear. He's probably still awake, working on some commission or the other. But we'll have to keep quiet through here… The Central Market night watchman is an especially foul breed."

We found Encho Nipalto's International Doll Shop and saw, indeed, a light burning within. By way of knocking, Olio slapped his palm against the door three times, producing an authoritative thumping.

From within I thought I could hear whispers.

"Nipalto," called Olio through the door. "It's me—Olio! Open up."

"Begone, you fool," came a voice from within. An unusually raspy voice, I thought. "Nipalto is not here."

"Who are you, then?" asked Olio with a frown.

This is when I became aware of two uniformed men with halberds hurrying onto the scene. "Here's your watchmen," I said quickly. "Come on, let's scram."

"Just a minute," said Olio, his frown deepening. He stepped back into the street and peered through the front glass window, trying to see who was there. "Who are you? Identify yourself!" demanded Olio.

The watchmen were now at hand, breathing heavily under the burden of their mail and pole-arms. "What's this now? Come away from there, you!" shouted the younger of the two men.

I started to apologize but held my tongue when I noticed the second watchman, a stocky middle-aged man, staring hard at me. *He does not like what he sees.*

"There's an impostor in Nipalto's doll shop," declared Olio, stepping away from the window and pointing back at it emphatically. "I demand to know who's in there!"

"He is drunk," called the raspy voice from within. "See that he does not return here again."

That voice. Something about it sent shivers down my back. Was it… a woman? A child? Some smallite?

The watchmen needed no further urging to point their halberds at the two of us, thrusting at us impatiently. We had no choice but to retreat rapidly to avoid being poked. "Hey!" complained Olio. "Careful with that, you miscreant!"

"Out you go," said the younger watchman, and the two guards drove us through the street to the archway that marked the entrance to Central Market.

"I've seen your face, fleggar," said the middle-aged watchman, staring directly into my eyes. "I don't want to see it again."

*Fleggar? I suppose the war never ended for some.*

"You can't talk to my friend that way," objected Olio.

"Quiet, you…" said the younger watchman, making another jab at Olio.

This time, instead of cringing back, Olio stood his ground and batted the halberd aside with the flat of his hand. "I swear, if you poke that thing at me one more time…"

I pulled Olio away. "Come on, we're going now." We retreated rapidly from the two watchmen, who stood under the arch watching us go.

"What did I tell you," grumbled Olio. "A foul breed, these night watchmen. Not even real guards. Did you see how they were holding their weapons?" And he burst into laughter. "Did you ever see such a thing?"

"Shush, will you?" I hissed. "You'll get us both killed."

"What, you're worried about those two? Never mind about them. They are nothing. Less than nothing. We've got bigger problems."

"What do you mean?" I thought about the voice in the doll shop.

"Something's not right. I can feel it. Come on, lad, this way."

"Seriously, stop calling me 'lad.' Where are we going?"

"To the House Nipalto, to get to the bottom of all this."

# CHAPTER 29

# Chickens to Eggs

I hurried after Olio. How did he get so spry all the sudden?

It was not far to the House—just a few blocks uphill. I kept looking behind, watching for a tail.

"Relax," said Olio. "Those ones don't leave the nest."

We passed an open-air drinking establishment, full even at this hour. "Sure we shouldn't wait till morning?" I said, gazing longingly at a pair of hens rotating on a spit.

"Suit yourself," said Olio without slowing his pace.

"Olio. We don't even know what we're up against here."

"I have a pretty good idea: Alakhar," he said, spitting. "With Hava out of the way, I'll bet you chickens to eggs that old fraud has swindled Encho out of his shop somehow. We'll see about that."

We turned a corner and I found myself impressed by the old stone buildings lining either side of the avenue. More than one tree lay split open, and someone's tent was tangled high in the upper reaches of a great oak. "Storm damage," said Olio. "That twister must have come straight through here." He picked up his pace then, like maybe he was afraid the House Nipalto had been hit.

He needn't have worried. The House itself appeared indestructible, with its outer stone wall and solid stone construction. In front of the House was a gatehouse, illuminated by two torches mounted on either side and guarded by two enormous men with swords and mismatched leather armor.

Olio slowed his pace as he approached these two rough-looking fellows. "Who are you then?"

The two enormous men closed ranks in front of the gate and put their hands on their sword hilts. "Who wants to know?"

"Easy," I whispered. Those two fellows were *both* bigger than Olio.

"You don't work for Alakhar," said Olio slowly, looking them up and down. "I demand to speak with Alakhar!" he shouted, raising his voice up toward the windows.

"There is no Alakhar here," said one, and behind him through the gate I could see the front door opening and another mean-looking fellow headed our way.

"Time to go," I said to Olio as the men drew their swords.

Olio drew his own sword in response, looking at each of the men in turn before joining me in a hasty retreat.

The men chased, but only half-heartedly, and only to the end of the block.

"This way," said Olio, leading me down an embankment into a low-lying creek bed—mostly dry at the moment—a foul-smelling place that caught the city's drainage. "This will keep us off the streets and take us out to the desert."

I made a sour face but followed my friend without hesitation. "And why do we want to go out to the desert again?"

"You can bet the city guard will be looking for us by now. If the night watchmen didn't already report us, that little dust-up back at the House will catch their attention for sure. I know those city guards. They don't tolerate armed men chasing each other through the streets, not in this part of town. Best we stay out of sight. Also, my caravan is camped out this way."

"Right—the singing girls."

"Go ahead, have your laugh."

"I'm not laughing. It's respectable work."

We exchanged no further words for several minutes, the only sound the occasional squish of one of our boots coming unstuck from the mud.

"Something's gone very wrong with the Nipaltos," said Olio finally. "Those guys at the House were not Alakhar's men. They weren't any kind of respectable men. Underworld types. Something's happened to Alakhar. Maybe to Encho and little Ichito, too. I don't like this. I don't like it one bit."

"This is why she brought me here," I said to myself.

"What's that you say?"

"We've got to help Hava's family. But we need to recover ourselves first. We're no good like this."

"You're right, lad—er, Ejertine. We lay low for the night, then see what we can find out tomorrow by the light of day. I know a couple guys I can talk to."

"Olio, from what you've told me, I wonder if Elevaer isn't involved."

"Elevaer?" Olio glanced over his shoulder at me in surprise. "But she's just a girl."

I put my hands in my pockets, leaving Olio to work out the math.

"Well, if she is mixed up with this, she and I are going to have words. It would be just like her, wouldn't it, falling in with the criminal element."

We walked in silence several more minutes, using starlight to find our way along the creek bed.

"Do you hear that?" I said, touching Olio on the shoulder to get him to stop. We stood in silence, listening to the night. I could definitely here it: Voices, raised in song. I held my breath.

"That would be my singing girls," said Olio and started walking again.

"You can hear it, too? Isn't it a little late for singing?"

"Not if there's paying customers, it ain't. Come on!"

# CHAPTER 30

# He Knew the Lighthouse Before It Was Made

A pack of groundlings scattered as we came up out of the creek bed.

At once we saw the lights of the Mystan caravan a few hundred yards away—an unusually bright and steady light, such as I had not before witnessed. The light originated from lamp-posts driven into the ground in a semi-circle around the camp.

Colorful wagons made a backdrop for the singing girls. More than a dozen of the girls were arranged in three rows with the taller ones in back, all wearing matching uniforms. Bats swooped to and fro at the periphery against the night sky, feasting on the light-lured bugs.

I caught a few words of the song. Something about twine in the sky?

"Here," said Olio, unbuckling his sword hilt from his belt as he walked. "Put this on."

I was reluctant to take the heavy steel object. "What for?"

"Fewer questions. She'll just assume you're part of my security team."

"She?"

The girls finished their song and the conductor turned to face her audience. This conductor was a substantial woman, draped in a sweeping cloak of faded blue.

"That would be Mother Etebe. She likes to think she's my boss. Very fond of waving contracts in my face. Just let me do the talking, if there's any talking to be done."

The audience consisted of a few old fellows lying on their sides smoking pipes around a fire, a couple huddled amorously together under a blanket, and a few men standing at the periphery or tending to the horses.

Olio took a few more steps toward the light, then stopped and turned to take hold of me as I was trying to hang the sword on my belt. "Listen, Ejertine. This is me at my lowest, my friend. Relegated to security for a bunch of little girls, and failing at that."

"Olio—you didn't fail. It wasn't your fault, what happened with the girl."

"Of course it was. That's why I was out drinking. I may have told Etebe I was going into town to ask around, put out the word about the missing girl. I did some of that, sure, but the real reason I went to town was to get myself good and drunk. Maybe I had in the back of my mind that I would take a walk off the pier and just keep walking."

"Well, then I'm glad I came along when I did." I squeezed the big man's shoulder and lay his sword across his chest. "Now take this back. It just pulls my pants down when I try to hang it on my belt. I've never been much of a sword person. Olio, listen: I was called here for a reason. That's what I believe. And maybe part of that purpose is to remind you who you are. What you're capable of. I always remember you as the man who fought off crocodiles and then took off on your own into the rain with a make-shift spear to hunt down that barrakapa while Hava and I lay hunkered down in that old hollow tree."

Olio's eyes widened at the memory—and then suddenly he burst into tears. "Oh, Ejertine! I'm a fraud. I've always been a fraud."

"That's not true."

"It is. That night I went out after the barrakapa? I didn't tell you what really happened."

"Olio, what are you talking about? It doesn't matter." We took a few steps back away from the light. The girls were lining up for another song.

The tears flowed freely down his cheeks now, but Olio's eyes were focused far away. "It *does* matter. I lied to you and Hava both. I told you I couldn't find the beast. Well, I did find it, all right. Just over the hill from where Hava stabbed it. That barrakapa was good and dead. Hava was right, she skewered it right down the throat."

"Well, then why–?"

"I couldn't handle it. I was sworn to protect Hava, to lay down my own life for hers. But what good was I against that thing? It tossed me aside like a rag doll."

"No man could stand against that thing!"

"But Hava could and did. She bested it! She didn't need me. I couldn't handle that. So I spent most of the night rolling that thing back down to the river, where finally the crocodiles took it off my hands. I washed up, came back to the tree and fed you a lie. I let you believe it was still out there, hunting us. That's how I finally convinced Hava to call it quits, to leave the Deep Valley behind. I marched us out of there as fast as I could, because I was scared. I never wanted to go back. So now you know the truth of it: I was a coward and a liar."

"You were right to be afraid," I said. "Maybe you were right to lie. And we should never have gone back. But you, sir, are no coward. If you had come across that barrakapa still alive and snapping, you would have not hesitated to throw yourself at it and finish the job. In a fair fight, you could have taken it."

"Yeah?"

"Yeah. And if that desert twister dares show itself around here again, my money's on you to take it down."

"We shall sing 'Lost Lighthouse Remembered'," announced Mother Etebe to her audience.

"Come on," I said. "It's been a long night."

Olio refastened his sword to his belt and wiped his eyes on his sleeves.

"Don't worry," I whispered to Olio, clasping him on the back. "I'll let you do the talking. I don't suppose they have anything to eat."

"Mystans always have food," said Olio.

I recognized the melody of the girls' song. Something Hava used to hum on the trail.

I hung back as we approached, drawn in to the song as one of the girls' voices rose above the others. Clear, beautiful, perfect, her voice made the old men lounging around the fire sit up and listen.

Olio grabbed my shoulder fiercely and he croaked, "That's her!"

She was standing in the back row of the choir, lost among the taller girls, eyes closed as she sang. The other girls kept looking sideways at her. Although she was just a girl, her voice was that of a mature woman. She had the voice of Hava.

"By the gods," said Olio, falling to his knees. "I'm saved. She's alive. She's all right. She's singing!"

I listened, enraptured by the voice, so uncannily like Hava's:

Your hungry sea swallows all light and reason,
Old Sava Ka Shan! But nothing is truly lost, nothing truly
   gone,
Not when the tumbled stones await their season,
Not when the lighthouse lives on in sacred song.

She sang with her eyes closed, this girl—Layona Tower, Olio had called her. But as the verse ended and the other girls bowed their heads, Layona sang on alone:

Nothing's forgotten under Phaltak's watch,
Our every slight and slip carefully inscribed,
Written forever in his great book of naught.
Still we cry, Rise again, lighthouse, rise again—rise!

The other girls, blinking in confusion, stepped away from Layona. Etebe motioned hastily for them to form a semicircle behind. Eyes still closed, Layona sang on. Under the lights, her uniform was torn and smeared with dirt, in sharp contrast to the other girls' crisp, clean outfits.

O, Lost Roksfort was known as Nomin's seat,
And there he sat even as the tower swayed,
And so you see Lost Roksfort was never lost to he;
And, yes, he knew the lighthouse before it was made.

We all stood in stunned silence a moment. Then, all at once, the small group of onlookers burst into applause and rushed forward excitedly. "You were wonderful!" "Where did you learn to sing in such a way?" They shook Mother Etebe's hands and pulled coins from their purses, saying, "Spectacular!" "Where did you find her?" "Wonderful how you brought her in at the end."

Etebe glanced over at Olio and me before throwing herself into shaking hands and accepting coins. "She is the daughter of Mizen Tower, you know. Our star singer. We will be touring next in Dashvar, you can see us there next week. Thank you, thank you all, good night."

I kept my eyes on the girl Layona. How could she have the voice of Hava? The other girls were talking to her, asking her questions, but Etebe planted her hands on the girl's shoulders and pulled her away from the girls and from the adoring crowd, which seemed to have suddenly grown. Etebe shot Olio a meaningful glance as she steered Layona to one of the painted wagons, unlatching the door and letting it swing open as she waved and smiled to the onlookers.

Taking his cue, Olio stepped in front of the wagon and waved everyone off. "Thank you everyone. Thank you. We're closing down now. It's late, folks."

I stood beside Olio, trying to look intimidating; the crowd began to disperse. One of the girls—the youngest by far, perhaps seven or eight—went round touching the lamp posts, turning them off one by one. Behind me from within the wagon I could hear the murmured voices of Etebe and Layona.

Olio was beaming with happiness. "Hey Mae," he said, pulling one of the girls over. "Any leftovers for my friend here?"

"There's bread and bacon," said the girl. My heart leapt.

"What happened to Layona? When did she get back?"

Mae shrugged. Another girl offered, "She just showed up. Like just now, while we were in the middle of performing."

"I'm gonna check on her," said Olio.

"It's better if you didn't," said Mae.

"Is that right?"

"You've been drinking. Etebe has the matter well in hand. You would just be in the way."

"I haven't been drinking."

Mae rolled her eyes and walked away. "Come on," she said in my direction, "I'll fry you some bacon." She was perhaps fourteen or fifteen, about the same age as Layona. I followed, and two of her friends shadowed close behind, keeping an eye on me. They were all about the same height, same black hair, same suspicious eyes.

"Thank you," I said.

"And who are you, exactly?" She took me to the back of a supply wagon, and I waited while she climbed up into the wagon and started rooting through boxes.

"Ejertine," I said. "An old friend of Olio's."

"You've been drinking, too."

I shrugged. "Just trying to be supportive. Olio took it pretty hard, losing Layona."

"Well, that's foolish." She jumped out of the wagon with half a loaf of bread, four strips of bacon, and a frying pan.

"That's what I told him. It wasn't his fault what happened."

She raked me with her glare. "No, I meant it was foolish, your trying to be supportive by encouraging his drinking."

"Oh."

"Come on," she said, shaking her head sadly. Her friends took the frying pan and bacon, and we all went over to the fire, where a few other girls were gathered in their blankets.

"What do you think they're *doing* in there?" one girl was saying. They were all staring at the wagon where Etebe and Layona were shut away. Olio lingered nearby, washing his face in a bucket.

"Move over," said Mae, nudging the girls away from the fire with her foot.

"Who are *you*?" said one of the girls, looking at me and wrinkling up her nose. Now all the girls stared at me.

"Move over," repeated Mae, shooing the girls, who wriggled caterpillar-like in their blankets, to make room for us. "This is Ejertine, an old friend of Olio's. He's drunk, and he's hungry."

I sat like some kind of specimen among them. The warmth and smell of the girls all around me was slightly embarrassing.

As Mae built up the fire, I said, "I can do that, Mae." But she silenced me with a rude hand gesture and accepted the frying pan from her friend.

The door to the wagon opened, and everyone, thankfully, took their eyes off me. Etebe slipped out the door, closing it quickly behind her, and the light inside winked out.

"I guess she gets to spend the night inside while we shiver out here," said one of the girls from her blanket.

My bacon was starting to smell like bacon. "She was sucked up into the sky by a twister," said Mae. "Give it a rest, will you?"

"Why are you always defending her?"

"I'm not even sure it *was* her," said Mae. "It certainly didn't sound like her."

"So. Weird."

Mae split open the bread and packed it with bacon, and my mouth started watering. I asked, "So she doesn't always sound like that?"

All the girls erupted at once. "No way!" "She's the worst." "She's the *least* talented among us." "Did you hear her? She sounded like an opera singer all the sudden!" "She's only here because of her father."

"What's going on over there?" said Etebe, turning our direction.

Mae passed me my bread and bacon. "Thank you, Mae, very kind!" I said, rising to escape.

"Who's that there then?" demanded Etebe, and a spotlight of blinding light centered on me, half-crouching with bread in hand.

"Oh," said Olio, hurrying over. "He's one of mine. He's one of mine. Don't shoot!"

*Shoot?* Etebe took the light out of my eyes, but I was still functionally blind. I stood very still in case anyone was still thinking of shooting. Evidently, this Mystan wielded light as a weapon.

"Then what's he doing mixing with the girls?" demanded Mother Etebe.

"I asked Mae to feed him, that's all."

"Well, let's all keep our voices down," said Etebe. "It's the middle of the night. Our girl has had a blow to the head and needs to recover."

"I'm just glad we got her back," said Olio.

"No thanks to you." Etebe scoffed and turned away.

My vision was starting to return. "Thank you again," I whispered to Mae, who repeated her hand gesture.

Olio took hold of me and led me away. "We sleep over here."

"That sounds glorious," I said, biting into my bacon bread. "The girls seem nice."

"Heh." Olio nodded to a man standing sentry in the dark and led me around to his flatbed wagon, open to the elements. "Room for two in here," he said, patting the wagon bed.

"Olio, I gotta ask you something."

"Yeah?" He peeled off his shirt, and a whole garden of wiry white chest hairs confronted me.

"Oh. Um, about the girl. Layona."

"A miracle, that."

"But when she was singing earlier. Did you notice anything... unusual?"

"Like what?"

"Her voice?"

Olio unbuttoned his pants. "Now that you mention it, she sang very well tonight, didn't she?"

"She sounded just like Hava."

He nodded vacantly. "I didn't know she had it in her. To be honest, I don't listen to the girls much, but she did seem better than usual tonight. Listen—I'll scrounge up a blanket for you."

"Olio—that voice, that song. That was *Hava*."

Olio glared at me. "What do you mean?"

"I mean it was her, somehow—channeling through the girl."

"Ejertine, listen–"

"No, you listen. I'm not wrong. First her spirit appeared to me at sea, summoning me here. Now this."

"Ejertine." Olio struggled visibly to keep his emotions in check. "You've got to let her go. There is no ghost of Hava floating about. End of story."

"She called me here for a reason, Olio. You said yourself something wasn't right with her family. I came to help. I think she wants us to work together."

"Fine, fine," said Olio. "We'll work together. But please—no more talk of ghosts. I'll speak with Etebe in the morning. I'll tell her I'm taking a leave of absence. She doesn't need me, she's got plenty of hired muscle. I'll see the caravan off in the morning, and then you and I will head back into Kortholomoth to see what we can find out."

I did not press Olio further. But as I lay next to him in his flatbed, staring sleeplessly at the stars, the song about the lost lighthouse reverberated in my memory. It was the same melody I'd heard out at sea, standing next to Semetrius on deck.

The girl Layona Tower was somehow mixed up with the mystery at hand. Forces were at work far beyond my comprehension. Strange theories rotated through the theater of my mind as I lay half-awake next to the snoring walrus of a man who was Olio.

I'm not sure if it was a dream or a vision or something else, but I saw the sky as a great wheel turning, and the wheel spoke to me in the voice of my long-dead father, saying, YOU SEE WHAT OTHERS DO NOT.

It was not the first time I'd experienced an unusual hallucination, but it was the first time it was accompanied by my father's voice. "Odeker?" I said, invoking my father's name.

I WAS ONCE THAT.

"You named me Ejertine."

YES.

I could have woken myself up then, I could have sat up, I could have fallen into dreaming. Instead, I decided to stay where I was, to see if I could extend the conversation with my dead father.

"I don't know how to help Hava."

SHE IS LIKE ME, GONE BUT NOT GONE.

"How is this possible?"

WE LEARNED FROM THE KORIESKI.

"I don't understand."

YOU NEVER DID.

"I want to understand."

NO, YOU DON'T.

"Tell me what to do."

STAY ALIVE. MANUFACTURE A BONE KNIFE WITH YOUR OWN HANDS ON A BOAT. TELL NO ONE.

"What?" I wasn't sure if I heard that last part right. "I don't understand." I sat up, wide awake now. Clouds occluded the stars in silent races across the sky. "Wait, come back! I don't understand."

# CHAPTER 31

# A Good Leader Knows When to Follow

Dawn arrived unpleasantly soon. People were already awake; a man walked by our cart. I sat up and saw the girls all gathering in a wide circle around Etebe, draped this morning in a brilliant blue-green robe. She opened her arms to the sun, rising now over the distant harbor, and led the girls in prayer. I looked from face to face but did not see Layona among them.

Olio snored.

Over the next few minutes, half a dozen hired men roused themselves and set to work packing up, brushing down the horses, digging up the lamp posts.

I poked Olio. "Hey. It looks like everyone's packing up."

"Eh?" He groaned and rolled away from me. "What did you *do* to me last night?"

The smell of biscuits and eggs got us both on our feet. Mae and some of the older girls passed around the hot biscuits, and Olio and I each got one, which we devoured happily while waiting on eggs.

Etebe came over and I tried to make myself scarce while she and Olio talked. But almost immediately their conversation escalated to an argument.

"That's what I'm trying to tell you, Etebe. I'm not going to Dashvar."

"You most certainly are. Have you forgotten your contract, sir?"

"How could I possibly forget when you bring it up daily? Look, Etebe. Something's come up. My friend and I need to go into town on urgent business. I just need a few days' leave of absence. I'll catch up to you before you've finished in Dashvar."

"I hope you don't expect to be paid."

"Well, I expect payment through yesterday."

"But here you are eating our rations today."

"Fine! Dock me for one biscuit. And three eggs, please," Olio called to Mae at the fire. "Not too runny, mind you."

Etebe shook her head. "And what am I supposed to tell Mizen Tower when he asks why you abandoned his daughter?"

"I'm not abandoning her. And I can speak for myself. Relax, Etebe, it's just a few days."

"Well, you should know I shan't be recommending you."

"Nor I you," growled Olio.

"Keep your voice down. Layona is still asleep."

The girls gave us our eggs, exchanging glances and barely suppressing their amusement as Etebe departed in a huff.

"Insufferable woman," said Olio.

"So what's our plan?" I asked.

Olio chewed his eggs. "Well, a few discrete inquiries about town. I'd like to find Alakhar for one thing. He frequents the club we were at last night, as a matter of fact."

"No more drinking." I made eye contact with Mae who was now cleaning up after breakfast.

"No more drinking," he agreed. "For today."

"Can someone explain to me who Mizen Tower is and what makes him so important?"

"How can you not know who Mizen Tower is?" blurted out one of the girls.

"Ejertine's not from here," explained Olio.

"Mizen Tower," said Mae, "is the oldest, richest, meanest and most powerful man in all the world. He's like best friends with Morphid."

"She's not far off," agreed Olio. "He is the greatest among us, more famous than the King. And he happens to be the one funding this tour, to help drum up support for the Mystan School in Ragne. And to give his daughter Layona some worldly experience."

We all turned our heads when the door to Etebe's wagon opened, and Layona finally emerged, blinking in the light. She looked at us and the landscape all around with equal fascination, like she was seeing it all for the first time.

Mae and another girl went to intercept her.

"Come on," said Olio. "How are you with horses?"

"I don't know the first thing." I went along with him reluctantly. I was more interested in Layona, and I cast a backward glance at the three girls standing close to one another, talking.

"We need to claim my horse before Etebe tries to keep her as collateral. I own my wagon and horse outright. Ejertine, this here is Feirne." Olio introduced me to a stolid black mare eating her breakfast from a feed sack tied round her neck. "Best horse I ever had."

"Pleased to meet you," I said, putting my hand on her neck. A brown eye considered me, an ear turned.

"Not to rush your breakfast, Feirne, but let's just walk you over this way. Here, you take her," said Olio. "I need to grab a few things. Meet me by the wagon."

I led Feirne to Olio's wagon and looked over again at the cluster of girls. "No!" cried Layona and broke away from Mae and her friend. She ran through the horses to an outcropping of rocks and called, "Goat!" She shielded her eyes from the sun, scanning the landscape all around. "Goat! Where are you?" There was an edge of panic in her voice. A voice that sounded like a teenage girl, not Hava.

"What's going on?" asked Olio, toting a harness and gear for the horse.

"Not sure. Something about a goat?"

Mother Etebe went and laid a gentle hand on Layona's shoulder.

"It's always something with that kid," said Olio.

"Layona?" I asked.

"Full of japes and jeers, that one, and always expects to get her way. I'm glad we got her back—but truth be told, I'll be gladder still to have a few days' respite from that overactive mouth of hers."

"Did you find out what happened to her?" I asked. Mother Etebe was kneeling now and talking earnestly with the girl.

"Best I can tell, the twister set her down somewhere out in the desert, and she found her way back here by following the singing and the lights." Olio untied Feirne's feedbag and set to work fastening the harness. "Help me out here, can you?"

Feirne cooperated as we strapped her into the harness and set her to the wagon. I hazarded another glance toward Layona and saw that she had climbed to the top of the rock outcropping and was debating Etebe from the high ground.

The other wagons were all packed up now, and the men were harnessing their horses in preparation for departure.

"So you've really never used a sword?" asked Olio.

"I have not."

Olio shook his head sadly. "Don't know about horses, don't know about swords. What does that leave?"

"I can tie a mean knot."

Etebe and Layona were walking together now in our direction. "Uh, oh," said Olio.

"Olio," said Etebe. "You said you were going into town, did you not? Please take Layona with you and see to her safety. She has an errand for her father."

"Not possible, I'm afraid." Olio glanced over at me. "Etebe, I'd like you to meet Ejertine."

"I believe we met last night."

"Well, Ejertine and I go way back. He knew Hava."

"Is that so? Well, a friend of Hava is a friend of mine."

"Ejertine and I have an urgent matter to attend to. Wouldn't be safe to take Layona along."

Etebe looked back and forth between us. "Would this urgent matter involve heavy drinking, by chance?"

"It's not like that—"

"I can still smell it on you, Olio." She raised a hand to stifle his next words. "I do not judge you for going out drinking with your friends on your own time. But today, all I'm asking is that you fulfill the substance of your contract with Mizen Tower. He selected you specifically to accompany and protect his daughter. Shall we return to Dhalmadhi and tell him you were unwilling to take his daughter into Kortholomoth on his official business?"

"I thought you were departing for Dashvar."

"We've had a slight delay due to this new business."

I was watching Layona during this exchange. She kept her eyes averted, mostly looking down at her shoes. "It'll be all right, Olio," I put in. "Let's take her. Maybe she'll be a help to us." This was my chance to get some time with Layona, this girl who sang in Hava's voice.

Olio turned to me with his jaw thrusted out in wounded astonishment. Layona looked up from her shoes, first at me, then at Olio, her eyes glimmering with hope. "Fine," said Olio. "But you're the babysitter." He poked me roughly on the shoulder and climbed up into the wagon.

"Hooray!" cried Layona and set out immediately walking toward the city. Mae and another girl ran after her, handing her some biscuits wrapped in cloth.

"Come on," said Olio, and I joined him on the seat of his wagon. He urged Feirne out of the line of the caravan and circled around to where Layona was walking. "Get in," he commanded.

"Oh, no thank you," said Layona. "I prefer to walk. It's not far."

I smiled at Olio and hopped down to follow the girl. "Remind you of anyone?"

"Olio," said Etebe, catching up to him. "You're not planning to take that wagon, are you? That harness belongs to the Mystan School. And who paid to fix your axle?"

"You don't own me, woman."

"Just the same, I'll keep the cart as collateral, to make sure you come back."

Olio abandoned his cart in frustration. "Have it then, you penny-pincher! But we are hardly going our separate ways yet, are we? You aren't going anywhere so long as I have your star performer under my wing."

And so we walked in the direction of Kortholomoth, with Layona in the lead, myself a few steps behind, and Olio bringing up the rear, cursing to himself.

# CHAPTER 32

# Jarmalade

The trail soon joined a proper road choked with ox carts and foot traffic coming and going from port. The way ahead was blocked by a herd of goats.

Layona rushed ahead when she saw the goats. When I caught up to her, she was standing amongst the herd, inspecting each, one by one. "Goat! Mr. Goat, are you here?"

Olio came up behind me, shaking his head. "Explain to me how you are all right with our mission being waylaid by this fool child?"

"She's part of this somehow," I said, watching the girl move among the sea of goats. "I'd like to keep an eye on her and see what I can learn. Maybe we should split up. You go make your inquiries, I'll stay with the girl."

Olio sighed. "Naw. Etebe's right. The girl's my responsibility."

Layona approached the goatherd with his beard and staff and I heard her ask, "Excuse me, sir, but have you seen a goat, with a spot on her left flank about here, and long horns and a big belly?"

"Japes and jeers, I tell you, Ejertine. This is how she amuses herself."

"Never mind," said Layona to the goatherd. "You would remember this goat, I think. One other thing, sir, if it's not too much trouble. Do you know where I might find the Ig?"

The herdsman lifted his arm and pointed up the road toward the city.

"Oh, thank you! Come on, Olio. And… Ejertine, was it?"

"That's right," I said with a smile.

A weathered-looking man who had been adjusting his boot on the side of the road stood up suddenly and said, "Excuse me, miss."

Olio stepped between them, instantly suspicious.

"Easy there," said the man pleasantly. He and a companion wore headscarves and they were covered in dirt, as if they had been digging or working in a field. "I couldn't help but overhear the young mistress asking about the Ig."

"So what?" said Olio, fingering his sword handle.

"So… we work for the Ig. My friend here, he can take you to him."

"Oh," said Layona. "That would be most kind. Thank you."

The filthy man bowed. "We are your humble servants." He scowled at his companion until he, too, bowed. Rising from the bow, he told his companion, "Take them back to the Ig's tent… I will meet you there by and by." Turning back to us with an unctuous smile, he explained, "I would take you myself, but I have an errand for our wise master. Good morning, lady, gentlemen." He bowed again and hurried along his way, leaving his companion standing a little bewildered before us.

"Well," said this fellow, wringing his hands. He was pudgier than the other but no less filthy. He smiled amiably toward Layona. "This way," he said, gesturing in the direction of the city. The goats had cleared the way now, and traffic was beginning to move again.

"You first," said Olio, hand still resting on his sword hilt.

The man looked longingly after his associate disappearing up the road. "Yes, of course." He smiled nervously. Sweat ran down his brow. "I am Aduan, by the way. We are all friends here, yes?"

Olio kept his hand on Layona's shoulder to keep her from following too close. "And who is this Ig fellow exactly?"

"You've never heard of the Ig? The All-Knowing?"

"A carnival charlatan, you mean?" To Layona he asked, "And this is the man you have business with?"

Layona looked down at her shoes.

"Your first time in our fine city?" inquired Aduan.

"It is," answered Layona without hesitation.

Olio rolled his eyes again. "She was just here yesterday."

"See here, this is called the Old Gate," said Aduan. Two crumbling stone columns flanked the road. "See the gargoyles up top? Ancient guardians, forever on the alert for evil."

"Oh, my," said Layona. "I'm glad they are friendly."

"Oh, they're not friendly at all. But luckily they are made of stone. They would consider us intruders, no doubt. Holdovers from the old days. Long before Kortholomoth there was an ancient fort here. See that wall on the hill? That's all that's left of the old fort. I went up there once with my brother, Achero," he said, pointing over his shoulder. "We thought maybe we could find some old tombs with treasure. We were young and foolish, what did we know? Well, we didn't find any tombs but did we find these huge murals. Flying elephants and cloud kingdoms. Giants of old, that's who lived there. Now it's just scorpions and monkeys and birds up there."

"Wow," said Layona in astonishment, staring wide-eyed at the crumbling wall on the hill.

Olio was unimpressed. "Every hill in Lagin has the same story."

"As you say, sir," said Aduan, puckering his lips. "And look there, you can see our fine baphl."

I looked where he pointed and saw through the thicket a windowless, slope-walled clay structure, half-submerged in the earth.

"What's a baphl?" asked Layona.

Aduan shrugged. "That's where they keep history, I think."

"You know perfectly well what a baphl is," groused Olio. "What are you playing at, girl?"

"And do you see that giant rock rising over the city?" asked Aduan.

"Yes…"

"That's Prowbeam Rock. That's what divides the South Port from the North."

"I see," said Layona.

"She's acting like we didn't see all this yesterday," said Olio.

Aduan chattered on through the city streets, obviously flattered by Layona's rapt attention.

"You talk too much," observed Olio.

"Oh, do try and be polite, Olio," said Layona.

Olio put his hand on Aduan's shoulder. "This is me being polite. The gentleman will know it when I become impolite."

Aduan tittered nervously.

"Where did you say you were taking us?" I asked. I was beginning to share Olio's suspicions.

"To see the Ig." Aduan kneaded his fingers.

"And where does the Ig reside?"

"In a tent, on Prowbeam Rock."

"Prowbeam Rock? That's over there. Why then have we taken this route?"

"Oh. Well, it's no slower to go this way. And I just thought, I thought maybe the young lady would like a scoop of jarmalade from the market."

"Jarmalade?" said Layona. "That sounds like something quite delicious."

"Quite delicious doesn't begin to describe it." Aduan grinned uneasily toward Olio.

We walked on and almost at once the city closed in around us. Here the way became narrow and crowded shoulder to shoulder with people in a hurry to be somewhere. "I didn't know there were quite so many people in all the world," said Layona, swiveling her head left and right.

"Stay close," said Olio, taking her hand.

"Here we are," declared Aduan. "Four scoops of jarmalade, please." Aduan flipped a coin to the vendor, a man with a vacant stare and an underbite.

Layona smiled up at me. "I can't wait to try some jarmalade."

Olio squinted at her through one eye. "What business does your father have with the Ig, little miss? You better not be taking us on this fool's errand just so you can have yourself some jarmalade."

"Here we go," said Aduan, passing out the treats. I accepted one and looked at it with just as much amazement as Layona. It was half an orange, with the fruit scooped out and replaced with a ball of smooth, glistening cream. "They don't know how to make it right, except in this one place."

Olio frowned down at his. "I don't want it."

"I'll take yours," I offered. I had never experienced anything like it. It was the best thing I'd ever tasted.

Layona tested the jarmalade with her tongue, and instantly her eyes came to life. "Mmm."

"You see? It's good," said Aduan, tipping his orange rind back and slurping up half the dollop. Abruptly, he seized up. He threw a stiff hand to his mouth to stop from spitting.

"What's the matter?" asked Layona. "Did you get a bad one?"

Aduan shook his head from side to side in quick, small motions. His eyes welled with tears. With effort, he swallowed.

"That good, eh?" said Olio. "I think I'll pass." I accepted Olio's with all eagerness.

"Let's go," he growled, and it sounded enough like a threat that we were all quick to begin moving. We climbed toward Prowbeam Rock along a jagged street full of herbalists and tinkerers sitting idly in front of their stores, yawning and shooing flies. Olio looked sidelong at me. "Enjoying your jarmalade?"

"I am."

"Good, good. I'm glad we're all having a good time."

"What sort of a person is the Ig?" asked Layona, looking up at the great rock towering over the port.

"The Ig?" said Aduan. "Oh... everyone around here knows about him. He is older than the mountains. He knows all there is to know." Aduan spoke without enthusiasm and, sighing, he passed his remaining jarmalade to Layona. "Here, you can have the rest of mine," he said, miserably.

"Are you sure? Thank you!" said Layona. "The Ig sounds like just the person I need to see..."

Layona stopped then in her tracks, fretting. "I'm afraid there is something I must clear up with you, Mr. Olio and Mr. Ejertine. My conscience is just not feeling right."

Olio turned and narrowed his eyes.

"It's all right," I said. "Why don't you tell us what's on your mind?"

Layona swallowed. "Well, you see… I didn't exactly tell the truth, about my reason for coming to Kortholomoth. It wasn't for my father."

Olio folded his meaty arms across his chest. Aduan lingered nearby, feigning disinterest.

Layona hurried on, "I had to say that, because Mother Etebe would not have understood the real reason. She would never have let me come. She would have thought it was nonsense. But, please, you must believe me—it is important. I need to speak to someone who is wise."

"Go on," I said.

"There has been some kind of a mix-up. I don't understand it. I certainly can't explain it. All I can say is, I don't belong here. I'm not Layona Tower. I am someone else entirely. And as if that weren't bad enough, now I have lost the best friend I ever had. Do you see now why I must speak with the Ig?"

"Someone else entirely," I said breathlessly. "Who is that, might I ask?"

"Well, if you'd asked me yesterday, I'd have introduced myself one way. But now I'm not so sure. My memories are all jumbled up with someone else's. The same thing happened to my friend goat. It was the witch's twister that got us all mixed up, you see."

Aduan thrust himself into the conversation. "The witch's twister, you say?"

"You stay out of this." Olio shifted his weight uneasily from one foot to the other, scowling down at the girl. "You're telling the truth now, aren't you? I can always smell it, dishonesty." He looked sidelong at Aduan.

Aduan cleared his throat nervously. "Shall we?" He motioned us up the winding hillside road. "We will miss the Ig if we don't go soon. He sleeps in the afternoon."

Layona followed. I exchanged glances with Olio and we matched pace alongside her.

"And what makes you think this Ig person can help you?" asked Olio.

"Can't he? I was referred by a friend."

The road sloped up to the pass, a notch separating Prowbeam Rock from the rest of the mountain. Here the city thinned out, with only a few houses and shops hidden among the pines and boulders. Little traffic moved on the road during the lazy noon hour.

Layona paused to admire the view over the city. "Look at all those ships! Where do they all come from?"

"Greatland, Sarta, Tross—everywhere," said Aduan. "And that's just the South Port. Once we reach the pass you'll see the North Port."

"I can't wait," said Layona.

As we climbed the steep trail up toward the pass, a family of picnickers were coming down. The man of the family was holding a towel to his face. His wife fretted over him, ignoring the wailing children. They paid no heed to us as they hurried down the trail past us.

"What is it?" said Layona.

"I don't know," said Olio. "But stay close, something's not right."

I eased my knife from its sheath and stooped to pick up a couple of well-balanced throwing rocks. Just in case.

When we reached the pass, a long narrow place between the Rock and the mountain, Olio stopped us. "I don't like it."

I was alert, watching behind for any sign of trouble.

Aduan mopped beads of sweat from his brow. "Oh, it's perfectly safe. I come through here every day."

"You go, then," said Olio, keeping Layona behind him.

"As you wish." Aduan straightened his jacket and strode ahead through the pass. When he arrived at the far end, he turned and called, "You see? Perfectly safe."

"I'll go next," I offered.

"No, we go together," said Olio. "Stay close, girl." Olio took deliberate, even steps, keeping his eyes on the figure of Aduan waiting at the end of the pass. As he approached Aduan, Olio's hand edged toward his sword handle.

Aduan took a step back, smiling.

I saw movement above. Two men dropped from the rocks, casting a weighted net over us.

I dropped and ducked, trying to avoid being caught. Olio threw up his arms to catch the net as high as he could, while simultaneously hip-bumping Layona, sending her flying into the dirt, free. One of the weights clobbered me in the back of my head and all I could see was stars. I heard Olio shout, "It's you they're after, girl. Run for it!"

As my vision returned I saw boots. Men with masks. One of my arms was free of the net. I still had my knife.

Layona found her feet and hesitated. At the far end of the pass, I saw two men blocking the way. "Not that way," I said.

"This way!" shouted Olio, and he hurled himself at the two masked men, dragging me with him. I clung desperately to my knife.

There was an impact and a crunch. The wind was knocked out of me; the crunch had been someone else's body breaking. We were all in a pile now with Olio on top, all of us hopelessly tangled in the net. "Run!" commanded Olio.

Aduan alone stood in Layona's way. He crouched and spread his arms, ready to grab at her. The men at the far end of the pass sprinted our way. I began cutting the net with my knife. One of the men in our pile groaned; the other began to struggle.

"Run!" repeated Olio.

So Layona ran. She feinted right, making Aduan dive that way, then she bolted left. She scrambled off the path and up onto the rocks over the pass where the men had set their ambush. There she stopped and looked down at us. "I can't just leave you!"

I said, "Don't worry about us—oof!" Olio pressed his elbow into the struggling man's neck while the poor fellow kicked his legs, trying in vain to throw Olio off. My feet were pinned at the bottom of this pile. "Just go!"

Aduan was climbing up after her. I cut for all I was worth, freeing much of my upper body from the net, even as the two sprinters bore down upon us, clubs in hand. "Olio!" I shouted by way of warning.

Olio rolled off his man, releasing the weight from my legs. It was almost enough for me to escape. But the men, breathing hard through their masks, were already here. "Stay down," warned the first one, pointing his club at me. The second sprinted by and threw himself up the wall of rocks to chase after Aduan and the girl.

"Sure," I said, staying down. "What's the problem, guys?"

"Drop the knife."

I dropped the knife. He moved to kick it away, and I chose this moment to strike, sweeping his leg with mine, bringing him to the ground. After that—well, Olio took care of things from there: He rolled onto the stunned man before he knew what was happening.

I was free of the net and on my feet now, but Olio didn't need me. He was pressing his elbow into the newcomer's larynx.

I looked up and saw Layona high above, cresting the top of Prowbeam Rock. I didn't see her pursuers, but I knew they were up there somewhere.

The other men had stopped kicking, submitting to Olio's persuasion, by the time I knelt and cut him loose from the net. Olio rose to his feet, dirty and bleeding, then turned to give the pile of groaning men a solid kick. The three of them lay tangled in their own net, broken and battered.

With a grunt, Olio started up the rocky slope. "I'm going after the girl. You look after these ones. Find out who they work for."

"On it," I said, putting my foot on top of the pile.

"I'm getting too old for this," grumbled Olio, his breath coming heavy as he pushed himself uphill.

I looked down at the three men. One was out cold, the other two moaned in pain where Olio had broken them.

I knelt to start cutting them loose when I became aware of a small but growing gaggle of spectators in the pass. Presently three city guardsmen, swords drawn and armor flashing, appeared on the scene. The spectators pointed.

I swallowed. "Hi," I said, looking down at my knife.

"Come away from there," commanded one of the guards, a big fellow with a golden eagle on top of his helmet. I guessed he was in charge.

I stood slowly, putting my knife away. "It's not what it looks like." I backed away as the three guards fanned out to flank me. "These guys jumped us. They were trying to kidnap a girl."

"Hey Benzel," said one guard to the other. "Didn't we have a report of a tall Soofian making a disturbance last night in Central Market?"

Benzel unlooped a pair of bolas from his belt. "So we did, Samu, so we did."

"He attacked us! He threw this net on us," interjected one of the thugs in the net, suddenly coherent.

*This is not good*, I thought. *Better get while the getting's good.* Before they had me completely surrounded, I bolted downhill toward the North Port, hoping to outdistance them.

"I love it when they run," I heard Benzel say.

*Shit*, I thought, dodging side to side, all too aware of those bolas. I conjured the speed and cunning of a rabbit. I ran like I had never run before.

# CHAPTER 33

# The King's Mercy

I don't remember being captured. I must have hit my head. I remember shackles in the back of a wagon. I remember rough hands transferring me from the wagon. I remember sickly weeds doing their best to push up through the mortar between the courtyard stones. I remember an oversized portrait of the king, gazing down at me without mercy.

They took me to a bare room and tied my feet, just as my head was starting to clear. "Hey," I said, "let me explain."

One of the men turned a crank, and I felt a tug at my ankles. Benzel, the one with the bolas, watched me with mild curiosity. "You speak pretty good Laginese for a fleggar."

Click, click, click went the crank as I was hoisted up by my ankles from a pulley mounted to a beam high above. There they left me dangling, my head a few feet above the floor. "I am a friend of the Nipalto family," I said. "Those men were trying to kidnap the daughter of Mizen Tower. Didn't you see their masks?"

"I did not see any masks," said the man with the eagle helmet, and he turned to go. His men followed, Benzel lingering just long enough to say, "You know, my father fought in the war." Then he too left, closing and barring the door behind him.

"I wasn't even born then!" I shouted.

The room was empty except for myself and the rope-and-pulley mechanism. A solitary ray of sunlight spilled in through a gap in the roof and slanted down to the floor near my head. I watched the dust swirling in the sunlight, I listened to my labored breathing. I looked at the drain centered below me and the dark stains on the surrounding floor.

"This is not good," I said to myself. "These guys are not going to listen to me. This would be a really good time for Olio to come to my rescue."

I returned my attention to the ray of sunlight and the pattern of dust drifting on currents of air. I blew a puff of air to disturb the pattern. Such was my entertainment.

I don't know if you've ever hung upside down for a long time. After the first hour, it becomes increasingly difficult to breathe. My head pounded. My eyeballs wanted to explode.

The ray of light crawled closer, such that it shone directly in my eyes. Unfocused, the play of light and dust and delusion created fantastical imagery for my benefit. I hoped perhaps to see Hava somewhere in the mix. Or hear from my dead father again.

I am not normally one to doubt myself, but in this moment of despair I did wonder whether I had made the whole thing up. Maybe Olio was right, there was no ghost of Hava watching over us. But I thought of that day at the river with my father, how he heard Hava's expedition coming before I did, though he was largely deaf. He had heard with a different ear. I, too, had this ear, it seemed.

*Stay alive.* That advice from my dead father resonated.

Finally, after what seemed a very long time, I heard voices outside the door. I heard them lifting the bar and pulling open the door.

A young woman strode in, beautiful, with dark black hair. She looked a great deal like a young version of Hava. Was this then Elevaer?

Benzel and another guard came behind, looking considerably smaller without their armor. Benzel held a long switch, which he proffered to the young woman. "Law says eleven lashes, Lady Nipalto, but Samu and I don't mind if you want to give some extras. Also, if you'd like, you can use that one," he added, nodding to the metal bar in Samu's hand.

Elevaer glanced with interest at the metal bar but returned her gaze to me. She tilted her head to the side to get a better look at my face. "Poor dear. Look how red his face is. Are you sure you have the right one? He is rather scrawny and harmless looking."

Benzel exchanged looks with Samu. "Ma'am, don't let him fool you. He's a dangerous man, that one. Had himself a rampage through the city last night. We found him this morning attacking picnickers on Prowbeam Rock."

"That's really not at all what happened," I said calmly.

"And I suppose," said Elevaer, taking the switch from Benzel and testing it with a practice flick, "I suppose that wasn't you who attacked my family's shop in Central Market last night and then tried to force your way into my home?"

"We didn't attack anyone."

"Of course you didn't. You're innocent. I believe you." She looked to the guards. "I really do believe him, actually. Now that I've seen him, I find I pity him. I've decided to drop all charges."

"Ma'am," said Benzel. "You're not the only victim of this man's rampage."

"Oh? And where are these other victims? Will they too be giving out lashes today?"

"They were too seriously injured," said Samu gravely. "They're in no shape to be lashing anyone."

"They attacked *me*," I pointed out.

"Likely story," said Benzel loudly. "We'll see what the Magistrate has to say about this."

"By all means," said Elevaer. "The Magistrate is a good friend."

"Look, Lady Nipalto, the King cannot just allow Soofians coming over here thinking they can go rampage through our cities with impunity."

"Now you're bringing the King into it? All right, let's do that then. You may recall His Majesty signed a treaty with Bvossoly. We enjoy an enduring peace, gentlemen. An enduring peace. I have been to Soofia. Some of my best friends are Soofians." Elevaer handed the switch back to Benzel. "Your authority may stem from the King, but do not presume to substitute your judgment for his. His will is clear: Peace with Soofia. You have no basis to prosecute this man simply because he is Soofian. Now, please: Cut him down."

"Ma'am," said Benzel. "With all due respect to your family–"

"This city would not even be here if it weren't for my family. Now do as you're told and cut the man down. You will not like it if I have to ask again."

Benzel opened his mouth but thought better and closed it again. He exchanged glances with Samu.

And that was that. They lowered me gently. Benzel even cupped my head as I came down.

They returned my bag of silver and my knife.

I couldn't quite walk on my own, but Elevaer took me by the arm and we made our exit from that unpleasant guard station. Walking arm-in-arm down the street, I said, "Wow, thanks for getting me out of there!"

Elevaer patted my hand. "I couldn't just leave you hanging there like that. They wanted me to hit you with a stick! Can you imagine? Not really my style."

"And I'm not especially fond of *being* hit with a stick."

"This whole thing has been a giant misunderstanding. Why don't you come by the House right now and we'll sort it all out?"

"I'd love to. Only–"

Three men hopped from a passing carriage, threw a bag over my head, and forced me into the carriage.

"I won't take no for an answer," said Elevaer pleasantly.

# CHAPTER 34

# The Cellar Reek

This was turning out to be a very bad day. I sat sandwiched between two hard bodies, firm hands grasping my upper arms on either side. The hood over my head limited my breathing, and it took all my concentration to avoid panic. I felt the carriage dip as Elevaer came in after me, and then I felt her hands on my legs, feeling, probing, removing my knife and my bag of silver. Her hands lingered longer than necessary, exploring my inner thigh. "I'm looking forward to getting to know you better."

The carriage lurched forward. I must have fallen asleep, I was so exhausted. I don't remember the ride.

A high-pitched squeak shattered my delirium. I heard the driver talking to the horses and felt the carriage turn slowly to the left and up over a hump.

"We're here," announced Elevaer. "Why don't you take our guest down to the cellar and see that he is comfortable." I felt her step out of the carriage while it was still in motion.

The horrible squeaking sounded again—the closing of a gate, I realized. The driver brought us to a full stop, horses stomping irritably. "Keep a good hold of him," came a man's voice close to my left ear. The grip on my upper arms tightened on either side.

"Easy, fellows," I suggested.

They more or less lifted me by my arms and hauled me out of the carriage. "Walk forward," commanded the man on the left. He sounded like one of the guys that Olio provoked at the entrance to House Nipalto last night. Hard to believe that was only last night.

*This would be another excellent time for a rescue,* I thought to myself, hoping Olio was out there watching for his opportunity. Not that I had any reason to hope that Olio even knew where I was.

No, it was up to me to rescue myself, I realized. They hadn't bothered to bind my hands or feet, but their giant hands were so well clamped upon my arms I could feel their fingers digging into my bones.

Peering down through the opening of the hood, I could see a little of the bricks of the courtyard passing underfoot. We would come soon to the front door of the House; this might be my best opportunity.

"Stop here," commanded the man on my left just as we reached the door—but by the time he said it, I had already planted my foot and pivoted myself like a top away from him, breaking his grasp.

This maneuver did not, however, free me from the man on my right. Instead I spun around and collided with him belly to belly, his left hand still stubbornly locked around my right arm.

And that was that. He took hold of me with his other arm, and before I knew it, I was backwards over his knee. The courtyard bricks came up to meet me and knocked the breath out of me. An immediate and immense pressure was atop me.

"Don't squish him. Elevaer wants him intact. Let's get him inside."

I heard the door open. Rough hands seized me and picked me up.

"Help," I tried to call, but no sound came. I flailed out at them, ramming my hand into the door jamb. They stuffed me through the door while I kicked and struggled. My hands fell on someone's knife hilt and suddenly I had a knife.

"Watch out, he's got me knife!" This made them drop me.

Quick as a bouncing ball I was up again and thrashing blindly with the knife. This bought me enough space to rip off my hood, just in time to tumble backwards onto a sweeping staircase. Three ogres of men were upon me at once, pinning my arms and pummeling me in the face.

I never had a chance against those guys. Once they were sure I had no more fight left in me, they picked me up, one at my feet and one at my shoulders, and they carried me, bleeding, along a curving corridor. Exquisite silver statuettes were sequestered in mirrored alcoves to the left and right, watching my passing. Hava's house was even fancier than I'd imagined.

"That's him, all right," said the third man, coming along behind. I heard the knife scrape against the floor as he stooped to pick it up.

They carried me through a swinging door into an enormous kitchen built around an impressive circular hearth. We waited by the hearth, and I feared they were going to toss me into the fire—but they were just waiting for the big man to come around and open the door to the cellar.

A sickly, sour stench greeted me as we descended a wooden staircase into the dark, cool cellar. The stairs creaked ominously under the weight of these men.

"Grab that chair from the kitchen," said the man at my feet, calling up to the big man still at the top of the stairs.

"Guys," I said. "I think we may have got off on the wrong foot."

"You're right," said the man with my feet—their leader, I think. He set my feet down gently at the bottom of the stairs, while the one holding my shoulders simply dropped me onto the stone floor. My head and shoulders collided with the floor, stars flashed before my eyes.

From very far away, I saw the big guy coming down with the wooden chair from the kitchen. There was yet another man, thin and disheveled, standing silhouetted in the doorway at the top of the stairs, feeding lengths of rope through a knot.

It was dark down here, and it reeked of some horrid batch of alcohol gone wrong. I could make out metal shelves on either side, stacked with coal. What might lay in the shadowy recesses beyond I could not say.

I sat up, raising my arms defensively. "Easy. I'm a friend of the family. No need for unpleasantries."

The big guy arrived with the chair and set it down forcefully beside me.

"Sit," said their leader.

"Sure," I said, rising slowly and deliberately. I parked myself carefully in the chair, not making any sudden moves. "What can I do for you guys?"

The thin man came down the stairs with his rope looped in his hands. There was something about him I very much did not like.

"You can put your hands behind the chair, to start. My associate here is going to tie you up."

"Is that really necessary?"

"It's for your own protection. Just to make sure you don't try anything slippery again. That's how people get hurt."

The thin man, smiling and licking his lips, slipped his knots around my arms and legs and through the chair with practiced ease. How often had he done this before? When he was done, he pulled everything tight, wrenching my joints cruelly. "Too tight!" I complained.

"We don't want that," said the leader. "Lank, ease off a little on the knots, eh?"

Lank's smile quivered. "Sorry, Uncle. These ones, they don't loosen. They just go tighter. The more he struggles, the tighter they be." He showed me a mouthful of decayed teeth.

"Try not to struggle," said the uncle to me. "All right, boys, clear out. Elevaer will be down when she's ready." As his men departed, he produced a crumpled cigar from his pocket and held it up to the light for inspection. "Leave the door open," he called after them.

He looked down at me sympathetically. "They're good boys. They mean well. Kerig and Jekub, I mean. Lank—well, that boy ain't right. Very, very useful, mind you. But a rotten apple for a heart." Older than the others, and only slightly smaller than the two ogre-men, this man was still easily the size of a bear. "You crushed my cigar, you know."

"I am sorry about that. What is that horrible stench?" This was somehow the question that came to my lips.

Putting the broken cigar in his mouth, he glanced over to the far wall of the cellar. "Sour mash. My idiot nephews spilled a barrel earlier. Worthless on the market, as it turns out. But it's not so bad. Want some?" He went over to a wall of stacked barrels and took hold of a pry bar hanging on the wall.

"No, I'm good."

"Sure? It might help you get through this interview a little easier."

I blinked when I realized he wasn't going to hit me with the pry bar. "Well, all right. Why not? It can't taste as bad as it smells, right?"

"Why not, indeed." He found a barrel already standing and pried open the lid. "They call me Uncle Baz. I'm your friend down here, remember that. Elevaer can be friendly, too, but not if she's scared."

"Scared! She didn't seem very scared to me."

"Sure she is. She's scared of your Mystan friends." He dipped a ladle into the barrel.

I shook my head in confusion. "Mystans? I'm not friends with any Mystans. Do you mean those singing girls?" My elbows and shoulders felt like they were about to pop.

Blinking thoughtfully, he brought the dripping ladle over. "Singing girls?"

A light appeared at the top of the stairs; here came Elevaer carrying a silver candelabrum with all its candles lit, flooding the cellar with light. "You didn't start the interview without me, did you?" She had her hair pulled back and had changed into a black dress with a plunging neckline.

"You didn't miss nothing," said Uncle Baz, putting the ladle to my lips.

Tentatively, I accepted some of the liquor, with immediate regret. Cloying it was, and vile. It soured my face. "Is this part of the torture?"

"Torture!" cried Elevaer, descending the stairs. "What's going on down here? I said to make him comfortable."

Baz shrugged and downed the remainder of the ladle for himself. "This is Lank's version of comfort."

She set the candelabrum on a shelf. "And, look—you've bruised his pretty face."

"Gosh," I said, trembling with the pain. "You really think I'm pretty?"

"Sure I do. From the moment I saw you hanging upside down in the gaol, I said to myself, now there is a man lithe and lanky. I am rather in the mood for a lithe and lanky man."

"Well, if you really wanted to make me comfortable, might I suggest relocating to the den perhaps?"

"All things in time," said Elevaer, putting her index finger to my lips. "I want to have some fun with you here first." She leaned down and gave my left ear a little kiss. "Baz, you may leave us."

"You sure? Don't let him fool you. He's a feisty one. Gave us a heap of trouble on the way down, he did."

Elevaer smiled at me. "Just the way I like 'em."

Baz sighed and eyed me sadly. "Good luck, my friend."

"Thanks," said Elevaer. She came closer, standing astride my knees, as Baz made a production of returning the ladle, closing up the barrel of sour mash, hanging the pry bar in its place.

"You certainly *smell* like a man," observed Elevaer.

"I've been at sea seven weeks," I said. "I slept in a wagon last night. Though how you can smell anything through that fermenting liquor is impressive."

"Oh, but I *like* that smell," she said. "Sweet and powerful, just like me. You may *leave* us, Baz."

"I'm going, I'm going."

# CHAPTER 35

# A Thing for Sailors

"I don't really understand what is happening here," I said.

Elevaer put her hands on my shoulders and brought her face close to mine, arching her back. "Don't worry. I just have a few questions. Then we can decide what happens next." Over her shoulder she shouted, "Close the door!"

"Great," I said. "Fun. Maybe we could hurry it along a little, eh? I can't feel my arms."

Elevaer's smile deepened. "Eager, aren't you? Well, all right." She stood up straight and ran her tongue along her teeth. "Tobias has told me many things about you. But there are some troubling gaps I'd like to fill."

"Tobias?"

"You said you came on a ship. When, and what ship was that?"

"Yesterday. The Spirit of Lanark, under Captain Graby."

"A Sartan ship? Where were you coming from?"

"Lanarkia. I served as a crewman the past two years."

"On a Sartan ship?"

"Why not?"

Elevaer pursed her lips and shrugged, pacing back and forth in front of me. "Very well. So why did you leave?"

"Leave?"

"You just said you 'served' as a crewman. Past tense. So I surmise you left the crew?"

"My contract was up."

"Why Kortholomoth? Have you been to Kortholomoth before?"

"What sailor hasn't?"

She came back to me and sat on my lap, resting her hands on my shoulders. "I have a thing for sailors, you know." Staring into my eyes, she asked, "And how long have you plied the seas?"

"Twenty years, give or take."

She put her finger in my face, narrowing her eyes. "You were there. Twenty years ago. You met my father."

A chill ran down my back. She went on: "You were there, weren't you? You worked for Hava. You *still* work for Hava."

I shook my head. "What are you talking about? I haven't seen Hava in all these years. I thought she was dead."

"She *is* dead. Isn't she?"

"How should I know? I just got here."

"Where is your friend? The other one?"

"Who?"

"When you attacked the shop last night. When you showed up here at the gate, demanding to speak with Alakhar. Who was that guy with you?"

"First of all, we didn't attack the shop. We just knocked on the door. We were looking for Encho."

"Encho? Why Encho? Do you know Encho?"

"No."

"Then why were you looking for him? In the middle of the night?"

"I don't know. He was drunk."

"Who was drunk?"

"The guy I was with. I don't know his name. Some guy I met at a bar."

She shifted on my lap, running her fingers through my hair. "Olio. His name is Olio. See, I already knew that. I was testing to see if you would lie."

"I swear, I just ran into him at the bar. He offered to let me sleep in the back of his wagon. He's the one who works for the Mystans, not me. I don't even know what Mystans are, exactly."

"Pompous killjoys is what they are." She stroked my cheek sadly. "I was so hoping we could make a connection, you and me. But the telling of untruths is just not something I can abide."

"I'm sorry," I said. "I knew his name was Olio. I just didn't want you to hurt him."

"Hurt him? Why would I do that?" She stood up again and returned to her pacing. "Wait a minute—Olio! I remember him now. That creepy, sweaty guy who used to show up at the shop and want me to sit on his lap. What a pervert!"

"He cares about you."

She laughed out loud. "What?"

"Just something he said. He wanted to make sure you were safe. He told me that Hava had kind of lost it over you. That she thought the worst of you. That she was out to get you."

"Yeah," she said, looking at me with fresh eyes.

"Olio didn't come to the shop to see you because he was some pervert. He did it because he was worried about your well-being. He thought Hava might do something to you."

"She always did have it in for me. I'm glad she's dead." She turned and plucked a candle from her candelabrum. "She really is dead, isn't she?" she asked before jamming the burning candle into my face. She was aiming for my eye, but I jerked my head when I saw it coming and took it on the cheekbone instead.

"I don't know!" I shrieked. "That's what I came here to find out."

Elevaer looked at me sidelong, deciding what to do next, holding the broken stub of a candle in her hand as if it were a knife. "Go on," she said.

"My contract was up. I had a little spending money. I thought I would enjoy a lark in Kortholomoth. I thought I would look up Hava. You're right—I used to work for her back in Soofia. Not that she ever paid me. But she was so pretty, you know? I liked her. So I thought I'd look her up. I thought, who knows? Maybe I had a shot. I just wanted to lay eyes on the husband first, you know? To size up the competition?"

A slow smile came to Elevaer. "You dirty dog. You had a thing for my mother."

I shrugged. "Not that I ever acted on it. She would never. But you, on the other hand…" I raised my eyebrows, looking her up and down. "You look better than she ever did."

"That's true, isn't it?" said Elevaer with a purr, returning the candelabrum to its shelf, to my relief.

"You seem way less stuck up than her, for one."

"Yes," said Elevaer, biting her lip. "I recognize when people are telling the truth. And you, my pretty sailor, are now speaking truth. Pray continue."

"Hava would never say what she meant, so I never knew where I stood with her. But you: You are very direct."

"Exactly."

"You are like a much better version of her."

She pursed her lips. "If you weren't tied to that chair right now, what would you like to do to me?"

I swallowed, not sure what I was supposed to say. What was the thing most likely to get me untied? "Elevaer," I started, not sure where I was going with this, "I would do things, all right."

"What kind of things?" she asked, tilting her head.

"Um, kissing. Other things. Things to make you feel better. I think you deserve it." I swallowed again.

"Hmmm," said Elevaer, considering me. "For a sailor, you sure are bad at talking dirty."

"I'm in a lot of pain right now. My poetry will improve when you undo these knots. Please?"

"There's a good boy, asking nicely. But no—not yet. I am enjoying you like this," she said, stroking my face. "Tell me about my father."

"What?"

"My father. Tell me about him."

"What do you want to know?"

"Anything. What was your impression?"

I took a deep breath. "Um. Intimidating."

"Yeah," she said with a grin.

"Um, how much do you know about your father?"

"I met him, just a few months ago."

"You did?"

"Not that he was easy to find."

"No," I said, wondering whether we were talking about the same being. "How did you? Find him?"

"I am a very determined person, Mr. Sailor Man."

"My name is Ejertine."

"Ejertine?" She put her hand on her hip, and only half of her mouth smiled. "Soofian for All Eyes? That's what they called my father, back in the day."

I swallowed. "I guess I am named after your father. How about that?"

Her mouth hung open in delighted astonishment. "Well, I can't very well kill you now, can I? I was already starting to like you. Now this?"

"I like you, too," I said. "And I don't want to die."

"Of course you don't." Elevaer returned to my lap and snuggled up close, resting her face against my chest. "What if you could live forever? Would you like that?"

"I don't know about that," I said cautiously.

She lifted her head, her face close to mine, our mouths almost touching. "What if you could serve me forever? Wouldn't you like that, All Eyes?"

"Um."

"We have found a way. My Pretty and me."

I blinked. I didn't know what she meant, but whatever it was, I didn't like the sound of it.

She kissed me, long and deep. What could I do? I kissed her back. Hoping that if I played along, maybe she would untie me. But it was during this long kiss I began to face the reality that she was not going to release me. She was not going to hire me on. She had some other, more sinister intent.

When my mouth was free, I asked, "Where is Encho and his daughter? What has become of them?"

"Hmm? Oh, have no fear. They are safe. They are well." She tilted her head. "Why do you care?"

"I don't."

Elevaer searched my face for a long second. "You do." She pursed her lips. "You think I would do something to hurt them. My own family."

She shook her head sadly. "Listen. Hava always thought I was out to get her precious Ichito. Ichito had to be kept separate from evil Elevaer or she might become corrupted.

"The truth is, I always wanted a little sister. I never wanted to hurt her. I only wanted to help her. She and I had a bond, and the adults' determination to keep us apart only made our connection stronger.

"I used to sneak out of the shop in the dead of night and come up here to the House. They kept the gate locked at night, but it was easy enough for a little person like myself to slip between the bars. Once you're in the perimeter, the House itself is easily scalable.

"I found Ichito's window. We used to talk to each other through the chimney. I was her sky princess. That's what she used to call me. We talked almost every night, about all kinds of things. I would tell her about my adventures. She ate it up. She loved me. She loved having a secret friend.

"One time I went up to the ancient fort on the outskirts of the city. I saw murals forty feet tall with storm giants and winged elephants, and when I told Ichito about this place, she wanted to see for herself. She was very determined; she would have tried to go on her own if I didn't help her. And that wouldn't be very safe, would it?

"So one night I helped her get her window open, and we climbed down the House together. The plan was to take her up to the old fort and show her the murals. But it was a clear night, and once her eyes fell on Prowbeam Rock, she got it in her head to go there instead. There was no convincing her that the cloud kingdom I had spoken of was a different place. The adults had kept this poor child so locked up that she had never been to Prowbeam Rock. So what could I do? I took her up to Prowbeam Rock.

"Now, I don't know if you've ever taken a little kid to the top of Prowbeam Rock before, but it involves a lot of stopping and resting. By the time we get to the top it's already almost morning and she's cranky and tired and wants to go home. 'You can't go home yet,' I said. 'First we have to look at the view.' So she's just about to peek over the edge to drink in the view of the ships below, when all the sudden Encho swoops down on us out of nowhere and grabs us by the napes of our necks. Poor Ichito! She never did get to look at that view from the top. Does that seem fair to you?"

"No, it doesn't," I said.

"Apparently this was some giant scandal to the adults. Oh, no! Ichito got out of the House and almost had a fun time with her best and only friend. Poor Encho, you should have seen his face! He was so serious. He gave me money and told me I had to lay low. That there were search parties out looking for me. That they would arrest me if they found me. Can you believe it?"

"That does seem like an over-reaction."

"I was just a kid!"

"I'm sorry that happened to you."

Elevaer returned to her pacing. "From the beginning Hava filled my head with lies. She pretended I was not hers. What kind of mother denies her own flesh and blood? She told me I was the bastard of her cousin Yerve in Tross. I couldn't go to Temple with the other kids, she said, on account of being a bastard. What did I know? I believed her lies. So when things got too hot here in Kortholomoth because of Hava's so-called search parties, what did I do?"

"You went to Tross, to track down your supposed mother."

"That's right. All I had was a name—Yerve. And a city—Shamp. At least that's where Hava's brother Belchamp lived. He was a big deal in Shamp. Palace, servants, piles of money. I had a pretty strong notion Yerve could be found somewhere in Belchamp's orbit."

"But that's a thousand miles from here. How old were you? How did you get to Tross on your own?"

"I had some connections. One learns a few things in the streets of Kortholomoth at night. That's where I first met Uncle Baz. Back then he was just Big Baz. All the other street kids looked up to him. Followed him around like little puppies. If he had his way, he would have taken me in, added me to his gang. But I've never been much of a follower.

"But as it happened there was a girl Baz knew. Ezel Ostrack." Elevaer smiled slyly. "Oh, I liked her right away."

# CHAPTER 36

# The Namer

Ezel and her brothers had the use of a boat, which they employed for minor acts of piracy. Robbing fishermen and the like.

I had bigger ideas, and the Ostracks were all ears. I laid out my scheme for them: I was a bastard Nipalto, I told them, and I could gain entry into the house of Belchamp, if only they would take me to Shamp. I would be their inside gal, and together we would rob Belchamp blind.

They, too, were eager to depart Kortholomoth, so we left right away. We were light of supplies, and these were hungry days for us, but we were happy and free. I found the open sea agreed with me.

But it was a long way to Shamp, so to sustain ourselves along the way we went from port to port, stealing from warehouses and careless dockmasters. It was from these Ostracks I learned the rules of the sea and the basics of sailing. I also learned how to sneak aboard an anchored ship without being heard, slit a few throats, and plunder the hold while most of the crew were out drinking and whoring in port. Good times. It was fun for me... appealed to my mischievous side, you know? When we got in trouble it was usually the girl, Ezel Ostrack, who saved us with some quick thinking or a good trick. I liked her, a lot. She was smarter than her brothers, and a lot prettier, too. It was for her sake I felt bad when I had to betray the Ostracks in Hajan port; I left them to take the fall for a botched robbery. By then I didn't need them anymore. I had money enough to book my passage the rest of the way to Shamp.

But Shamp proved a terrific disappointment. After Kortholomoth and Astina and Wahl Dahldin, this was no proper port at all, just a pitiable wharf with less than a dozen berths. No warehouses, no sleazy establishments, no nothing. Just a bunch of trees and the glow and murmur of the town hidden behind the ridge. A slow, lazy river joined the sea here, but the channel was so choked full of silt there was no passage for sea-faring ships.

Just a few steps from the dock and you find yourself in this wooded spot. There's a spring feeding into a tidal pool, and everywhere there are these little frogs. I hate those little frogs. They just seem so happy all the time. Birds singing. Absolutely dreadful. Then you crest the ridge and there is Shamp, a bunch of moss-covered houses clustered like mushrooms on a grid of crisscrossing canals. I felt entirely repulsed by the quaintness of the place. I could tell at once this was no place for a person like me.

Happily, my business did not take me into the town proper. Belchamp's palace was farther up the ridge, overlooking the town. It was not hard to find. You could see the place from a mile away.

When I arrived at last at Belchamp's house, I did not exactly find the warm reception I expected. Belchamp was not home, and his wife Meida, she disliked me at once. You'd think a person would be glad to see her long lost granddaughter. "I suppose you want money," is what she said to me.

"I wouldn't mind some," I said, "but really I just came to meet my mother." Turns out, Yerve had been disowned by the family and now lived in scandal with a band of lewd players who circulated up and down Tross putting on shows. The more I learned about my supposed mother, the more I liked her.

"And will I find my father with her, do you suppose?"

"Your father?" She gave me a long, searching look. I could tell there was something she wasn't telling me.

"Look," I said. "I'll go away and you'll never see me again; isn't that what you want? Just tell me what you know. I was born in this house, sixteen years ago. I have come seeking the truth. Tell me, and I will go."

After a moment's hesitation Meida pulled me outside, away from the ears of her servants. "What happened, I don't know," she said in a conspiratorial whisper. "I wasn't here. Belchamp sent you away before I returned from my annual retreat in Naul." But she did give me the name of someone who was there, the wet nurse they hired to care for me. Sveka was her name. "Seek for Sveka at the lacemakers shop in Shamp. If it's the truth you want, ask Sveka."

So I walked down into Shamp and asked the first person I met where I might find the lacemakers shop. As it turned out, the first person I met was this old man with sideburns out to here, smoking on the biggest pipe I'd ever seen; it must have been six feet long, resting on the porch where he sat. "I don't know a thing about lace," he said, "but if you sit with me a spell, I'll show you how to catch the moon and put it in your pocket."

"No thanks," I said. Tross was full of wizards, they said, and he was probably one of them. My gut told me to steer clear of such. I turned to walk on.

"To go forward you must go back," said the maybe-wizard.

"What's that supposed to mean?"

He just shrugged and gave me a stupid grin and went back to his pipe.

I walked on, annoyed. *To go forward, I must go back?* Back to Belchamp's house? Back to Kortholomoth?

I walked aimlessly through the mossy streets and arched bridges of Shamp. Everything was so orderly and clean. It made me queasy. Where were the roaming bands of dogs fighting in the streets? Even the children were well behaved. There was no mischief afoot anywhere at all.

Completely on accident I stumbled onto the lacemakers shop. I went in, all too aware how filthy I was compared to the elegant women stepping through the shop like those tall fisher birds stalking the shallows for their dinner.

A heavy-set Soofian woman in the back saw me and motioned me over. She sat behind a counter, working her hands. I looked her over. "You Sveka?"

She set her work aside and looked at me. "Well... could it be Elevaer?"

"You know me?"

"I recognize all my babies. Come 'round here." Sveka stood up and pulled me into her embrace. "I was the one named you, you know."

"No—I didn't know that."

She sat back down, blinking. "What brings you here, Elevaer?"

"Meida sent me."

"Did she now?"

"She said you would tell me the truth."

She let out a big, long sigh. "Did she now… Well, I suppose you have a right to know."

And so I heard the truth at last. I was not in fact the daughter of Yerve. True, Yerve had a bastard daughter, but that had been months earlier. No, my mother was Hava. It seemed Hava had returned from Soofia very pregnant and very sick—just showed up like that at Belchamp's gate one day.

Well, they hushed it up. They hid her away in the back of the house. And after I was born, they hired this Sveka to take care of me, because Hava wouldn't touch me. Wouldn't even look at me.

"I always knew you would make a lovely young lady," said Sveka.

I have to admit, I was a little impressed she could recognize me from when I was a baby. To me, babies just look like little raisins. I can't tell 'em apart.

So now I knew the truth, or part of it: Hava was my mother. Of course, my next question was, "Who then was my father?"

Sveka shook her head. "Your father, I don't know, he was something bad. Something so bad they thought you would be bad, too…." She gave me a long look and added, "*Are* you bad, Elevaer?"

Ha! "Of course I'm not bad. In fact, I'm very, very good."

"Some priests came looking for your mother, but Belchamp protected her—protected you, too."

Why would we need protecting from priests, I wondered? I wondered what she meant when she said my father was "something bad." She didn't say "someone." I was intrigued.

I pressed Sveka for anything she knew, but all I got were a few names of places where Hava had traveled in Soofia. It wasn't much to go on, but it's all I had. I decided then and there I would go to Soofia and follow in the footsteps of Hava to see if I could find my father.

I turned to go, but Sveka stopped me. "Wait," she said.

So I waited. She just sat there wringing her hands.

"Well?"

"There was a man, maybe you know him." I didn't know who she was talking about at first. Turns out, it was that very same fellow you ran into at the bar. Your Olio.

When I realized who she was talking about, I said, "You mean that guy with the big hands who smells bad?"

"That's the one," said Sveka, licking her lips.

"Well, out with it. What about him?"

Turns out, she had a son from Olio. That's right—yet another bastard enters our tale. Little Lukas is his name, a strapping tyke old enough now to've got himself entangled in some local trouble. She wanted to know if I'd take him back to Lagin and deposit him with Olio. "He needs a father to raise him proper," she said.

"I'm not going to Lagin," I said. "I'm going to Soofia."

"Soofia?" She frowned at that. She tried talking me out of it. "No good can come from this," she said.

"Thanks for the advice," I said and took my leave.

# CHAPTER 37

# Demon Spawn

"Hold on," I said. "Just wait a minute. Olio has a son? Does he know this?"

Elevaer shrugged. "How should I know? Don't interrupt, I'm just getting to the good part."

"Elevaer, I want to hear your story. I really do. It's just I can't feel my arms."

"That's good, you don't want to feel your arms. If I untied you now, it would hurt a lot. I have to say, I rather enjoy having a captive audience. Don't get me wrong: Baz and his boys are a delight, but they're not like you and me, All Eyes, are they? You're a good listener."

"Yeah, I get that a lot."

"It feels good, you know? To have someone to confide in."

"Your candles are burning out," I said.

"Bother! Good thing I have this other one." She picked up the candle she had tried to thrust into my eye socket earlier. "Now shut up. You will like this part."

•

Just as I was coming out of the lacemaker's shop, they were waiting for me. I didn't get a good look at 'em. Maybe three guys. They took me by surprise, threw a sack over my head. Before I could do a thing, they had me hogtied.

"Hey!"

"You will be silent, demon-spawn," boomed a man to my right. *Demon-spawn.*

I felt rough hands seize me and drag me over the cobblestones. They seemed like they were in a hurry.

My mind raced. Who were these guys?

They dumped me into a wagon, none too gently, either. I lay there, head ringing against the floor of the cart, and then I heard the driver's whip and I felt the cart jar forward.

The sack over my head smelled like something rotten and made me retch a little in my mouth. My head banged against the floor as the wheel hit a bump.

Someone was muttering something. "What?" I said. "Is there someone there?"

"Silence!" commanded a different voice and gave me a hard whack across the back with something heavy.

I was going to say something smart, but the breath was knocked out of me, so I just lay there opening and closing my mouth like a fish, trying not to gag on the smell of the sack. These guys were starting to make me mad. These were no gentlemen, to treat a lady like this!

The muttering sound was still droning on in this strange monotone, and then finally I realized this must be the sound of praying. That's when it hit me: Priests! That's who had me.

On the heels of that revelation came another: Meida had betrayed me. She must have sent me ahead to the lacemakers shop, then told the priests where to catch me.

I'd never had any experience with Morphidians up till then. I never received a blessing, never went to Temple, never hurt myself bad enough to need healing. So this was my introduction to Morphidians. And now that I'd met 'em, I found I didn't care for 'em at all.

You know what was going through my mind as I lay there hogtied, bouncing around in the floor of the cart? The words "demon-spawn." Is that what I was—demon-spawn? I tried the words on for size and I found I liked the implications. I'd always known I was different. Better than others, you know? Now I had an explanation: My father was a demon. Now I wanted to find him even more.

But first I had to get away from these unfriendly priests. The prayer-mumblings were starting to get on my nerves, and I was about to open my mouth and get myself in trouble again when the cart lurched to a stop. I felt man-hands all over me, dragging me out of the cart. I smelled the sea and heard a ship's bell. They'd brought me back to the wharf! I smiled under my sack, glad if this meant I got to leave Shamp behind. They meant to put me on a boat, but we stood around for a time while the priests negotiated with someone who I can only presume was the captain. "We depart at dawn," I heard him say at last.

They carried me aboard and stowed me below-deck. Someone, one of the men who'd carried me, stayed with me. He pulled the sack from my head, and boy, was I glad to have some fresh air! I tried to focus my eyes on the man as he untied my elbows and legs. He left my wrists tied together behind my back.

He was not a bad looking man, this priest, if you like 'em broad-shouldered with thighs like tree trunks. "Are you going to cooperate?" he wanted to know.

"For you? Sure," I said, blowing the hair out of my face. I must have looked a mess. "You're not the one who clobbered me, are you?"

"No," he said. I knew it wasn't him, because if *he* had hit me, I would be broken. "I apologize for the behavior of my colleagues. They didn't know you were just a girl."

"What, did they think I was a rhinoceros?"

"We take demonic threats very seriously."

"Do I look like a threat to you?" I arched my back a little so he'd get a good look at my chest. With most men I could tell if they wanted me or not, but this priest, he was indecipherable, which made him interesting. I couldn't help it; I found myself wondering what that muscular body of his looked like under his robe.

He turned the loops of rope over in his hands as he considered me. "Looks can be deceiving."

"So it's just the two of us," I said, crossing my legs.

"Three," he said, putting the rope over his shoulder.

I looked around. We were in a drab little holding cell with a slit for a porthole that let in a little light, enough to see we were alone. "What do you mean, three?"

"Morphid, myself, and you."

That's when I knew I wasn't flirting my way out of this situation. "There's just the one bunk," I pointed out.

"That's for you," he said. "Morphid and I will be outside."

Seems the plan was to ship me to Wahl Dahldin where, apparently, the High Priest would know what to do with me.

I got to know my captor pretty well over the next few days. Yezimeyer, that was his name. The son of a Yhari horse lord.

Called to the priesthood when he was but a boy. I've never met a more solid man. He was just a wall of a man, all bristling with integrity, he was. It made for a tedious voyage back to Wahl Dahldin, with nothing to do but peer out the slit at a featureless gray sea or talk to Yezimeyer, who never seemed to leave his post outside my door.

"Yezimeyer, don't you ever have to take a wee?"

"Actually, no," he said. Apparently that was the power Morphid had granted him, along with the power to bore people to death.

# CHAPTER 38

# A Useful Man

I was glad when we finally arrived in Wahl Dahldin. Even if the High Priest planned on sending me to Hell early, at least that would be better than spending another day with Yezimeyer. When the big priest brought me out of my cell and up on deck, I was blinded by the sunlight but I could feel the breeze on my face and the smell—ah, the sweet perfume of Wahl Dahldin— ditches full of human waste, rotten fruit, dead fish… the smell of a proper city. I couldn't help but smile, even with my wrists tied behind my back and Yezimeyer's firm hand guiding me through the throng of eager crewmen, all scrambling to unload the cargo even before the boat was made fast.

Well, you can imagine my surprise when Yezimeyer was wrenched suddenly upward, and I found myself unexpectedly free. I spun round, still half-blinded by the afternoon sun, and caught sight of Yezimeyer's boots rising overhead. Someone had put a hook through his belt and now he was hanging from a crane line wearing a startled expression on his face.

"Come on," urged a young crewman who rushed me quickly down the ramp to the docks, while most people's attention was distracted by the spectacle of the dangling priest.

"Stop there!" commanded Yezimeyer, pointing down at us. But by then we were on the docks and sprinting into the welcoming arms of Wahl Dahldin's blessed, reeking alleys. We were soon well away and free.

We hid ourselves in an empty shed, and I let out a yop of joy. "That was great! Did you see his face?" I looked to my liberator. "Who are you anyway?" He was smiling and leaning on his knees, trying to catch his breath. A mixed-blood lad, no older than myself.

"I'm Lukas," he said.

"*You're* Lukas? Son of Olio?" Somehow I'd pictured a snot-nosed kid toting a slingshot. But here was this broad-shouldered guy with chest hair bursting out his tunic and a long knife on his belt. I'd be lying if I said he was good-looking, but he did exude a certain man-appeal, in that sweaty kind of way.

He shrugged. "I needed outta Shamp. My mom said I should help you."

"So you joined the crew of the ship what took me. Well done! How about untying me?"

"First things first."

"What, you want to take advantage of me while I'm all helpless and tied?"

He wrinkled his nose. "No. When was the last you bathed?"

Now I was offended. No man wrinkles his nose at me.

"You and I have to get one thing straight," he said, putting his finger in my face. "I've done for you, now you gotta do for me."

"I don't owe you nothing. I didn't ask for your help. I had the situation under control."

"Shh!" There were voices outside. Lukas drew out his knife and cut my bonds. "Come on, let's keep moving." He took my hand and led me back into the maze of alleys.

It felt good to be free, and I found I didn't much mind holding onto Lukas's big strong hand. "So what is it you want? What would you have of me?"

"Well," he said, leading us into the crowded Barber's Market. "I understand you know my father."

"Barely."

"He's an adventurer, yes? An explorer, a brave warrior?"

"I guess so. How should I know?"

"I want you to take me to him."

"I told your mom, I'm not going back to Lagin. I'm going to Soofia."

"See? We are the same, you and I."

"How's that?"

"We are bastards both, each searching for our father."

He had me there. "All right, look. You seem okay. You're welcome to come with me to Bvossoly. I could use somebody to watch my back. But I make no promises, not about your father or anything else. And—just to be clear—do not take this to mean you can take liberties with my body." I looked him up and down again.

Five minutes later I found myself in another alley, pressed up against the wall, with Lukas taking his liberties. Poor lad was overeager and clueless, but my, he was a lot of man and I decided on the spot I would keep him.

The weeks that followed were sweet ones. Lukas proved himself useful in any number of ways.

We kept a low profile, took what opportunities presented themselves, doing odd jobs, a little burgling here and there, till we had enough coin to buy Lukas a sword. Then we stole a boat and made the crossing to Harta. I didn't speak the least Soofian, so Lukas had to do the talking. No one was going to listen to me anyhow; I was just a girl. By Bvossoliad Law, I was his property just by merit of traveling with him.

Bvossoly, the Kingdom of Soofia, is a big place. I had come chasing the memory of Hava, a woman who'd passed through sixteen to nineteen years before. Sveka had given me the names of places: Aymad, Terade, Ucheti. Places that were scattered over a thousand miles. And yet I found people, all the length of the River Flegmarn, I found people who remembered Hava. She'd made an impression, clearly, everywhere she went. The Singing Angel, they called her. An ambassador for Laginese culture, the first Laginese most of them had ever met, or at least the first who wasn't trying to kill them. In Riez Nohl I heard a song about the Singing Angel, which told how she had come upriver full of hope and song and returned downriver sick and broken. It was the jungle what broke her, according to the song, but something told me it was in fact my father who could claim credit for taking the singing out of the angel.

Lukas asked every time, but no one had any memory of Olio. "The Singing Angel's protector and companion," he would prompt them, "a great warrior." They would squint their eyes and stroke their beards, trying to remember, or just stare blankly. I guess Olio just wasn't as memorable as Hava.

Most versions of Hava's legend agreed she had come floating down the Durez, a great wild jungle river that flows down from the high mountains. The Durez being the tributary no one follows, because upstream there is nothing to be found but places where no man should tread. In the rainy season, when floods come sweeping down from the mountains, the gargantuan corpses of terrible beasts come floating among the logs and rafts of vegetation, the discharges of a vast high valley between snow-capped mountains, a valley choked full of monsters and old magic. The Deep Valley Durez. A place only a fool would go.

And rafting *up* the Durez is a different matter entirely from floating down it. There are stair-step falls and rapids, places where you have to leave the river and carry your raft up or down sheer rock faces. I was glad of Lukas for that labor. There were certainly no other fools around willing to come with me to the Deep Valley. We were just young enough and stupid enough to think we could do this on our own.

Lukas had a sword, sure, but he was untrained and untested. The first real fight we got into, we quickly lost. It was just some little groundlings. Lukas beat back the first few, but we were quickly surrounded and overwhelmed. They barely touched me, but they tore up poor Lukas pretty good. I had to watch while he thrashed around on the ground with three or four of the little things attached to him by teeth, claws, or hooks. Evidently, I was to be their hostage, and so long as I sat still they didn't bother me.

Well, the next thing I know these huge, green, shaggy dogs come sweeping through, scattering the groundlings, head-butting a few of them and sending them flying. And then just as suddenly the dogs were gone and so were the groundlings. Where did they all go? It's like they just melted into the ground. Lukas is gasping for breath and bleeding all over, and it's just the two of us. What the hell just happened?

Then all the sudden there's this kent girl standing on a high rock, holding her bow and looking down at us. "What's the matter with you? This is no place for you," she says, speaking Westongue.

Oh, I liked this kent girl right away. She was so sure of herself and deadly looking. I think I might have said, "Hi," or something equally insipid.

"What is your purpose? You have no business here if you can't manage a pod of groundlings." She seemed genuinely dismayed by Lukas's injuries but did not move from her spot on the rock and kept her bow at the ready.

Lukas was trying to talk, but only managed to gasp.

"He's bleeding," I said. "Can you help?"

The kent girl narrowed her eyes. I could see her trying to make up her mind whether to shoot or help. She notched an arrow. "Tell me why you have come."

"I'm looking for someone."

She searched my eyes, then put away her arrow, leapt down from her rock, and sauntered over to Lukas. "Help me get him down to the river."

"But he's bleeding!"

"Trust me, you'll want to wash those bites first. Sometimes it's better to bleed out than bleed in."

So we pulled poor Lukas up to his feet and supported him on either side, and walked our way back down to the river, some hundred feet or so from the place we were attacked. Laboring so close to the kent girl, I could *smell* her. She smelled beautiful; Lukas did not.

We washed out his wounds and laid him unconscious on the bank. A couple of long crocodiles came along, drawn by the sounds in the water and the taste of blood on the current. The kent girl showed them her bow, and the crocodiles faded into the river and did not return. Smart crocodiles.

I was rapidly falling in love with this girl. "What is your name?"

She shot me an evil glare. How was I to know kents consider that a rude question? Then she whistled, clear and loud, and all at once the huge green dogs came bounding back on the scene. They circled eagerly around Lukas and descended upon him.

"Hey! They're eating him alive!"

But they were not eating him alive. They were snuffling at his wounds, licking away his blood. After a few moments of the dogs' attentions, Lukas was no longer bleeding. The dogs circled away then, making room for the kent girl to have a good look at him.

"He'll live," she declared.

I regarded the huge dogs, circling with their energy. I counted six of them. "These are your dogs?"

She shot me another of her looks. "Bind up his injuries. Keep his bandages clean. I will be back in a week to check on him."

"In a week? I'm not sticking around here a week. And I don't know the least thing about bandages. You'll have to do it for me."

This provoked her to draw out her knife and put it against my throat. "You are lucky to be alive, foolish girl child. I have helped you more than I should. Your man is not my responsibility."

"I love you," I said to the kent girl.

She sheathed her knife and turned away in disgust. "Who is the person you seek?" She began to unravel a cloth from around her forearm. It was such a fine material, I hadn't even noticed she was wearing it. Kent-silk.

"In truth? My father."

She crouched over Lukas and bound her silk around his wrist, where he'd lost the most blood. "Most of your kind who come here are criminals fleeing human justice. Usually the best thing for it is an arrow to the neck."

"Well, we're not criminals," I lied.

She shrugged. "Whatever you are, you're no use to me." She bandaged Lukas up, pouting the whole time. I just watched her, enchanted at the way she moved.

When she was done, she said, "We'll need to move him one more time, away from the river. On account of the crocodiles. But after that—no more moving. He needs to stay still and rest." And she started in with all these instructions for me.

"Look," I said, cutting her off. "Just so we're clear, I am not staying with the boy. I mean, he's been great. But now—well, he's not much use to me either, is he? In fact, he's a liability and a distraction."

"What, you will leave him to die?"

I shrugged. "It's not my job to fix people when they get hurt. Why don't you stay with him?"

"Forget it."

"You're a kent, right? You must have knowledge of healing. For goodness sake, you've got green dogs with magic saliva."

"I told you, your man is not my responsibility."

"So, you would just leave him to die?"

She stood to go. "I saved his life. And yours. You should be grateful."

"Thank you," I said. "Well, I guess this is good-bye. I figure I can make another mile or three tonight. I sure hope the lad makes it and doesn't get eaten by the groundlings."

The kent girl glared at me. "You are a bad person, to leave him like this."

I threw up my hands. "Why does everyone think I'm bad? I'm not the one with the gift for healing. That's *your* job, lady. What good is it for me to sit around here? I've gotta keep moving. My father's not gonna find himself."

So I left. Sure, I missed Lukas. Especially when I had to carry my own boat. But I left him in good hands. I'm sure that kent girl stayed with him, nursed him back to health. The two of them probably ended up in love and married, and by now they have little half-breeds scampering about.

Well, after a couple days trying it on my own, I gave up the river route. I'm just not built for all the climbing and toting. So I sought other routes to the high valley country.

Oh, I had some crazy times in that country. Had myself some close calls, I did. Stories for another night. But let's skip ahead to the good part. The part you're waiting for. The part where I found my father.

CHAPTER 39.

# The Black Fortress

It was the rainy season. I'd made it to the Deep Valley, but I'd given up searching. I just hunkered down and waited for the weather to turn. The whole jungle was more or less a river, and I settled down on an island in that river, a jutting rock and a few trees I shared with a family of monkeys. Well, I was just sitting there, miserable with the monkeys, watching the river go by, when I saw something float by—a cloth twisting in the current. I went in after it and pulled it out.

It was a scarf, coarsely made but intact. And it hadn't been in the water for long.

The next day I made my way upriver and found myself an actual damn fortress. I don't know what else to call it but a fortress: tall walls of black stone, a solid gate closed and locked, battlements and everything; but it was strangely out of proportion, too small for a garrison.

No roads, no other signs of people—just a fortress in the jungle. And it was a strange thing, those black walls made of a stone not native to this place, surely.

I sat in front of the dark fortress, watching. Nobody came, nobody went, nobody showed themselves on the walls. That quickly became boring so I went up to the gate, a wall of wood reinforced with metal, and I banged on it with a stone. "Anybody home?" I waited, I banged some more.

Finally, a man peered over the wall at me, his hair all disheveled and black. Not a Soofian by the looks of him but a westerner. He looked down at me with a strange combination of contempt and curiosity.

"Well? Will you let me in?"

His head disappeared, and moments later I heard the lock disengage and then the gate began slowly to open, lifted by some unseen winch. The gate lifted only a little, just enough for me to squeeze underneath.

The man was waiting for me on the other side, pointing this crazy staff at me. There were these two living snakes growing out of the top of his staff—truly! I sat there on the ground, having just crawled under the gate, and I looked up at those snakes and they looked down at me, and I thought, now here's a role reversal.

And oh, how I wanted a staff like that.

"Hi," I said. That same rush of attraction that made me swoon for the kent girl was back but multiplied again. Something about brandishing that wicked staff just really worked for me, you know?

"Speak," he commanded. "What is your purpose here?"

I tried to judge the age of this severe but handsome man. Could he be my father? "I'm Elevaer," I offered, batting my eyelids.

The eyelid thing seemed to work on him; he lowered his menacing snake-staff a little and hung on my next words.

"Do you think we have the same eyes?" I asked him.

"What?" The poor dear looked very confused.

"Never mind. Will you tell me your name?"

"I am called Korieski. Do you know me?"

"I do now." I made to rise up, and when he did not stop me, I found my feet and stood up straight. "Tell me, Master Korieski," I said, gently pushing his magic staff aside, "do pretty girls often come calling at your castle?"

"They do not," he admitted, smiling a little but narrowing his eyes. I could sense him ready to tense if I tried anything. He smelled not unpleasantly of aromatic smoke.

"Well, how about some hospitality for your guest?"

"This is no guest house," said Korieski, planting his staff on the ground, and it stood straight up without him having to hold it. That impressed me mightily. The two serpents stopped their writhing and they turned to face one another, a little sullenly I thought, and froze in place.

"What kind of a place is it, then?"

Korieski seemed amused. He lowered the gate back to the ground by turning a giant crank, then he turned a second, smaller crank to engage the lock with a satisfying thunk. "If you'd really like to know what kind of place this is, follow me and see for yourself." He clasped his staff again and led me into a narrow, curving space between two forty-foot-tall walls. The space was barely wide enough to accommodate Korieski's broad shoulders. I followed him one hundred, two hundred feet through this strange curving walkway, never passing a door or window—just walls of strange black stone on either side. I ran my hands along the walls and found the stone coarse and warm to the touch. There was something... unusual about this place. I looked at the back of Korieski's head, his shoulders, and his double-serpent staff. I decided he must be some kind of dark sorcerer who'd constructed this place with his spells. I decided that was incredibly sexy.

But was this man a demon? my father? The answer, I shortly learned, was no. Korieski was not the demon, but he was the demon's master. He showed me into the heart of his fortress, a large vaulted chamber built round a great pit—the pit where he kept his demon. "I bring a visitor," announced Korieski and from the pit came a roar that shook the stones in the walls. "He likes you," said Korieski with a grin.

I went straight up to the pit to have a look for myself. The pit was covered in a metal grating and through this grating I could see, some forty feet below, the demon himself, his eyes glowing up at me. He was so—beautiful. Full of teeth and rage and elbows. "Father?" The demon shifted positions and I heard his breathing quicken as he stared up at me.

"What did you say?" demanded Korieski.

I turned back to face Korieski, all the more impressed. "How does a man master such a one as this?"

Korieski smiled and stepped up to the pit beside me, returning the demon's gaze. "With a power greater than his." Korieski spat down into the pit, and the demon roared up at us, showing us his gullet, so large it seemed to fill the whole span of the pit. His breath reeked of Hell. Though the force of that howl rattled our bones, Korieski laughed. "He *hungers.*" He turned to look at me with curiosity. "Are you not afraid?"

I shrugged. "You're not afraid. Why should I be?" I looked back down at the demon. "He really is magnificent." The demon paced back and forth in his space, his breathing tortured.

Korieski's gaze lingered on me. "Who *are* you? Where did you come from?"

"My name is Elevaer." I ventured out onto the grating over the pit. "Tell me, Master Korieski, is it just the two of you with this whole fortress to yourselves? Or is there perhaps a Mrs. Korieski stashed away somewhere?"

"There is no Mrs. Korieski," he said rather hastily. That's when I knew I had him. I heard the demon snort down below.

"Come," I said, urging him to follow me out onto the grating. "Tell me more about this power you spoke of, Master Korieski." I could tell he liked it when I called him master.

Korieski smiled, glancing down again at the demon. He left his staff standing where it was and came out to join me, careful with his footing so as not to step through the grating. "I've never met anyone quite like you before."

"Likewise," I purred, taking his hand and pulling him closer. I lined up my face with his and captured his eyes.

"Mine is the power of Kaphador," he said. A low growl came up from the demon. "He does not like it when I speak his master's name." And the demon barked up at us, a series of syllables, like he was trying to speak. Korieski only smiled.

Then we kissed. I don't know who started it, me or him. Doesn't matter. We wanted each other. And we wanted each other right there. The demon howled up at us, we tore at each other's clothes. Korieski pressed me down onto the metal grating, his hungry mouth never leaving mine. And he took me, flesh slapping against flesh, right there in full view of my father.

Afterward I lay in his strong arms and stroked the carpet of black hair on his chest. I thought I loved him. But in truth it was his power I loved.

*Mine is the power of Kaphador*, he'd told me. "Tell me of Kaphador," I asked. I'd heard of Kaphador, of course. Morphid's perfect offspring, the Prince of All, disfigured by lightning, ruler of Hell, god of the dead. But his was a name I'd only heard used as a curse, never spoken in reverence the way Korieski did.

"Kaphador is power, pure and simple. If it is power you seek, Elevaer, you need only ask Him for it. Ask Him three times and the power is yours."

Sounds too good to be true, right? Oh, don't look so shocked. Kaphador's not half so bad as people make him out to be. What had *Morphid* ever done for me, other than send his priests to kill me? I liked my treatment at the hands of this Kaphadorian far better.

Ask three times, he said. I was intrigued. I wanted to try asking right away but felt a fool in front of Korieski. I wanted to be like him: Full of power and confidence and possessed of fantastic toys.

I had much to learn from him, and happily he was entirely agreeable with my staying. A little clingy, actually.

He showed me around his strange little fortress. I remember a laboratory with a giant oven. And in an adjoining room the corpse of an ape was spread over a table, next to a saw. "I found her in the jungle," he explained. "That's what I was working on when you came knocking. She'll feed the beast for a week."

"Really? He looked like he could have swallowed her in a single bite."

"Of course he could. But I do not give him the whole ape, do I? He gets maybe a forearm, just enough to keep him alert. I like to keep him hungry."

"What for?"

Korieski smiled. "Hunger makes him angry."

"And that's a good thing?"

"Oh, yes. My fathers before me, they did all they could to suppress his rage. My fool father actually sang him little lullabies to make him sleepy, if you can believe it. This Korieski has a different approach. I want an active, angry demon. I don't want to suppress his power, I want to *maximize* it."

I could tell he really liked saying the word *maximize*. "You're cute," I observed.

Something caught my eye. "What's that over there?"

Sitting slumped in the corner was... a doll. A little girl of cloth and wire and teeth. I loved her at once.

Korieski gestured dismissively. "She is as yet unfinished."

"Look at her, with her little fangs. Adorable. Can I pick her up?"

"Do not touch the homunculus."

He urged me on to the next room, but my eyes lingered on the doll. Now, I'd seen my share of dolls growing up, I think you'd agree, but this one was something else entirely. She was just like me, somehow, discarded in the corner. I felt a connection with that little misshapen girl.

There was really only one other portion of the fortress, a sprawling lair where Korieski made his quarters. "You will stay here with me," he said. "Make yourself... comfortable. Touch nothing. I must attend to the ape before the flies finish their work." This is why I liked Korieski, because he would utter sentences like that one.

He left me in his room, so of course I had to go through his stuff. I found an alcove with a shrine and the dual-face of

Kaphador—half skeletal, half flesh—staring back at me.

*Ask three times.* I went to the shrine and touched the face of Kaphador, half smiling. "Kaphador, I come to you seeking power."

My smile disappeared when the dual-face glowed red hot, burning my finger. And a voice—the most beautiful voice I'd ever heard—said to me, YOU ARE WELCOME HERE, DAUGHTER OF ENYIN.

I found my eyes locked with Kaphador's, one eye gleaming with life, the other a socket of infinite black. In his gaze, I understood: He knew me. He loved me. He accepted me.

"I want to serve you," I blurted. "As Korieski does."

YOU HAVE ASKED ONCE, said the beautiful voice.

And then I was looking at Korieski's shrine—no longer the true face of Kaphador, but just a crude mask.

Wow. I sat heavily on Korieski's bed, a vast semicircular stone covered in layers upon layers of furs. I lay my cheek against the musky softness of his bed and smelled his scent on the furs.

I wanted to be a Kaphadorian. Nothing had ever made more sense.

When Korieski returned, covered in ape's blood, we made love again, taking our time to do it properly this time. Then we spoke of Kaphador late into the night. Korieski was nothing if not a zealot, and he gladly answered my questions. "Kaphador accepts all who come to him. He does not care who you are or what you may have done. He shares His power with any who ask. In return, you must be willing to give yourself over to Him, just as He gives Himself to you. Once you belong to Kaphador, you will always belong to Kaphador, even after death."

The way I saw it, I was going to end up in Hell sooner or later. All the better if I could go in as a servant of the Prince, instead of just another lost soul. And me, with demon blood… maybe Hell was where I belonged. Maybe Hell wouldn't be so bad for the likes of me.

When at last we slept, we slept well and long. When I woke, sprawled on Korieski's furs, I could not say whether it was night or day. I'd lost all sense of time within those windowless, black walls.

I rose before Korieski, desperately thirsty. We'd finished his cistern during our endless talking and I knew not where in the fortress to fetch more. So I went wandering.

The fortress had at its center the great room with the pit, and it was impossible to remain unaware of the demon, no matter what room I found myself in. I could hear him stirring down in his pit; I could hear him snorting from time to time, impatient. Was he just as aware of me, tiptoeing about the fortress?

I found myself drawn into Korieski's laboratory. And once in the laboratory, I found myself drawn to the doll. She sat slumped in the corner, her head tilted against the wall, looking up at me.

"Hello," I said. "You are a pretty little thing, aren't you?"

Though she made no reply, I could tell somehow she wanted to. There was an intelligence pulsing behind those beady little eyes, I was sure of it.

Behind me there came a faint hissing, scaring me half to death. I turned to see… a shadow. Something half-seen shifting. I saw something—a figure?—cross out of the laboratory. What the hell was that? I turned back to the doll, half expecting her to have moved, but still she sat where she sat, inert in her corner.

Whatever it was, it was gone now.

The opposite end of the laboratory opened onto the central chamber, and from the pit I heard the demon make some kind of a popping chortle sound. Was he laughing at me?

Well, I don't much like being laughed at. I came out of the laboratory and walked right up to the pit. I guess I must have thought it was a good time for a father-daughter talk. Maybe I wanted to show him I wasn't afraid.

Only that's not what happened. What happened was this: When I stepped up to the pit, the demon was *right there.* He'd climbed up to the top of the pit and was wedged there just beneath the grating, and he had his enormous mouth-flap open. And even as I was stepping up to the pit with some smart remark on my lips, the demon Enyin—my father—breathed in. He inhaled.

Understand. This is a mouth that could swallow a moose at a gulp. This is a mouth like a cavern, and his breath was a wind, drawing me in. I was already moving forward, and the sudden suction was just enough to pull me down.

This is a moment I shall not forget. This moment of falling toward that mouth. *Mouth* is not the right word for it. It is a hole, ringed with teeth. A pit. And the pit was depthless. I saw things in the pit of Enyin's mouth-hole. Things... moving around in the abyss. Things that did not make sense. And into that madness I was falling.

Happily there was a nice solid grating between me and that abyss. I threw out my hands to break my fall, but one of my hands slipped and I jammed my wrist pretty badly, and my arm slipped through the grating. I also banged up my shoulder and the side of my head, but none of that was concerning me at the moment; what concerned me was my arm inside the mouth of a greater demon.

I yanked back my arm with a speed I didn't know I possessed, even as Enyin's hell-mouth closed with a terrible *whump*, close enough I felt the needle-like hairs around his lips brush the back of my hand. I rolled onto my back, trying to get away, but the demon shifted himself and he got hold of my hair in some secondary mouth I hadn't noticed before—a tiny little mouth to the side of his big one.

So there I was, lying on the grating while the demon had a mouthful of my hair. I thought to myself, this is a fine predicament. I also found myself wondering, just how many mouths does this guy have?

I could feel him working his mouth, keeping a tight hold of my hair while pulling more and more of it into his mouth. I couldn't lift my head, and I felt him tugging, tugging, tugging. His breath came in excited little bursts. And let me tell you, the stench of his breath was a thing far worse than the pain I felt in my wrist, shoulder, and head.

Well, if there was one thing I learned from my days with the Ostracks, it was this: Don't go anywhere without your knife. I'd learned that lesson well, and with my good hand I took out my knife and began to cut at my hair.

A few seconds later I was on my feet glowering down at my father. "Bad demon!"

"What are you doing?" demanded Korieski.

I turned to see him, half clothed, his jaw hanging open.

"Oh, nothing," I said, trying to play it cool. "Just checking on the big fellow." I put my knife away and tried to smooth out my hair where a giant chunk was now missing.

"Dak dak dak dak," called the demon, barking or laughing, as he slid down the wall, scrabbling and scratching, throwing off sparks, on his way back down to the floor of the pit.

Korieski stood next to me and gaped down at his pet demon. Enyin circled eagerly and hunkered down with intense interest. "Your hair," said Korieski.

I rubbed my sore shoulder. "I was ready to change my look anyhow."

"You've got him excited," observed Korieski. Then: "I want to try something. Go, quick—fetch the homunculus."

"The what? Oh!" I realized he was talking about the doll. So I ran to retrieve her from Korieski's laboratory while he hurtled off on his own errand. I was increasingly aware of the throbbing pain in my wrist and head, not to mention the still unquenched thirst which had drawn me out of Korieski's lair in the first place. But seeing the little doll in the corner looking up at me with a little twinkle in her eye helped me forget these discomforts. "You and I will be friends," I decided.

Korieski met me back in the great room. He was lugging a heavy glass bell jar. "Put her down there," he said. I gave the doll a little kiss and put her down where Korieski had pointed, a few feet from the lip of the demon's pit. Korieski raised an eyebrow at me before lowering the bell jar over the doll.

"Go to him now," commanded Korieski and gave me a little shove toward the pit.

"Hey," I complained.

"Please," implored Korieski. "Hurry. Excite him further."

So I went and looked down at the demon. He snorted up at me, tilting his head as he considered me.

"Hey ugly," I said. "Want some more hair?"

"Yes," said Korieski encouragingly. "Give it to him!"

So I took my knife and cut out another clump of my hair. Enyin circled in anticipation as I held it over the pit. "What's he going to do with it?"

"Eat it. He is a Devouring Demon. He eats everything."

"Oh." I worked the hair between my fingers, letting it rain down while Korieski busied himself marking the floor up with chalk. "Might as well finish the job," I decided, and I stepped out onto the grating and set to work hacking off my hair, letting it rain down on top of the demon, until I was more or less bald. For his part Enyin was silent during this operation, accepting my offerings with open maw.

I glanced over at Korieski, saw him with upraised palms, eyes open wide, mouthing some incantation.

"What exactly are you doing?" I asked him.

"I am making life—behold!"

And the little doll in the jar twitched a little.

"How about that?" I went over to have a closer look, ignoring the demon below who now began to wail, utterly dissatisfied with the meal of my hair.

Beyond her initial twitch, the doll remained motionless. Korieski stared hard, waiting. When she showed no further movement, he frowned deeply. "Hmmm," he said and stalked away, disappointed.

I reached out to lift the bell jar but over his shoulder Korieski commanded, "Leave it."

I was getting a little tired of his ordering me around and was about to say so, when the doll smiled at me.

Ha! She *was* alive, but too smart to show it. I followed after Korieski, savoring the little secret I shared with my new friend.

# CHAPTER 40

# Daughter of Enyin

Korieski was cranky after that and, truthfully, not nearly as much fun to be around. He blamed me for the failure of his experiment.

"What were you doing with the homunculus, earlier?" he demanded. "Did I see you *kiss* the homunculus?"

"What, are you jealous?" I tried to lure him to the bed, but it was no good. He pushed me away.

He pointed an accusing finger in my face. "What were you doing skulking about my laboratory earlier?"

"I wasn't skulking. I was looking for water."

"Do not lie to me, girl. You're up to something. Who are you, exactly? Who sent you? I'll have the truth." And behind him, all around us in fact, the shadows on the walls shifted, and I sensed the presence of unseen others—beings without substance, others like the one that had spooked me in the laboratory earlier.

I looked around, feeling impressed again with Korieski. "And who are these?"

"They are my creations, those whose hands built the walls around us, an army to do my bidding. My loyal servants. Shadows of Enyin."

"Shadows of Enyin," I said, raising my voice to be heard. "Meet daughter of Enyin." And I threw up my arms, just for dramatic effect.

Well, they reacted to that. There was a certain amount of rustling and hissing, and I could see them jostling about—vague primitive forms, almost rectangular, sliding along the walls like kites or very fine veils made of smoke.

"Daughter of... That is not possible," said Korieski, drawing back and looking a little uncertain.

"I am Elevaer, teller of truths. My mother was Hava, my father was Enyin." I crossed the chamber to Korieski's shrine. "I am Elevaer, daughter of Enyin, declaring myself a second time for Kaphador." And I reached out to touch the mask of Kaphador.

And I felt a warmth, not on my finger but within my heart, a warmth that radiated out to encompass my whole body. YOU ARE HEARD, DAUGHTER OF ENYIN, said the idol mask—and all the shadows went crazy, leaping off the walls and flapping madly about Korieski's lair, squeaking excitedly.

Korieski, utterly taken aback, fell on his rump in the chaos, throwing up his arms to protect his face against the frenzy of his disobedient minions. He gawked up at me in amazement as the shadow beings swirled around me. I saw fear in his eyes.

I took a step toward him and glowered down at him, enjoying the moment. You know what he said to me? He said, "I've never met a woman like you before." The poor devil was smitten with me.

Well, after that I had him wrapped around my finger. I gave him what he wanted—plus some extras he didn't know he wanted—and left him spent, asleep in his bed, while I slipped away to see my baby in the bell jar.

And there she was, waiting for me just where I left her. Too weak to lift the bell jar on her own, she had waited patiently for me. As soon as I lifted it, she leapt up and ran circles round the demon's pit. I laughed to see the cute little thing go. I put the bell jar down and clapped with delight. Enyin, for his part, was strangely quiescent down in his hole.

The homunculus leapt onto my shoulder and whispered in my ear. Such sweet things she whispered. She told me she was bound to me, not to Korieski. She told me I was pretty and how much fun we could have together. If she had her way, we would have killed Korieski and freed Enyin from the pit. But I didn't see the profit in that. Besides, I rather enjoyed Korieski. I may have been bored with him, but I didn't want him dead. I just wanted to steal his fantastic toys.

So I did. I took his staff with the twin serpent heads and I took his little homunculus. I would have taken his shadow minions, too, had they not been bound to the place. They grieved to see me go, I think, but they obeyed when I commanded them to open the gate. I found Korieski's boat and stole that, too. By the time he woke, I would be miles downriver.

My little Pretty ran up and down the boat, alive and free. We soon abandoned the boat and set it adrift. The jungle became our playground. The rainy season was still in force, but I didn't mind so much because my precious little Pretty made everything fun again. The world and everything in it was fresh and new to her. In her I'd found a true kindred spirit at last. Don't get me wrong, I'd enjoyed each of my playmates in turn: Korieski; poor Lukas the bastard son of Olio; the Ostracks whom I left to the gallows in Hajan port. But none of them compared to my precious little Pretty.

It was with my Pretty in the jungle I came into my power, sealing the deal with Kaphador under the cloud-shrouded moon in the slackening rain, witnessed by tree apes and chub toads.

If it weren't for my Pretty I would never have puzzled out the secrets of Korieski's staff of power. Once I learned the knack of it, I could summon myself another true friend: Tobias the bat. An infinitely useful fellow. Gleeful he was to call me master, glad to have escaped Korieski and just as eager to leave behind the Deep Valley Durez.

With Tobias our guide, my Pretty and I were never lost, for Tobias knew all there was to know of the Deep Valley Durez, knew enough certainly to live in terror of the many ways a little bat could meet his end in that place. He showed us a secret way out, a hidden way through the maze of caves and crevices in the southern wall of the valley.

And so we came out of that valley, and out of the Ucheti, and out of Soofia altogether, and by ship to ship to ship, all the way back to Lagin, back here to claim my birthright.

# CHAPTER 41

# The Elephant

"Wow," I said.

"I think it was destiny," said Elevaer, "you and I crossing paths here in Kortholomoth."

"I don't disagree."

"You must meet my Pretty."

I swallowed. "Is she… here?"

"Not at the moment, no. She comes around at night, mostly. I'm so excited for her to meet you. I'm dying to know what she thinks of your name. How did you come to have this name—Ejertine?"

I was beginning to wonder the same thing. Why would my father choose that name? "My dad was friends with Korieski's dad."

"Really?" She came and sat astride my lap again. "I guess we run in the same circles. Have you ever thought of becoming a Kaphadorian?"

"It had not occurred to me. I am, after all, a pagan."

"Still? Even after all you've seen, you doubt the power of the Alyonic gods?"

"I never doubted their power. It just never occurred to me I could be part of it. Being a Soofian."

"Kaphador doesn't care where you come from. As long as you have a soul, he wants it."

"So it can belong to him forever."

"Sure, but he doesn't collect until after you're dead. And if you stick with me and my little Pretty, you can live forever."

"How's that exactly?"

She smiled, leaned forward and covered my mouth with hers, smothering any further questions with a long kiss. Behind this kiss lay an insistent desire. My mind chased itself in circles.

It came as something of a relief when the door at the top of the stairs opened, and in irritation Elevaer gave me a chance to come up for air as she turned her head and called, "Yes?"

"Uncle asked me to check on you," said Kerig, the larger of the two ogres, a flaming torch in his hand.

"I'm *fine*," said Elevaer.

Kerig took in the scene and hesitated on the stairs. "So, should I go? Or you want I should work on him some?"

"I think you've worked on him quite enough, the poor dear." Elevaer climbed off my lap with a heavy sigh. "You might as well come down. The mood's ruined anyhow."

"Also, you wanted to know when the eagle left the nest."

"Well, finally," said Elevaer. "Out of curiosity how much did it take?"

"220, plus travel expenses."

Elevaer whistled. "It'll be worth it if they get Belchamp and Meida both."

Kerig came down and looked me over with his torch. "He'll be all right. What're we gonna do with him?" No malice in his eyes, just a cold professionalism.

Elevaer pulled at a tangle in her hair, considering Kerig's question. "Nothing. Little Pretty will come tonight. Let's see what she makes of our new friend. I, for one, like him and want to keep him."

I was out of witty things to say. I was too tired even to hold my head up.

I heard Elevaer sigh again and start upstairs.

"You need something?" asked Kerig. "Some water?"

I opened my eyes. I hadn't realized he was talking to me. "Water," I said.

"Or there's some swill down here," he offered, angling a thumb toward the barrels of sour mash. "It's not half bad."

"No, no," I said hastily. "Just some water. That would be lovely."

From the top of the stairs I heard Elevaer exclaim, "Papa! What are you doing down here?" just before she disappeared through the door, closing it quickly behind her.

*Papa? Surely she didn't mean...*

Meanwhile Kerig was helping himself to some sour mash. "Sure you don't want some?"

I closed my eyes again. "I thought you were getting me water."

"Naw. I never said that. I just asked if you *needed* some."

"Ah."

I listened to him sip loudly from the ladle.

"So this little Pretty," I said.

Slurp.

"You've seen her, have you?" I asked.

"Oh, yes."

"You can untie me, you know. I won't make trouble."

"Yeah, you will." Slurp.

"What's going to happen to me?"

"No idea," said Kerig. "She seems to like you, though. So does Uncle."

"So why am I being treated this way?"

"How should I know? I just work here."

It was around then I finally passed out, I think.

I awoke some time later to total darkness. That kind of absolute darkness one can find only underground.

There was no knowing how much time had passed. Only that smell of sour mash anchored me. Even my pain had become abstract, distant. I felt a floating sensation, like I was gently bobbing, weightless, in a sea of night.

Had I been dreaming? Someone was with me. Another presence, I was sure of it.

"Hello...?"

I tried moving, but the only thing I could move was my head—and when I did that, the bobbing sensation worsened. I was spinning through space now. No up, no down, only a void of nothingness.

I bit down on my tongue, to have something to focus on.

"Father...?" That was the presence I felt.

"I'm in a bad way, Father. I need some help."

The dark and silence persisted.

"Why did you name me Ejertine?"

SEE WHAT I SEE. What came then to my eyes was a vision of an opulent chamber. A bed loomed large before me, as if I were sitting on the floor at the foot of that bed looking up at it. And on the edge of the bed sat a man in his nightgown, hunched over and diminished, clutching a raggedy, dirty doll to his breast and weeping bitterly. HERE IS YOUR SAVIOR. HERE IS WHO HAVA CHOSE.

I leaned into the vision, looking carefully at the weeping man. Was this then Encho Nipalto?

"Is this upstairs? What am I seeing?"

A new spasm of weeping overtook Encho, and he lay down in the bed. Now I was looking at the soles of his feet.

The vision faded. I felt my father slip away. I was left alone again in the cellar.

What had I been dreaming about?

I was with Odeker, my father, crossing a great desert. But it was not Odeker as I knew him; this was a much younger man. My father when he was my age, when he still wandered the earth, having his adventures.

There was an elephant, dying in the dirt. But my father whispered into her ear, "There is no need to go, not when you can stay with me forever."

There was someone else there, someone other than Odeker or me or the dying elephant. But who was that other person? I tried to turn my head and look, but my head did not want to turn. Or maybe I did turn my head and the world turned with it, preventing me from seeing who was there. But there was a *smell.* I could smell him.

Perhaps it was the sour mash invading my dream. But no: It was the musk of the dwerrig I smelled.

Having identified his scent, now I had the power to see him, and I forced my head to turn and look at him, even though it really didn't want to.

That's what woke me from the dream. The sight of the dwerrig, that same dwerrig I'd encountered on the trail over my village so long ago. His knowing look, gazing back into my eyes, was something terrible. He was *awake*, an invader watching my dream from afar.

Had there been someone else there as well? Just as I wakened myself in a panic, I thought I saw a figure on a dune perhaps a thousand yards out, watching us. A queer-looking fellow, bolt upright and tall with a hat, dressed in gleaming white.

# CHAPTER 42

# A Voice in the Dark

When the door at the top of the stairs opened, I could only assume they were coming to mistreat me further.

The light of morning blasted into the cellar, blinding me. I couldn't see for the light, but I could hear them on the stairs, grunting and shuffling. They were hauling something heavy—and as my eyes adjusted to the light I saw it was a dead Laginese woman, naked, withered and wet. They flopped her unceremoniously at my feet, her head lolling in my direction. Some violence had been visited across her eyes, deep scratches having destroyed the orbs in their sockets.

"That's what's waiting for you," promised Kerig with a laugh, starting back upstairs.

In that space of time during which the men ascended the stairs and the light remained, what I noticed in the woman was not so much the ruined eyes as the calm lines of her face. A face to which joy visited easily and frequently. She, the dead, and I, the nearly dead, regarded one another for a moment before we were shut in the darkness together.

*Who was she?* I wondered. Even then a part of me knew, or at least suspected, I was culpable in her death. It was my decisions, my words, my deeds that triggered a series of events leading up to this moment. Such dark thoughts chased one another around the inside of my skull.

Only seconds after the cellar door closed, I became aware of an unusual clicking sound. Not a mechanical click, but something organic. I thought nothing of it at first, but the sound repeated itself several times at irregular intervals, and I thought I could hear something else—a high wheeze between the clicks. Then there came a voice, very quiet but very angry. "Now you listen to me," said the voice.

The voice startled me badly and I jumped, bound though I was. This was not a voice in my head like my dead father's, but a real voice, speaking in my native Soofian. As my mind raced for explanations, I could only assume it was the dead woman who had spoken.

I fell backwards in my chair, a terrible moment of free-fall followed by a flash of white light as my head collided with the floor.

# CHAPTER 43

# Not My First Homunculus

I was someone else, walking. A woman. Muscular legs propelled me effortlessly, my easy strides passing slower persons in the street. The sun was shining down on my hair and shoulders. I was healthful and young, with no memory of Ejertine or coal cellars.

But slowly, a muffled, darkened world of pain returned to me. Someone very far away was poking me with his boot. "Hello?"

"Forget de Soofian," said the same little voice that had spooked me so.

I tried to open my eyes.

"I can't just leave him here like this," said the other voice, a man's, gentle but insistent. "Go and keep an eye out. Let me know if anyone is coming."

Who was standing over me? I tried to see, but he had turned away now.

Why was my hair wet?

I closed my eyes again. The effort to keep them open had exhausted me. I may have momentarily fallen asleep again, but was startled awake again by the motion of my chair being lifted from the floor.

I tried to say something but only a grunt came out. The room was spinning.

I tried to focus. My chair had been spun round to face away from the stairs. No one was in front of me, but behind me I sensed movement. A puddle of dark fluid on the floor. My own blood, I realized dimly. "What's happening?" I said, finally.

"I think I'm rescuing you. This may hurt."

It did indeed hurt. Blood-flow returned to my arms as my rescuer cut my bonds, one by one. I tried to swallow as much of the pain as I could, but my vision darkened around the edges and I lost a few moments.

"My name is Encho Nipalto," said the man behind me.

The name brought me out of my haze. "You're Encho? Wow! I'm Ejertine," I said hurriedly. I paused, waiting for him to recognize my name. Surely Hava had spoken of me. "From Soofia. Did Hava never mention me?"

"No," said Encho. Then, sensing my disappointment, he added hastily, "Perhaps she did and I forgot. She had a great many friends, you understand."

*Of course she didn't talk about me.* "She talked about *you* all the time."

"She did?"

"Oh, yes."

I was startled when he came around and I caught sight of him for the first time, his nose badly broken, blood streaming down his little beard. The front of his nightgown was saturated with blood, clinging wet to his frail little frame.

Having freed my arms, Encho rotated my chair to face me toward the light, so he could see the knots securing my legs to the chair. The dead woman was there again at my feet, still looking up at me with her ruined eyes.

I tried to move my arms, but to my horror they hung limp like dead things. Would they ever work again?

I glanced up at the stairs, several compelling questions competing for expression as Encho knelt and worked on freeing my legs.

Something brushed against my ear and hair, startling me. A quick motion and that voice again: "Papa man! Papa man! She's inna House! You gots to go! Quicky de quick!"

"I can't just leave him," pleaded Encho, glancing up at—something passing overhead?

The little voice came from a different direction now. "Run, papa man! She is coming to harvest dis one. You don wand to be heres for dat."

*Harvest?*

Even if Encho had had time to finish cutting me loose, I was in no shape to go anywhere. Encho needed to save himself while he still could.

"Go," I said.

"Go," echoed the little voice.

But still Encho hesitated, until at the top of the stairs there came a sound—a strange little voice singing, "Well, what have we here?"

Only then did Encho take his knife and hide himself behind the coal chute. It was good he did, because in that instant the rectangle of light at the top of the stairs was slightly disturbed: a scant sliver in the lower left corner showing the silhouette of a tiny figure.

"Awwww," called the abomination, mocking me from the top of the stairs. "Did someone play rough with you?"

I tried to understand what I was seeing. Some nightmare caricature of a child's toy, brought to life. Like one of Korieski's homunculi from the jungle, but cruder, larger, more menacing.

Down the stairs she came loping, skipping three steps at a time. "Tree heee heee, treee heee heee!" I nearly fell over backwards again, recoiling from her. Directly onto my lap she catapulted herself, latching onto my right thigh with needle-like claws.

The one advantage I had was this: My tiny adversary did not know I was partially free. With the rush of panic, some limited control of my arms had returned. I could use my large muscles, and use them I did, swinging my left arm, club-like, dislodging her from my lap and sending her tumbling gracelessly to the floor.

I did not hesitate then. I had to be Olio if I was going to get out of this.

Before she could recover, I used what mobility I had to tip my chair sideways, falling on top and pinning the demon-toy to the floor. This was not my first time fighting an evil homunculus; and if there was one thing I'd learned from Olio, it's that you've got to pin these little varmints down to have any hope of beating them.

But if Elevaer's little Pretty was now trapped under my chair, neither could I escape her claws, and she used them, frantically scratching deep trenches into my flank. "Eeeee! Let me go!" Both of us were screaming at that point. If no one upstairs had heard us yet, surely they would now.

My fingers were useless sausages, but I could use my thumbs sufficiently to get hold of the squirming nightmare with both hands. There followed searing pain as her fangs penetrated the fleshy part of my right hand. I cried out but did not let go.

Shifting my weight, I pulled her out from under the chair, squeezing for all I was worth. I had a tight hold of her now, and even now I was discovering new unpleasant surprises of the sharp and painful variety stuffed inside and sewn throughout her body. But I did not let go. She hissed, she cut, but still I held tight.

Desperately I tried to rise, but I had only one leg partially free of the chair.

"I'll bleed you out," promised the homunculus and went for my wrists.

What would Olio do? That's the question I asked myself in this situation. So I did what Olio would have: I took hold of her head with my teeth and I tore for all I was worth. I was rewarded with a ripping sound and a shrill scream. Wires and—spiders!— came spilling from the rend in the head of Elevaer's little Pretty. Despite myself I could not help reacting to the spiders—and I let her slip from my hands. Immediately I realized my mistake and made a grab, but it was too late, she was on the move.

Unnoticed by both the homunculus and myself, Encho had emerged from his hiding place with a pair of metal tongs, which he utilized with impressive dexterity to seize hold of the homunculus firmly by the torso. Kicking and screaming, her torn head dangling and flopping, she cried, "Eeeeeee! Let me go! I'll skin you alive. Let me go!" But Encho did not let go, even when the spiders came crawling up the tongs.

I was still desperately brushing away the spiders from my face and arms. With my arms free I started to right myself. The chair had broken on its last fall, and I found I was able to break it completely into two parts, and then stand with the broken chair still dangling from me. My legs, however, so much abused, were not ready to support me, and I fell once more to the floor. With all the noise, I was certain Elevaer or one of her unfriendly helpers would appear. But they did not. Perhaps they'd been trained to ignore screaming.

Seeing who had hold of her, Elevaer's little Pretty ceased her flailing and was silent for a beat. Then she erupted into an unearthly fit of giggles. "You? The cuckold? Tree heee heee heee heeee! Bleee feee beetle dee! Tweedle needle deeee! What'll it be, Papa Dear? I'll make a puppet from your bones, and we'll dance and dance, now won't we?"

With a sudden twist and lurch, she tried to break free—but Encho was ready for that and held firm to the grips. "Where's Ichito?" growled Encho, ignoring the several spiders of various sizes crawling up his neck.

"Crawl in his ears! Bite his eyes!" commanded Elevaer's little Pretty.

Encho was only slightly startled, and recovered quickly, when something fast and nearly invisible wicked away the spiders in rapid succession. His little talking friend—a bat!

By this time I had regained my feet, wobbling more than a little, with pieces of the chair still dangling from me. I saw a knife on the shelf and instinctively I reached for it. Seeing the wreck of my hands was a little off-putting, I must say. Wet red holes punctured right through, with blood welling up as I watched. Despite this damage to the flesh of my hands, my fingers (most of them at least) were starting to work, and so I picked up the knife and turned to the struggling homunculus at the end of the tongs. "You hold, I cut."

"No!" screamed the thing in evident terror.

I went to work. And sloppy work it was. At first I hacked at her with little effect, although I was able to shave off some claws and wire bits, and I tore some rends in her outer sack. What proved more effective was taking hold of an extremity and then sawing with the serrated blade. In this way I was able to remove whole pieces of her body. Sand and sawdust and nails and other debris came spilling out, collecting on the floor in a scattered heap, wet with my dripping blood.

Throughout, Elevaer's little Pretty screamed and pleaded and threatened, her puppet head hanging open. Even when I removed the head, the horrid voice continued unabated. Finally, when she was little more than a tangle of wires and a torn sack, her verbal assault trailed off into incoherent gurgles and growls, punctuated by occasional profanity. Then—suddenly, the voice changed. A girl's voice: "Father?"

Encho dropped the tongs, then, and cried, "Ichito? Is it you?"

With that, the tortured remains of the homunculus skittered away, disappearing beneath the coal shelf, tittering to itself. "Tree heee heeee! I can't believe you fell for that."

Wobbling, I turned to Encho and took hold of the sleeve of his bloody nightgown. "Let's go."

He stood, shaking, looking stunned. "Ichito?"

"Come on," I said, pulling him toward the stairs, shedding the last of my bonds.

"Not dat way, stupids! Up de coal chute wid de twos of you, quicky de quick!"

"Wait," said Encho, looking back toward the shelf.

"Leave it, papa man," said the bat. "Lil pretty gone get chew!"

"I'm not afraid of her anymore," said Encho, glaring into the space under the shelf where he expected the homunculus crouched, returning his gaze. "Let her come," he said, trembling though he was. "I'd like another turn with her to finish the job." With that, he approached the shelf and picked up a doll—the same raggedy doll I'd seen him clutching in my vision.

"Come on," I said, tugging on Encho's arm. I was keeping a wary eye on the rectangle of light at the top of the stairs. Amazingly, no one had come despite all the commotion.

Up the coal chute we climbed, myself in the lead since I was the more injured. At the top was a hatch, and when I pushed, it opened into daylight and fresh air. It was a bit of a squeeze, getting my shoulders through, but I was highly motivated.

And so it was that the castle of House Nipalto excreted two bloody and coal-blackened persons onto the floor of the back alley. Blinking in the sunlight, we struggled to our feet.

"Get you gone now," said the bat, fluttering around our heads. "Lil pretty gone wake up Elevaer. You gots to go!" Was this then Tobias? Elevaer's bat? Why was he helping us?

"This way," said Encho. "The Temple is not far." But my legs refused to support me, and I had to depend on Encho. He was much too short and I far too tall for this arrangement to work well for either of us, and our lurching forward progress was far from graceful or speedy.

The pair of us limped along unmolested, like some hybrid mutant. We made quite a pair as we emerged from the alley onto Green Street. Myself a tall Soofian with my breeches shredded and bloody, blood dripping from open wounds on my hands, my hair matted with blood; and my companion, a diminutive man in his blood-soaked nightgown and wrecked face, clutching a child's doll; both of us barefoot and covered in soot and looking half-dead.

I could hardly blame the family of passersby who gathered themselves close and crossed over to the other side of the avenue so as to avoid us; nor could I fault the gawking tradesmen in the back of a passing wagon or the driver who whipped his horses to speed past us.

"Why won't anyone help us?" asked Encho miserably. If he'd been alone, no doubt someone would have stopped and helped. But with a seven-foot-tall Soofian glued to him? That changed things, didn't it?

We had no choice but to lean on one another and make our way as best we could, falling frequently, crawling at times upon the hot pavement.

So it was that Encho saved me, rather than the other way around.

# CHAPTER 44

# The Mural

Now, this was my first time visiting a Morphidian temple. I'd never had occasion to enter one before. Never felt like a place I was *allowed* to enter, frankly. Seeing its great, golden dome looming, the largest I'd ever seen, I was not sure what sort of reception a pagan Soofian like myself could expect in such a place.

But to the credit of these Morphidians, when we arrived bleeding at their gate, three young acolytes, hardly more than boys, seeing our injuries, rushed to meet us, and I more or less collapsed into their arms. No words were exchanged, they merely accepted me and, with one of them cradling my head, they carried me.

Giving myself over to them, I sank into a dreamless stupor.

I don't know how long I was out.

I remember waking to the intricate mosaic tile-work embedded in the vaulted ceiling, scenes of filthy, naked, hungry wretches gathering to receive mercy, healing and food from gleaming priests in white, who drew their power from Morphid in the heavens.

When I rolled my head to the side, I saw that I lay in the first of a long row of simple beds, all empty except for one where a young lady lay sleeping. The ward was otherwise empty and quiet, a calm, steady light falling through high windows.

As my eyes returned to the mosaic on the ceiling, I couldn't help but notice, off at the periphery, a depiction of Morphidians with armor and swords holding back a Soofian horde, mixed with Grithis and dragons and… was that supposed to be an great bear?

I closed my eyes again. Where was Encho?

Morphidians were famous for their healing powers. But also for sticking their swords into pagans.

I wanted to look at my hands, to see if they had been miraculously healed. But I was asleep now, and in my dream when I looked at my hands, I was bewildered to see not my own hands but someone else's—the slender hands of a woman.

"Hello there," said the stranger, standing over my bed in the desert. How long had he been there? I recognized him at once as the white-clad observer on the sand dune from my earlier dream. Up close, he looked even stranger: his skin was translucent white, his eyes were without pigment, his hair was long and pure white and astonishingly well-brushed. He was dressed in an immaculate white suit.

"This is a dream," I observed.

"Indeed so. I must apologize for my intrusion."

I sat up in my bed, looked around at the sandy, scrubby terrain, the dim unearthly light. "What is this place? Why is it familiar?"

"That is for you to say, I expect."

"Who are you then?" I asked sharply, turning to the stranger and finding my feet. "I've seen you before."

"Ikkada Damada," he said, inclining his head. His hands grasped a tall hat, which unlike the rest of his outfit, appeared tattered and a little flame-scorched. "Mystan of the Third Orb, at your service."

"Mystan."

"Correct. Your friend Olio asked me to find you."

There was some good news! "Tell him I'm at the Temple of Morphid."

"He knows. He is there with you, at your bedside."

"How long have I been asleep?"

"Not long. Come—walk with me." He put on his hat. I noticed in his other hand a crystalline cane, sparkling somehow in the gloomy light.

We walked together over a cracked earth. "Why are you here?" I asked him. "In my dream?"

"Discretion. Expediency. Curiosity. Duty. This inquiry is part of a larger investigation."

"Investigation?"

We wandered without direction. There was no path. Just desert plants pushing their way up here and there at random through the meager, sandy soil.

"That was an interesting dream you experienced earlier. The one with your father and the elephant and… that other uninvited guest. That's what attracted my attention; it's not everyone who has a dwerrig eavesdropping on his dreams."

I swallowed. "What exactly are you investigating?"

"And that you *noticed* the dwerrig. And noticed me as well. Most impressive."

Up ahead I saw the elephant, lying on her side, her breathing labored. I stopped, not wanting to go closer. "But this is not even my dream, is it? This is my father's dream. One of his memories."

"How interesting," said the Mystan, turning his cane in the dirt thoughtfully. "Do you often share dreams with others?"

"I don't think so," I said. "Maybe?"

"Tell me about your father."

"Um." I glanced over at the dying elephant.

"A shaman, perhaps?"

"How did you know that? No, he was never a true shaman, but he aspired to be one."

"He must have recognized the potential in you."

I paused, looking the Mystan in his unusual eyes. Unaccustomed as I was to conversation with someone of equal height, I found myself a little surprised to find his eyes so close to mine. "What do you mean when you say, 'potential'?"

"Do you ever see spirits? Converse with the dead?"

My jaw dropped.

"I thought so. And what, pray tell, is your relationship with the dwerrig?"

I shook my head. "I don't have a relationship with the dwerrig. I mean, I had one encounter with him, some twenty years ago, back in Soofia, outside my village. I never saw him again."

"Did he not tell you about the curse?"

"What?"

"Why do you think he's been following you from place to place?"

"What!"

I moved quickly away from him, and away from the dying elephant. "This is just a dream," I told myself.

Up ahead, I saw my father coming down the hillside—young and energetic, toting a rucksack. He waved at me cheerfully, his eyes sparkling.

"She's over here," I called. My voice was not my own; it was Hava's.

Why was I having my father's dream?

Why was I *Hava* in my father's dream?

Drawn in by the dream logic, I took Odeker, my father, to the elephant. He knelt beside the elephant's head, lifting her ear, whispering.

I wanted to wake up.

"Wait," said the voice of Ikkada Damada. "Not yet!"

But my eyes were already opening. I saw the Morphidian mosaic on the ceiling. And there at my bedside, as promised, was Olio, his caterpillar-eyebrows knitted with consternation. When he saw my eyes open, his demeanor brightened all at once. "Thank the gods you're all right! You're at the Temple of Morphid."

"I know."

"He's all right," said Olio.

I heard a footfall and turned to see another man step up to the foot of my bed: a broad-shouldered Trossman wearing a breastplate and looking very much ready for war. Very much like one of the figures from the mural.

I looked away from the imposing Morphidian and then down at my hands. My skin was smooth, clean and unbroken. "They fixed me." Amazing!

"You're going to be all right," said Olio. "They said you just need to stay off your feet. You're gonna feel drained for a couple days."

"Do you think I could sit up?" I did not want to look at the ceiling mural anymore. I'd had my fill of symbology and craved engagement with the real world. With someone solid like Olio.

Olio helped me sit up. "Yezimeyer, could you let them know he's awake? See if they can bring him some of that broth. You'll like it, lad, it's got these dainty little mushrooms floating in it."

I looked at the big man at the foot of my bed, a heavy battle mace dangling from his belt. He made no move to comply with Olio's request. "Did you say *Yezimeyer?*"

"Do you know me?" he said, his voice resonant and powerful.

"No," I said, pursing my lips. "But I know *about* you. For example, you never have to pee."

Olio blinked and put his calloused hand upon my brow. "Are you feeling all right?"

"Your friend speaks truth," said Yezimeyer. "Like your Mizen Tower, I am sustained by Morphid and have no need of food nor water, nor elimination, nor any such base need."

"What are you doing *here?*" I wanted to know.

"I have come hunting a demon spawn."

"Ah."

"We can't talk here," said Olio, looking over his shoulder. "Ejertine, I should never have left you–"

"It's all right," I said.

"No, it ain't. What happened to you is my fault. If I woulda listened to you, none of this woulda happened."

"That may be true," I said. "But I'll have no apologies from you. I can't count how many times you've saved my life. But Olio—I must know. Did you find the girl? Is she all right?"

"Yes, she's safe and sound. Back with her singing troupe, and that's the best place for her just now."

"But–"

Olio sanctioned me with his finger. "Later. For now, food, water, rest."

"All right. But Olio. Listen. There's something you should know."

"Whatever it is, it can wait."

"Olio. You have a son."

The blood drained from the poor man's face. "What did you say?" He shook his head. "That's not possible."

"With Sieve Sveka. From Shamp."

Olio sat heavily upon the bed.

"His name is Lukas."

"Lukas," repeated Olio, staring off into nothing.

"He wants very much to meet you. But Elevaer left him wounded in Soofia. Now, I don't know for sure if he's even alive."

"I have a son..."

Yezimeyer folded his arms. "This man you speak of. Lukas. I know this man. He is alive. Or he was when I left him."

Olio and I both gaped at him. "Well, where did you leave him?" I asked finally.

"In King's Prison, outside Wahl Dahldin."

Olio put his hand to his head. "My son is a reprobate."

"No," I said. "He's got a good heart, Olio. He just got mixed up with Elevaer."

"Your son is the reason she escaped my custody to begin with."

Olio looked up at Yezimeyer through teary eyes. "My son... outfoxed you?"

Yezimeyer scowled.

My old friend regained his feet and wiped his eyes on his sleeve. "A chip off the old block, innit?" Half his mouth was smiling while the other half quivered.

We were alone in the long healing ward, but I could hear a murmured conversation on the stairs to my left. "How much time has passed?" I asked. "Where's Encho?"

"Encho! Have you seen Encho?"

"He was here, with me. He's the one who saved me from Elevaer."

"Shh," said Olio, glancing toward the stairs.

"Elevaer's not here, is she?" I asked, horror struck.

"No, no," said Olio. "But there are ears everywhere."

"The local High Morphidian does not share my philosophy," said Yezimeyer by way of explanation. "But I will not be shushed in the House of my Lord. If we cannot speak freely Here, then we should depart this Place."

"My friend can't depart," said Olio. "He needs to recuperate."

"I should like very much to depart," I said, glancing up at the mural. I knew if I lay back down, I would fall instantly asleep and be confronted again with dreams I was not ready to face. "What happened to my clothes?" I looked down at a flimsy gown scarcely long enough to cover me.

"They didn't have anything your size," explained Olio. "But we'll get you sorted. Come on, then, up with you."

My bones were weary, but it felt good to stand under my own power.

"I've got a place," said Olio, "where we can talk and be among friends. But we need to find Encho. He's not here at the Temple, or I would have seen him by now. Did he say anything to you?"

"He was in a pretty bad way himself. I'm surprised he's not here. To be honest, I don't even know what day it is."

Olio rubbed the back of his neck. "There's only two places he would go. But neither is a good option for us right now."

I patted him gently on the back. "No longer rushing in head-long, I see. You really *have* grown."

Olio growled slightly. "I'm going to carry you up these stairs now, and I'll have no argument."

# CHAPTER 45

# Broth Before Soup

"Olio, there's something else," I said as we walked together with Yezimeyer down the tree-lined street. I felt half naked in my gown but utterly safe with these two well-armed and intimidating men at my side.

"Wait'll we get where we're going," said Olio, glancing over his shoulder.

"We being followed?" I whispered.

"I don't think so, but not taking any chances. Come on." Olio turned us suddenly leftward onto a lesser street and made us wait in the bushes to see if anyone came after us. No one did.

Once he was satisfied, Olio led us down the street into the lower city. I was duly impressed by Olio's precautions, but Yezimeyer was not. "I agreed to come with you, sir, but I will not *skulk*."

"All right," said Olio. "Come on. Just don't want any of the wrong people taking notice. We've got people to protect."

The sun hung low over the bay, anchoring me in time. It would be dark in a few hours.

"You doing all right there, buddy?" asked Olio.

"Tired but good." It was good to be alive, to have survived my ordeal, to walk again in the daylight.

Olio led us downhill into the lower city, past a series of tall fences and warehouses, through a gap in the fence. Inside was a weedy lot where a gang of monkeys loitered amongst a heap of broken pottery, rusted metallic rings and discarded rotting rope encrusted with barnacles.

A solitary figure in a sailor's hat and a long, ragged blanket stood sentry at the far end of the lot and as we approached, Olio nodded to him. The whiskered, weathered man returned the gesture, looking past us toward the gap in the fence to make sure no one followed.

"Gusaf," said Olio to me. "A good man. He worked for Al-akhar before being put out of work by Elevaer."

We entered a dilapidated warehouse smelling of must and decay. Half a dozen persons were busy clearing out debris to make sections of the warehouse useable. I smelled ghorma stew, and through the open door at the far end of the warehouse, I saw a big lady stirring an enormous steaming pot.

A strapping, armed man about my age came forward to meet Olio, and they embraced fiercely. "Marden, old friend, I'm glad they were able to track you down. We have need of your sword arm." I felt only the slightest twinge of jealousy at the warmth of their friendship.

"You're looking pale," observed Yezimeyer, steadying me with his hand. "Even for a Soofian."

I did feel a bit light-headed.

"When's the last time you ate something?" demanded Olio. "Come on, there's a chair over here." He cleared a path, kicking aside some old, broken pallets. He beat the cushioned chair with his hand to raise a cloud of dust. "I told you you should have taken some of that Morphidian soup before we left the Temple."

I let the dust dissipate a bit before settling myself into the old chair.

"I'll check on yonder stew," said Yezimeyer.

"Yonder stew," repeated Olio when Yezimeyer was out of earshot. "Trossmen talk funny."

Marden asked, "Who've you brought us then? That Trossman looks solid."

"This Soofian's useful in a scrap as well," said Olio.

Marden considered me doubtfully. "Where's his clothes?"

"Shredded by a demented homunculus," I said flatly.

Olio shook his head. "What are you talking about?"

I sighed wearily. "Elevaer's a witch proper now. She's in league with dark powers. Olio—she's been to Soofia, she found Korieski, she met her father. She brought back a living demon-doll who wanted to harvest my soul."

Yezimeyer, returning with a steaming bowl, said, "What's this then?"

"Olio, you would have been so proud of me. I channeled you, I think, and that is how I survived. Encho and me, we destroyed it. Or maimed it, at least. There wasn't much of it left when we made our escape."

"Well done," said Yezimeyer approvingly. He knelt beside my chair, his mace dragging across the floor, and passed the bowl to me. "It's just the broth," he said. "She was reluctant to let me have this."

"Madam Kroduselentsi," said Olio. "Queen of the kitchen, long-time cook for the Nipaltos. She's out on the street now, like these others—thanks to Elevaer."

My hands, I found, were not steady enough to manage the operation of moving the bowl to my lips; and seeing my struggle, Yezimeyer took the soup back from me. "Allow me." He blew on the soup to cool it, and very gently, he held the bowl to my lips and allowed me a little taste. Not bad for ghorma stew in a back alley.

"It was a brave thing you did," said Yezimeyer. "If anything remains of that demon-shard, rest assured I will find and destroy it."

I took a little more soup, burning the roof of my mouth. But it was worth it. "And what about Elevaer? Will you find and destroy her as well?"

"The High Morphidian of Kortholomothamadhi has forbidden me."

"She has bribed him, the Magistrate, the Dock Master and everyone else who matters in this city," said Olio.

Yezimeyer shook his head. "One cannot *bribe* a High Morphidian. No, his obstinance on this matter derives from a sincere if misguided belief that the witch has her place in our society. His philosophy does not distinguish one brand of witchery from another."

"Call it what you will," said Olio. "She owns half this city, and she's got Baz's gang behind her, too. Feels like the whole damn city is under her thumb."

"Elevaer said something during my interrogation. I think she's sent a band of killers to Shamp to take out Belchamp."

Olio shook his head sadly. "She's not wasting any time. It makes sense. He is a direct threat to her. He can challenge the legitimacy of her claim."

"We're going to have to work together on multiple fronts to have a chance of stopping her." Olio looking meaningfully at Yezimeyer, whose whole attention now seemed focused on feeding me.

"Gather round, everyone," called Olio. "We need to do a few things before dark. Totsy and Erabeth—spread word to the urchins that there's a silver piece waiting for the one who finds Master Encho or our young Ichito. And check in with our eyes on the House and the shop. Franklin and Penny—measure our friend here, he'll need some decent clothes and a knife as well. Take what you need from the pot."

"About that," said Franklin. A small, dark-skinned man with fine features, Franklin tried to make himself smaller.

"Don't tell me we've spent the cash already."

"We've a lot of mouths to feed," said Madam Kroduselentsi.

"Madam, just have our supper ready for us when we return tonight. You are a blessing. I will see about securing some additional funds. Carrie, can you make sure Ejertine here has a pallet and a clean place to sleep, close to the fire?"

"I have the funds you require," said Yezimeyer. "Assuming you have the means to exchange a diamond?"

Olio's eyes lit up. "Marden, I want you on this," he said, pointing at Yezimeyer. "Take Gusaf with you."

I took the bowl from Yezimeyer so he could fish out a tiny black bag from within his breastplate.

I found I could feed myself now, and did so while we all watched Yezimeyer open his little black bag and extract a tiny glittering stone.

Olio whistled. "How many of those you got? We could hire a small army, eh?"

"Never mind," said Yezimeyer, tying his bag closed again and eyeing us all with suspicion. "I am entrusted with the resources to complete my mission successfully."

"Thank you," said Olio, holding out his hand.

Yezimeyer gave him the diamond, saying, "Consider this a gift from the Temple of Wahl Dahldin, a beginning to redressing the harms done by the Nominian menace." I didn't fully comprehend what he meant by *Nominian menace* but assumed he was referring to Elevaer.

Everyone went into action then. Penny made me stand for a few moments while she took my measurements with a twine.

I was impressed with how Olio had gathered and organized all these people. So this is what he had been doing while I was in the clutches of the city guard and then Elevaer. "Olio, How did you find me?"

"I would have found you, regardless. But one of Mother Etebe's queer friends found you first."

"Ikkada Damada?"

"That's right. You met him?"

"Sort of. Odd fellow, is he?"

"Odd as they come, I'd say."

"Elevaer is afraid of them, you know. The Mystans."

Yezimeyer chuckled.

Olio, a little surprised, asked, "Elevaer is afraid of Mystans?"

"Yeah. That's mostly what she asked me about. She was especially afraid of Hava."

"A demon-spawn afraid of a Mystan," laughed Yezimeyer. "Did she say anything about me?"

"Well, yes. But I don't think she knows you're here, in Kortholomoth."

Olio rubbed my shoulder. "Sounds like you extracted a lot more information outta her than she got from you, eh?"

"Olio, I'm glad you're being careful. She knows about you. She used your name. She's got her guys looking for you."

"I'm looking forward to our next reunion," said Olio.

# CHAPTER 46

# Our Dream in the Forest

Every part of me was weary, and when Carrie showed me to my pallet I lay myself down. Even I had to admit that I needed rest. Olio had everything well in hand.

The truth, of course, was that I was afraid to face my dreams.

I looked up at the overcast sky. A better view by far than that creepy Morphidian mosaic.

The day was still in motion around me. People coming and going, the shouts from the nearby harbor. Such commotion did not bother me. I was accustomed to sleeping in the raucous swaying belly of a Sartan ship.

And so I confronted my fears and surrendered myself to sleep, come what may.

The evidence of the past hours and days, the words of the white-haired Mystan: I could no longer deny that I was my father's son, that something of his shamanic ways continued in me. Olio didn't want to hear it, but Hava's spirit was here, trying to communicate.

Calm and with intention, I entered the realm of sleep. I walked along a curving corridor with many doors. I could open any door I desired, but the door I chose was the one that led to the desert and the dream of the dying elephant.

We'd been tracking her for days across the Hartan peninsula. She knew she was dying; she was probably trying to return to the jungles of her birth, impossibly distant though they were.

"Look there," said Odeker. A crater in the earth, recently enlarged. And within this hole a puddle of muddy water. "You can see where she was digging."

Odeker unshouldered his rucksack and took the opportunity to fill his canteen while I searched the immediate area. Tracks, elephant or otherwise, crisscrossed the surrounding land. Evidently this was a well-known watering hole.

There was a small hillock here with some old stones atop it, and as I crested the slope I saw ahead what I had been looking for. What I had dreaded.

She lay on her side, a gray heap, breathing, her ear turning itself slowly over.

My heart dropped. What had I been expecting? What had I hoped for?

I doubled back to find Odeker.

This is not my father's dream at all. This is Hava's dream. I am Hava.

Here he came, picking his way down the facing hillside. He waved at me cheerfully, his eyes sparkling. He didn't know yet.

"She's over here," I called, voice catching in my throat.

He tightened his mouth and came along. I watched him come. A pleasant man to look at, I had to admit.

I entertained the idea, for just a moment, of giving in to Odeker's charms. Would it be so bad, at the fire tonight, if his arms fit so nicely around me? Who would be harmed by this?

But it was just the elephant messing with my emotions. By the time Odeker closed the distance, the moment had passed.

We went together to the place where she lay. She tried to lift her head at our approach, but she was too weak.

Odeker took out his canteen and knelt, emptying its contents into her mouth. The elephant's eye looked up at me where I stood watching.

"Sing something," said Odeker. "It'll soothe her."

I woke then in the forest. How long had I been asleep?

The river, the dark canopy, the chill of night. Reality was slow to reassert itself. Wasn't I–?

Wasn't I someone else there for a minute? I shook my head to clear it.

Ejertine? Funny, I haven't thought of him in years.

No, it was Odeker. I was having the elephant dream again.

Groaning, I rose and went to the river. I lay on the bank and splashed my face with cool water. Still lying on my belly, I gave myself a laugh. Odeker? Really? I had one lusty thought about a man thirty years ago, and it was still weighing on my conscience. He was way too old for me, but he did have his charms.

Wait. Was I still dreaming?

The water's surface, an inky black, was a mirror, shifting imperceptibly, darkness within darkness gurgling quietly, folding in upon itself. I wanted to go into that water, to lose myself in it, to be swallowed.

"Time enough for that later," promised the river, using the voice of my mother.

Definitely dreaming. I wasn't even camped next to the river at all, come to think of it. That's several days ahead.

I noticed then the presence of someone else here in the dream with me, a ghostly white reflection in the water.

"Hava Nipalto, I presume," said Ikkada Damada.

I rolled over and sat up, surprised but not afraid to see the legendary Mystan standing in the forest of my dreams. "Master Damada? What brings you to my dream? Has something happened?"

"A great many things have, indeed, happened. I have been called in to investigate."

We looked at each other, his strange eyes searching mine.

Finally, he said, "I remember you now. You, too, were a Mystan, like me. We met once, years ago, at the Tesedog."

I could never forget it. The great master had made an appearance at the Tesedog for his Confirmation to the Third Orb. I was lucky enough to be a student in residence at the time.

"I never amounted to much as a Mystan, I'm afraid."

"True."

I winced. "Ouch."

Ikkada tilted his head. "You mastered none of the essential arts."

"You are right, of course." I shrank into myself. Has the master appeared just to shame me for dropping out of Mystan school?

"Are you aware you've been sharing dreams with a Soofian sailor named Ejertine?"

That didn't sound right. And yet—hadn't I just been thinking of me? Him. Wait—which am I?

"All the more remarkable considering you are dead."

"Master Damada, I've had a rough few days, but I can assure you I am not dead. Would I be dreaming if I were dead?"

Ikkada blinked as he considered this response. "Interesting."

"I wouldn't go without a fight. I would know if I were dead."

"I believe you," said Ikkada, turning his cane as his mind worked. "I wonder…" He looked at me sideways. "You know, shared dreaming needn't be concurrent. Especially as this is a recurring dream you've shared many times before. I do believe I am in communication with a Hava Nipalto *before* she committed the crime."

"So I am a dead criminal, am I?"

"Not yet, you're not." Ikkada's smile widened, its glow illuminating the clearing. "Most fascinating! Well done, Ejertine! A nice trick. A shared recurring dream. Brilliant."

"Is it really Hava? Of course I'm me, who else would I be? Ejertine? Is that me?"

"Listen, you two. Or should I say, three? Odeker, do not think you've escaped my notice. I will deal with you, by and by. But first, before we lose our connection, I am going to try something. Something I've always wanted to try. What, you ask? Retrotransubstantiation of a third party from a past dream. Yes: I am going to extract and project, reified, Hava, from her past dream, through Ejertine's current dream, into my presence, that she may answer for a crime she has yet to commit."

"If I stand accused of something, I'd like to know what."

"Come with me and I'll show you. Ejertine, I have her now. You may go. You have performed a great service."

"Wait! Are you saying you are bringing Hava back to life?"

"A mere short-term manifestation only."

"How short term, Ikkada? Can I talk to her? I need to see her."

"Hmm. My investigation takes precedence, but I will hold her as long as I can. It is unlikely you will get here in time, however."

"I'll come! Where is here, exactly?"

"The main square in Central Market. Hurry along now." He clapped his hands, and I awoke.

# CHAPTER 47

# The Ladder of Invisibility

I leapt to my feet, disoriented.

I was back at the warehouse. It was not yet dark.

"I have to get to Central Market."

I cast my eyes about for the closest person, which happened to be Madam Kroduselentsi in her apron. I rushed up to the poor startled woman, demanding, "Where's Olio? Which way to Central Market?"

"I beg your pardon?"

"Mr. Ejertine, sir, Mr. Ejertine," said Franklin, materializing behind me. Penny was right behind him, with new shirt and pantaloons draped over her arm. "Your clothes, sir."

"No time! Where's Olio? Which way to Central Market?"

"Sir, you are barely covered. You can't go to Central Market like this."

"They won't let you in," explained Penny.

I grabbed the pantaloons and, without grace, thrust one leg in. "Right. Central Market. Guys with long, pointy weapons. Still—no choice. I've got to go."

Penny diverted her eyes as I struggled with my second leg. Franklin said, "But sir, I don't think that is a good place for you. Why don't you wait for Mr. Olio? He'll be back soon."

"No time! Must go!" I was already going as I spoke.

"But sir, Central Market is that way."

"Your knife," said Penny, as I doubled back. She handed me a quality, general purpose knife and sheath. "Mr. Olio wanted you to have it."

"Thank you!"

"Just keep going uphill and left," said Penny. "You'll see the arches."

"Wait, sir," said Franklin. "See there, that ladder? Take that ladder, keep your head down, no one will stop you."

A serviceable wooden ladder, about eight feet long, leaned against the wall of the warehouse. "Not a bad idea, Franklin." I grabbed the ladder and ran.

I ran uphill, I ran left, carrying the ladder under my arm, sometimes over my head to avoid collisions.

My heart raced. Olio would never believe me, I knew. But Hava was there waiting for me. A spirit, a dream, a projection, perhaps—but definitely Hava. For a few minutes, I *was* Hava, our minds merged. Her memories, her lusty feelings for my father (gross!). Her familiarity with despair. I could not have manufactured these.

I ran faster, despite the risk of calling attention to myself. I was not going to miss her.

The warehouses gave way to shops and sailors' quarters. People on the street actually made way for me when they saw me coming. Somehow the ladder lent me more respectability. I should have carried a ladder from the start and this city might have been kinder.

I saw the arched entrance to the market at the top of the hill and knew I was getting close. I slowed my pace to a fast walk, so as not to draw attention. I picked out the two guards flanking the entrance.

I put my head down and slowed my breathing, tried to look like I belonged. Precious seconds were wasted as I forced myself to walk slowly, deliberately uphill toward the archway.

A barefoot urchin fell in step beside me, begging for a coin. He whispered, "Olio wants to know what the hell you're doing. He said get off the street, quick."

I glanced over my shoulder and made eye contact with Olio. He was poking his head out from behind a wall of barrels stacked in the alley. He motioned me over.

I shook my head and kept walking. "Tell Olio we have to go *now*."

By the time Olio caught up to me, I was nearly to the market entrance. He had his arms wrapped around a barrel, hiding his face as best he could. He hissed, "What the hell are you doing?"

I kept my head down, and the two of us walked unnoticed between the guards. *Amazing*, I thought. *Somehow a ladder renders me invisible to Laginese people.*

There was not much light left in the day, and most of the shops were closing down. I quickened my pace, crossing over to the main square.

"You gonna tell me what we're doing here?" demanded Olio.

"There," I said, pointing. Across the way, a crowd lingered around a man whose very tall hat and white hair made him stand out. He was putting on an illusionist's show for the customers:

colorful lights and wriggling dragons delighting adults and children alike.

We closed the distance at a fast walk. I dropped the ladder and pushed my way through the crowd. Where was Hava?

"That concludes our entertainments for today," announced Ikkada with a flourish of his hat. "Keep your pennies, keep your pennies," he said when a young lady tried to give him a coin. "A free show today," he assured a father holding his purse.

Hava was not here. "Where's Hava?" I demanded, a little frantic. Behind me, Olio shifted his weight, dropping the barrel to the cobblestone floor of the market.

Ikkada was even stranger in person than in my dream. His eyes were far away, like perhaps he was thinking of something else. I wasn't sure he heard me, so I was about to repeat myself, when he nodded in the direction of what used to be Encho Nipalto's doll shop, its windows still covered in paper. "Look there."

And there was Hava, approaching the steps of the shop, her gait hesitant.

I started after her, but Ikkada put a hand on my shoulder. "Let's give her a moment."

Olio, frowning, turned to look just as Hava climbed the three steps to the front door of the shop. Even from behind, Hava's faded blue tunic was instantly recognizable.

Olio turned back to me, his eyes suddenly saucer-like and moist. "What in the name of the gods have you two done here?"

Ikkada's smile was broad and boundless. "Retrotransubstantiation."

It was really her.

The door opened. There was some kind of commotion.

"Wait," said Ikkada, stopping Olio, who managed to restrain himself only with great effort.

But Hava didn't need our help. Ever a woman of action, she pulled Encho from the shop. Bleeding, he staggered out, bearing in his arms a young woman in a party dress.

Hava interposed herself between her family and the shop, just as Elevaer appeared at the door, eyes agog. Without hesitation, Hava struck Elevaer in the throat with a two-knuckled jab. "What have you done to my family?" Elevaer reeled backward, clutching her throat.

"Hava, don't go in there," pleaded Encho. Bleeding from a large gash in his back, Encho went down to one knee under the weight of his daughter. Passersby stopped to gawk as he deposited Ichito gently on the sidewalk. "You have to take her. Quick, before the guards arrive."

Olio surged forward, but again Ikkada stopped him. "Wait— let this be her moment."

"What have you done?" repeated Olio, not taking his eyes off her. Hava closed the door and then knelt, got her shoulder under her daughter and lifted.

"This way!" Encho tugged at Hava's sleeve and led her away from us. I caught sight of his eyes for a moment, alight with desperate giddiness.

The door to the shop cracked open, and I saw Elevaer peeking out again as the Nipaltos fled.

"Go on," said Ikkada. "I'll give them as long as I can."

I took up my ladder of invisibility, Olio hoisted his barrel, and we hurried together across the square. Olio admonished me with, "What the hell, Ejertine?" At least he didn't call me lad anymore.

Elevaer emerged from the shop as the Nipaltos disappeared around the corner. As Olio and I dashed across the square after them, Elevaer spotted us.

Her jaw dropped when she saw me. "Sailor man?"

I quickened my pace. Olio and I rounded the corner in time to see Encho and Hava bursting through an archway before the guard had a chance to object. "Halt!" he called after them but made no effort to pursue.

The guard turned around in time to see Olio and me coming at full speed. Behind us, we heard someone in a commanding voice call for us to halt.

"I go low, you go high," said Olio, rolling the barrel in front of him and knocking over the guard while my ladder deflected his pole-arm.

Ahead, Encho cut a sharp right at a double-tall building bearing the King's crest, disappearing into the sailor's quarter. Hava, struggling a little with Ichito over her shoulders, was a few steps behind.

Leaving our barrel and ladder, Olio and I hurried after, ignoring the shouts behind us. I hazarded a glance back at my ladder, missing it already.

"The city guards will be after us for sure," I said.

"It ain't them I'm worried about." As soon as he rounded the corner, Olio stopped and flattened himself against the wall of what turned out to be the Office of Disbursements. I hesitated, thinking to myself, *There will be guards right inside.*

On the street ahead I saw Encho and Hava turn into a narrow alley.

Olio peered back around the corner, watching for any pursuers behind us.

"We're gonna lose them," I said, watching the entrance to the alley where they had just disappeared.

"Go on, but watch yourself. Baz has eyes everywhere down there. I'll hold these others off here."

"Olio, come on. We need to stay together." Last time he deserted me, this city ate me alive.

"No—You go now, quick."

I didn't like it, but I went. He called after me, "All eyes!"

That stopped me. "What did you say?"

"Keep your eyes out, Ejertine. We're playing for keeps now, understand?" He drew his sword and stepped back around the corner.

# CHAPTER 48

# An Easy Place to Disappear

I didn't exactly know what Olio was up against, but from the sound of the crashing and shouting, it might have been a whole battalion.

I made speed for the alley. There was a little traffic on the street, and everyone was turned away from me, mostly people on foot headed away from Central Market.

Heeding Olio's advice, I did not go charging around the corner. Instead, I made myself one with the wall and peered carefully into the alley. This was the back of an inn for rich travelers, and here were porters, mostly young men, unloading crates from a wagon. I waited until none of them were looking to slip by the wagon and into the deeper alley.

The alley branched ahead. In either direction lay double-stacked stone apartments—penny accommodations for sailors. I'd spent my share of nights in places like this.

Scanning up and down the walls, I could see any number of spots where a spy might hide and peer through gaps in the walls to watch who came and went. Down one direction a sailor relieved himself against the wall; down the other I saw a family of rats running in single file. Neither way opened to the street, but instead turned inward: a maze of back alleys. An easy place to disappear. Hava and Encho might be anywhere.

I forced myself to wait and listen and watch, slowing my breath to the rhythm of this place. I heard someone coughing. Distant conversation and laughter.

I was too exposed here. A short distance in, I found a better spot, a nook leading into an empty apartment. Here I waited, unseen, watching the alley.

Someone was coming. A thin man with disheveled hair, smiling to himself. I recognized him: one of Elevaer's. The guy who tied me so cruelly to the chair.

Lank, they called him.

He would be on his way to report the location of Encho and Hava. My eyes narrowed, my hands closed around an iron bar.

Lank crumpled without a fuss. I dragged him into the vacant apartment. Someone's bags and clothes were here but it was otherwise devoid of furnishings.

Seeing an iron ring bound to the floor, I found a string and tied Lank's hands behind his back and secured him to the iron ring. "See, I'm pretty good with knots myself," I muttered as I found no fewer than six knives hidden about his person.

I was trying to find places to put all these knives when I heard murmured voices in the alley. I returned to the nook, waited and watched.

Who should I see coming down the alley but Olio, and with him the broad-shouldered Morphidian Yezimeyer.

"Fancy meeting you here," I said, emerging from the shadows. "I wasn't sure I was going to see you again."

Olio looked no worse for wear but was still breathing heavily. "Our boy Yezimeyer showed up in just the nick of time."

"I have little patience for these underworld types," declared Yezimeyer.

"This way," I said, leading them in the direction Lank had come from. "I think the Nipaltos may have gone to ground in one of these sailors' apartments."

But which one?

As I came around the corner, I had my answer: The one Ikkada Damada was standing in front of, with his donkey. He looked at me. "It's time."

"I didn't get to see her…"

"Might I suggest seeking her again in your dreams?" He took his hat in his hands and went through the door then, saying, "I am sorry. I gave you as much time as I could. May I come in?"

Encho, bare-chested and bewildered, opened and closed his mouth, finding no words. His eyes found mine as I came behind Ikkada. He seemed stunned but happy.

Ichito in her dress was slumped in the corner, eyes open and wide. Hava was nowhere to be seen, but in her place sat a beautiful cloth doll, perfectly crafted and clean, out of place in the squalid apartment. This could not be that same battered and torn doll, and yet—undeniably—it was.

Behind me was Olio, and upon seeing him Encho burst into tears and the two men embraced. "You're safe now," said Olio, his voice hoarse with emotion as he received Encho's embrace, gently for his injuries.

"She was here," wept Encho.

"I know, I saw her, too." Now they were both crying.

Yezimeyer waited outside with the donkey, daring any more "underworld types" to harass him.

Ikkada knelt beside the girl Ichito. "None of this," he said, drawing a circle in the air before her face. Ichito breathed in sharply and sat bolt upright.

At this, Encho pushed away from Olio and grabbed hold of his daughter. "Ichito! Ichito, speak to me!"

Ichito's mouth quivered. "It's all my fault. Everything that's happened!"

He held her tighter. "Oh no, sweetie. None of this was your fault. I'm so glad to have you back!"

Ichito pulled away. "Haley—I can't feel her anymore. But she was so angry! She's going to come for us, Father, there is no doubt."

*Haley?* The girl's name for Elevaer's little Pretty, I realized.

"You need fear her no longer," said Ikkada, rising back to his full height and putting on his hat. "That one had no life of her own. Without your link to sustain her, she is no more. Just a pile of parts."

Encho and Ichito sank back into one another's arms, profoundly relieved. They clung to each other for a long moment, overcome with emotion.

Olio wiped his eyes and glanced at Ikkada and me. He had forgiven us, it seemed, for summoning Hava.

"Let's get you somewhere safe," said Olio gently. "Elevaer's still out there. She more or less runs this town now. We need to stick together and move quickly and quietly. Don't talk unless you have to, keep your head down and follow me. I know a place."

"This is where I take my leave," said Ikkada.

Olio spun to face him. "Not so fast, bub. If we are going to take Elevaer down, we'll need your help."

"I will only call attention to you on the street. Also, I have no interest in, as you say, 'taking Elevaer down.'"

"Then why did you help at all? Why did you bring Hava back?"

"I did not bring Hava back. Let's be clear."

"Excuse me," said Encho, folding his arms across his naked chest. "Could someone please explain to me what is happening?"

"Forgive me," said Ikkada, removing his hat once more. "I am called Ikkada Damada. A Mystan. I met your Hava once, long ago, but I admit she did not make much of an impression on me at the time. I circulate very little with the other Mystans, please understand. I am something of an anomaly. A wanderer, a watcher, a guardian, and most recently: an investigator.

"My investigation has found your late wife, Hava Nipalto, guilty of breaking one of the most fundamental precepts of the Mystans. Mysta founded our order long ago to guard against the return of Koposs. Forbidden magic: death magic. Hava Nipalto on her deathbed did deliberately attempt soul transference, invoking an antiquated syllabic syntax that technically pre-dated Koposs. A sort of proto-Koposs, by which I suppose she hoped to avoid detection."

Chills raced down my spine. Soul transference. Death magic. She learned it from Korieski. As did my father.

"I don't understand," said Encho. "What does that mean?"

"Hava tried to cheat death," I said.

"She only wanted to protect us," said Encho.

"So it seems," agreed Ikkada Damada, returning his tall hat to its perch atop his head.

"But where is she now?" asked Ichito. "Where is my mother?"

"Incorporeal. And moderately distributed. You have some of her there in your doll, young lady. She can see you; she can hear you. She is here with you now."

"I knew it," said Ichito quietly, looking down into the eyes of the doll.

"Whatever you do, keep her out of sight of any Mystans. What you have in your hands is a forbidden artifact. By all the laws of my order, I am compelled to seize and destroy it."

"But you're not going to," I said, looking at him sideways.

"As I was saying, this is where I take my leave. Gentlemen. Ladies. Etcetera." Ikkada Damada bent at the waist and walked through the door.

"What an odd fellow," said Encho. "Have I met him somewhere before?"

"Here, cover yourself with this," said Olio, handing Encho a blanket. "We need to move."

Back in the maze of alleys, we moved as a tight group with Olio in the lead. Encho and I followed him closely, with Ichito behind us and Yezimeyer bringing up the rear.

I leaned down to Encho and whispered, "Thank you for saving my life."

Encho looked back at me, stricken. "Did I?" A slow realization dawned across his face. "I suppose I did." He held his head a little higher as he walked.

Olio led us back to the warehouse, where a great fuss was made over Ichito by the former servants of House Nipalto.

Olio pulled me away from the others and we stood together in the weedy yard under the darkening sky. "Ejertine, listen." He pulled on his ear and looked at the ground. I waited for him to find his words.

"I want to thank you for what you said to me the other day. For believing in me. I needed to hear that. You helped turn me round."

"You've done well, organizing these folks. They all believe in you."

Olio looked back at the ground. "Sooner or later, they'll have to fight. And not all of them are gonna make it. We'll see how much they believe in me then." He looked at me crooked and asked, "Why do you have so many knives?"

"Funny story."

"Ejertine, listen." He put his hands on my shoulders. "There's something I need you to do for me."

"Name it," I said.

"It's not a small thing."

"Go on."

"It's easier to show you. Come."

# CHAPTER 49

# The Lately Carrier

We walked a few blocks to the harbor, stopping at a wall overlooking an inlet.

"That there's the Lately Carrier," said Olio, nodding toward a two-master flying Laginese colors, docked in the inlet below. "Owned by the Nipaltos. She departs in two hours carrying new cargo, new orders, and a new captain, appointed by Elevaer."

"How do you know all this?"

"I spoke to the first mate, while you were sleeping. A fine fellow by the name of Plandus. He and the crew are loyal to Alakhar. It was Alakhar who always appointed their captains and issued their orders. For years they've had the same weekly route delivering documents and parcels between Kortholomoth and Port Morphid. The crew all have families in one port or the other, or both. But now—Elevaer's planning to send them off to Greatland and the Nohads.

"Plandus remembered me from the old days, when I used to be man-at-arms for House Nipalto. The law may say Elevaer is in charge, but true loyalties run deeper. Neither Plandus nor his crew are the kind to take orders from criminals. He instead trusted me to know what would serve the family best. In Alakhar's absence, he recognized me as acting steward.

"I want *you* on that ship, Ejertine. Once they're clear of the harbor, Plandus and the crew plan to mutiny against their new captain. You are then to immediately assume command."

"What?"

"As acting steward, it falls on me to appoint the captain of Old Nipalto's boat. There is no one better than you for this job. Your orders, Captain Ejertine, are to sail immediately to Shamp, reach Belchamp ahead of Elevaer's assassins and foil the plot against him. It is essential we keep Hava's brother alive. Do you understand your instructions?"

"I did not see this coming," I said, swallowing. My own command? "Yes, I understand. But Olio–"

"It's got to be you. You're ready for this." He squeezed my shoulder. "I have a secondary mission for you as well. This one of a personal nature."

Ejertine slowly exhaled. "Go on."

"I need you to find my boy. If he's still in prison, find out what it'll take to earn his release. If my flesh and blood truly walks the earth, I need to know he is all right."

Olio had entrusted me with these two all-important tasks. How could I refuse him? "Very well, my friend. I will do as you say."

*Captain Ejertine.* That would take some getting used to.

"You'll be paid, of course," said Olio. "Assuming we aren't all hanged by the time you return."

And so it was, only a few minutes later, after a few hasty farewell hugs, I found myself stepping aboard the Lately Carrier. My ship.

Even before I was aboard I could smell its cargo: acrid, fruity, overpowering. Olio had mentioned something about a new cargo.

They'd given me a scarf to blend in with the crew. Olio had encouraged me to "hunch down" so as not to attract attention. I hid my face behind the scarf, just in case any of Elevaer's men were about.

I needn't have worried. The crew, mostly soft middle-aged men, strangers to me, took me in immediately, and an earnest lad escorted me belowdecks to a hiding place they'd prepared for me. Along the way, I saw the hold filled to capacity with small, round Laginese fruits, green, yellow, and orange.

What was Elevaer up to? Why would she fill a ship with fruit and send it across the sea?

The boy left me in my hiding spot, a nook behind bundles of rigging. He placed another bundle to close me in, and said, "You wait here, cap'n, till the deed is done."

I hunkered down in the dark, resting against a rib of the ship. My body against hers, I could feel her movement. A flurry of boots on the deck overhead as the crew made ready for departure.

It was strange, leaving Kortholomoth so abruptly. Hava's spirit had summoned me to this place to protect her family; this I believed. And Encho and Ichito would be all right now, under Olio's watch; it was Belchamp who needed protecting now.

I couldn't ask for a better command. A clear mission and purpose, serving Hava's family.

It wasn't much of a ship, just a little mail carrier, but it was the first in Old Nipalto's fleet, and as such, served as a flagship, at least symbolically.

As for the crew, from what I'd seen, a hardy bunch they were not. But if they were as stout of heart as Olio described them, well—then, I liked my chances.

I felt them push away from the dock. As the Lately Carrier came about, I leaned with her. My own ship. It was hard to believe.

I would have time, at sea, I supposed, to contemplate the revelations of the past hours and days. This death magic Hava had gotten herself mixed up with, it had touched me as well, woven into the very fabric of my being. Odeker, my father, dead but not gone, still somehow resided within me. The dwerrig, too, had left his taint on me. Ikkada Damada saw all of this in me, but still sent me along my way, without judgment or intervention.

It was an odd thing, someone else seeing me and understanding me better than I understood myself. In a way, it gave me permission to reexamine myself anew. To open those doors and windows and blow out the dust from the rooms of my mind long closed away and forgotten. What did Ikkada see when he looked into those rooms? I wanted to see for myself.

Most of all, I didn't want to let Olio down.

I waited patiently, listening for any signs of trouble. I didn't know exactly what the plan was. I was too excited to sleep. The scent from all those Laginese fruits was making my eyes itch.

At last, I felt the ship find her rhythm on the open sea. *We've left the harbor. It'll be time soon.*

I prepared myself, not sure what to expect.

Finally, the boy came for me. Lifting the rigging, exposing my hiding place, he smiled and said, "It's time now, sir." His calm demeanor perplexed me. Had a mutiny been afoot? Where were the shouts, the clash of steel?

I followed him up top, where the crew, fourteen in all, were lined up for inspection. At the bow, facing me, was a Sartan flanked by prodigious sideburns. My first mate, Plandus, I presumed.

"The boat is yours, Captain," said Plandus, as the boy took his place at the end of the line.

The faces looking at me were set, determined, but trepidatious. Only one man was conspicuously armed.

I came among them, unwrapping my scarf to show them my face. "Thank you. I am Ejertine, assuming command of this vessel under the orders of Olio, acting steward of the House Nipalto. Report. What is the situation?"

"Well, Captain," said Plandus, motioning me toward the hold. "We have deposited our would-be captain down there for the time being."

A beefy man lay sprawled amongst the citrus, his eyes rolled back in his head.

"He'll be fine," said the sailor with the fighting blade. "Eventually."

"Poison?" I asked, surprised, looking to Plandus.

He pursed his lips. "The only poisoner on this ship lies there. Laid low by his own vile concoction, the same as they fed our poor Master Nipalto."

Surveying the grim faces, I hastened to reply, "Encho is doing much better; I saw him last night." This comment seemed to put them at ease.

"Listen, men," I said. "You don't know me. Heck, I don't even know me, if I'm honest. But I do know these seas, as well as anyone. Our orders will take us far beyond the Lately Carrier's usual Green Sea haunts. We will be asking more of her, and more of you, than has been asked before—more than any of you signed on for."

"We're with you, sir," said one of the sailors, a pock-marked youth.

"We signed to serve the Nipaltos—not some criminal gang," said a sallow elder.

I looked face to face; every man nodded his assent. "Very good," I said, pleased. "Now, listen, men: We're in a race with another crew. They have a head start, but the advantage is ours, because they don't know we're in a race."

"What's our destination, Captain?"

"Shamp."

Jaws dropped, glances were exchanged. "That's the far side of Tross, sir, a thousand miles from here!"

"And we have to get there first."

"We're not supplied for a trip like that," put in a portly, middle-aged man.

"We'll make straight for Fwerd-Aul and resupply there."

The sailors looked at each other, bewildered. Half of them probably hadn't heard of the Ckorrmanian port. Its obscurity was precisely what appealed to me.

"You heard the man," said Plandus, puffing himself up. "That's half rations till Fwerd-Aul. But all the gransapples you can eat."

Audible groans from the crew.

"Is that what you call these?" I asked, pointing to the hold. "Why is our hold full of gransapples?"

Plandus shook his head. "We were told not to ask questions, sir. They planned to offload them in Greatland, so far as I can gather."

"What do they taste like?"

"You've never had a gransapple?" asked an incredulous youth.

Moments later, an orange mottled fruit, small enough to close my fingers around, landed in my palm. Everyone watched me expectantly.

Taking my time, aware of their eyes, I selected a knife.

"Why do you have so many knives?" someone asked.

"A story for later," I promised, as I cut through the thick peel down to a hard core. "There's not much fruit to this fruit, is there?"

They laughed with me. It was true: A gransapple was mostly peel and core, with just a thin layer of juicy, fibrous flesh between.

I cut off a slice and put it in my mouth.

I don't know why I should have been surprised. It tasted like it smelled: overpoweringly bitter.

The crew had a good laugh as I spat my mouthful overboard. "Oh," I said, "that is truly terrible."

"You get used to it," said the portly man, taking the rest of my gransapple from me. "They'll make a fine glaze, you'll find."

# Epilogue

By the time we reached the rocky beaches of Fwerd-Aul, I knew all their names, and something of their families, their hopes and dreams. I knew which ones could fight.

And they learned about me. I told them about my village, about Hava, and how Encho saved me from the coal cellar.

The barbarians wanted nothing of our gransapples, but Olio had pressed one of Yezimeyer's diamonds into my hand when we parted ways, and in the markets of Fwerd-Aul this bought us salted meat, fresh water, and sundries enough to carry us to Shamp; as well as a few arms and weapons, ropes and gear; and lumber to repair and reinforce the ship against the harsher seas ahead.

Elevaer's man had mostly recovered from his poisoning, and I found work for him as a guano scraper. Six months or a year of hard labor would earn him enough for passage back to Lagin.

Before departure, as a treat for the crew, I arranged a leg of yak feast on the beach. A wonderful barbarian custom. We ate no more than half the leg, and we brought the remainder with us to devour the following day at sea.

When the meat was gone, I kept the leg bone for myself. Captain's gnawing privileges.

Another privilege of being captain: private quarters. A tiny bunk, too short for me to extend my legs, a table too small for unrolling a map—but private.

One of the things my father taught me was how to make a knife from bone. That night by the light of a hanging lantern, with the porthole closed, I set to work on the yak bone. It was really several different bones joined together, and my first task was to gently separate these into their components.

I spent most of that first night cleaning and scraping, using Lank's knives to good effect. All the debris, smaller bones and gristle I dropped out the porthole into the sea, with a word of thanks to the yak.

The second night, I cut the bone down and shaped it into a blade, grinding it down and sharpening it against a rough stone I'd collected from Fwerd-Aul.

On the third night I drilled a hole through the handle, wrapped it, and bound the handle tight, making a solid grip. I kept it well hidden in my quarters until I could get my hands on some remnant sailcloth. With this, the following night I sewed a simple sheath for my bone knife.

My dead father had told me, "Manufacture a bone knife with your own hands on a boat. Tell no one." I didn't trust Odeker or his motives, but nor had I forgotten his cryptic advice. When the knife was done, I felt him smiling within me, pleased.

From that day forward, I would keep this knife carefully hidden against my thigh. I became so accustomed to it, the knife became essentially part of my body. I put it out of my mind, for years, never unsheathing it, never showing it to anyone.

Having a secret knife, it's good advice. You, too, should keep one. But why on a boat? And why made of bone? I didn't understand, but nor did I linger on these questions. It wasn't until I needed the knife, when the moment arrived which Odeker had foreseen, that I comprehended.

But that is a story for another day. Today's tale—the story of how I came to Kortholomoth and left again a completely changed man—has come to its end.

You'll be wanting to know what befell the crew of the Lately Carrier, and whether we reached Shamp ahead of Elevaer's assassins; and would I find Olio's son; and what about the dwerrig's curse?

Patience, my friend. Ninety and nine more tales do I have for you.

# Glossary

**Alyon.** A bright purple planet in the night sky. Traditionally considered the seat of Morphid's power, Alyonic faithful believe that Alyon is a great palace in the sky, home to myriad deities and demigods constituting the Court of Morphid.

**Alyonic.** An academic and religious system centered around a pantheon of deities including chiefly Morphid (Morof), Nomin (Knomyl), and Bolderaft (Bvolo). Originating in ancient Lagin, Alyonic culture has experienced a modern revival in the New World, taking root in Greatland and Tross.

**Ancientongue.** A mostly extinct language, still used by historians and scholars. The precursor to modern Laginese, Sartan, and Westongue.

**Baphl.** Usually a low stone or mud building or complex where history is kept. Baphls are usually situated in places of little strategic value near population centers and are designed to be fire resistant. Often a baphl will house one or more orders of monks or scholars dedicated to recording local daily events and maintaining records of antiquity.

**Bolderaft** (Bvolo). A greater god of Alyon, brother to Morphid and Nomin. The god of storms and weather, he chooses to live on earth at the top of legendary Mount Idbig at the easternmost promontory of Moghia. He is responsible each day for sailing the Sun and Moon across the sky.

**Deilderaft** (Thima). Wife of Bolderaft, goddess of honor, duty, and duality. She was once a mortal, and now must spend her time riding a great dragon to the west, returning the Sun and Moon to her husband each night.

**Dwerrig.** An ancient species of foul-smelling, subterranean, solitary smallites. Dwerrig are infamous for their powerful magic and are feared and dreaded for their proclivity to place curses upon any who dare disturb them.

**Gathering, the.** The largest and most famous convention of unaligned witches, called once every ten years or so by the Great Witch (known variously as the Bone Witch, Crone Bone, Baba Yaga, among others).

**Gransapple.** A small, bitter fruit that grows in the arid hills of Lagin.

**Great War, the.** A 15-year conflict in which the western powers of Lagin, Sarta, Tross, and Logozha (Greatland) combined their forces to expel the occupying armies of Bvossoly from eastern Tross.

**Greatland** (the New World). A vast frontier on the Moghian mainland, across the Green Sea from Lagin. In modern times, settlers have converged on Greatland from Lagin, Tross, and

Sarta. These settlers have united against grithlings, dragons, and beasts who previously ruled Greatland, and formed a new national identity (see Logozha). The term New World is also used to describe modern Greatland, a blend of Old World cultures.

**Groundlings and Grithlings** (also called variously Gritz, Gritis, or Grithis). Groundlings and grithlings refer to two broad classes of subterranean species who find safety from humans in a vast network of caves and tunnels. Groundlings are a form of smallite which can be found everywhere, squatting in hidden dens and multiplying profusely. They live alongside humanity and survive primarily by avoiding conflict, though they are known to occasionally organize into armies under a so-called goblin king. Grithlings, in contrast, are much larger and are antagonistic toward humans after countless generations of warfare.

**Isthmus, the.** A vast mountainous land bridge connecting Lagin to mainland Moghia. Controlled by Lagin but sparsely populated, the Isthmus is a haven for those who wish to hide from the King's law, but also for freethinkers and independents. Hava told friends and family she was traveling to the Isthmus when in fact she was attending the Gathering in the Lokiswood.

**Kafati.** The sixth day of the week, named for Kaphador.

**Kanis.** A common psychedelic weed.

**Kaphador** (Kafa, Kafis). First born of Morphid, the Prince of All, god of personal power, King of the Underworld and Hell, god of death and destruction.

**Kents** (kentkind, kentish, kenti). An advanced and ancient civilization standing apart and aloof from humanity. Occupying deep wildernesses far from humans, they are masters of long life, song, healing arts, and magic. Although generally benevolent toward a human in distress, they are suspicious and guard their secrets carefully.

**Koposs** (Kopotok, Kopotik). An ancient form of forbidden magic. Also called death magic or soul transference, Koposs was abused by ancient sorcerer-kings as a means of attaining immortality.

**Kortholomoth**. A booming Laginese port in the north Green Sea, known as the Gateway to the New World because of its role in facilitating Laginese exploration and colonization of Greatland. Also known as the City of Crossing Paths, due to its reputation as a chance meeting place, where it is said that if you wait long enough, you will meet everyone in the world. The Nipalto family are prominent patrons and landowners who helped establish the modern port more than a century ago. Kortholomoth is really a cluster of several different communities, most notably the North Port and South Port separated by its most famous landmark, Prowbeam Rock. When the suffix "-madhi" is added to make Kortholomothamadhi, it refers to the greater region of communities surrounding the ports, all governed under a single magistrate representing the King.

**Lagin.** The westernmost kingdom of man, Lagin is a long peninsula, stretching from glaciated mountains in the north, a band of deserts in its middle, and tropical jungles in the south. The Dark Sea batters the inhospitable cliffs of its western coast, while the Green Sea laps more gently at its eastern coast, harboring trade and fostering migration to the New World. The ancient center of Alyonic culture, Lagin is the oldest and perhaps original human nation. Rich in holy sites, Lagin attracts pilgrims from many lands.

**Logozha.** The new national identity emerging across Greatland, named for the Order of Logoss, the order of New World knights patterned after the ancient Morosovan.

**Morphid** (Morof, Morov). King of the gods, creator of life. After defeating Nomin and casting him down into the earth, Morphid created Alyon.

**Morphidian.** A devotee of Morphid. Famous for their powers of healing, Morphidian temples can be found close to the halls of power in every community. In modern times, Morphidians have grown to become the most numerous, prosperous and influential of Alyonic cults. There are many distinct orders of Morphidians, but almost all are strictly patriarchal and community-oriented, operating schools, hospitals, and missions.

**Mysta.** A lesser goddess, daughter of a mortal (Havn) and Sava (Savakashan). Goddess of magic.

**Mystan.** A devotee of Mysta. Mystans are a small, scholarly order of mostly women who study magic and regulate its use in the world.

**Moghia.** The world supercontinent, mother to all nations. The known world, that is the Western World including Soofia, occupies a vast fertile corner of Moghia. But most of the Moghian landmass consists of uninhabited desert wastelands. It is generally agreed that other human civilizations exist somewhere beyond the wastes, in the Far South and in the Far East, and very occasionally an exotic traveler will appear hailing from one of these unknown lands. But the true scale of Moghia is unknowable. Some Alyonic philosophers subscribe to the theory that Moghia's coastline is in fact infinite, and that should one attempt to sail around, they would never find their way back home, but would be doomed to sail on forever, a notion satirized in a popular serial called Gerigo which tells of the never-ending misadventures of a sailor named Gerigo who is forever discovering strange new lands.

**Nomin** (Knomyl). The original, primordial god in Alyonic mythology. Nomin created the Sun, the Moon, and the Sea. Moghia (variously Earth, Rith, or Ulna) was made from the leftover bits. When Morphid sprang into existence from the Sun, Nomin and Morphid battled for supremacy of the heavens. Nomin was defeated and cast down into the earth.

**Rivanna.** Goddess of romantic love.

**Sarta.** Island nation to the south of Lagin, famous for its maritime prowess. Although their language is closely related to Laginese, Sartans are fiercely independent and largely reject Laginese religion and culture. Sarta is controlled by four city-states ruled by powerful merchant lords.

**Sava** (Savakashan, KaShan, Ksaka). Daughter of Morphid, goddess of water. Sava resides in the Fallen Sea beneath the earth. Her likeness adorns wells, fountains, and mastheads.

**Sieve.** A woman or girl who adheres strictly to Alyonic moral precepts of chastity, humility, and subservience.

**Smallite** (pip). Any of the numerous diminutive folk, including norks (norfs, nords), groundlings, zhums (gnomes), halfites, hobolgobs, and dwerrigs, among others. Smallite is an umbrella term for a small humanoid, used especially if the speaker is uncertain of the species. Pip is a pejorative, connoting condescension or signifying willful ignorance of smallite diversity.

**Soofia.** The eastern lands encompassing the Kingdom of Bvossoly (also Bvossolee, Bossoly), a confederacy of heterogenous tribes who form a linguistic and cultural family group distinct from the Western nations of Lagin, Logozha, Sarta, and Tross. Generations of animosity between Tross and Bvossoly erupted into the Great War.

**Tross.** Peninsula nation on the South Sea, the cultural and intellectual center of the modern West. A center of scholarship, sorcery, and invention. The standard Western currency, the Golden Crown, is minted in Tross. The international language of commerce and scholarship, Westongue, is the native tongue of Tross. The people, language, and culture of Tross came originally from Lagin.

**Westongue.** The language of Tross, spoken throughout the West. Like its cousin Laginese, Westongue derives from a common Ancientongue.

**Witch.** A broad term encompassing practitioners of magical arts, usually referring to a woman, often used pejoratively as an implicit disapproval of feminine power.

www.ingramcontent.com/pod-product-compliance
Lightning Source LLC
Chambersburg PA
CBHW061640190726
48289CB00006B/1681